BAANQUER'S POINT

BAANQUER'S POINT

EDWARD W. RAMSELL

AuthorHouse™ LLC
1663 Liberty Drive
Bloomington, IN 47403
www.authorhouse.com
Phone: 1-800-839-8640

Published by AuthorHouse **01/15/2014**

ISBN: 978-1-4918-5071-8 (sc)
ISBN: 978-1-4918-5072-5 (e)

Library of Congress Control Number: 2014900479

Any people depicted in stock imagery provided by Thinkstock are models,
and such images are being used for illustrative purposes only.
Certain stock imagery © Thinkstock.

This book is printed on acid-free paper.

Because of the dynamic nature of the Internet, any web addresses or links contained in
this book may have changed since publication and may no longer be valid. The views
expressed in this work are solely those of the author and do not necessarily reflect the
views of the publisher, and the publisher hereby disclaims any responsibility for them.

CHAPTER 1

The Library

Books, regular store-bought lower-case books, have a certain heft and whip to them, flexible in some dimensions and stiff in the others. These Books, rather, have more the aspect of a brick; they have no more whip than a stump.

The Books in this library rest proudly in dark oaken cases protected by leaded cut glass drop doors. Eons of patience have darkened the heavy woodwork beyond esthetics, even beyond woodiness. Were it not for their obvious design, the bookcases might well be taken for pillars supporting some wayward planet, or beams built to broach a rampart. Their design is obvious; skilled hands intended that the Books be both protected and contained.

The Books themselves are thick massive tomes really, things built rather than bound. The spines glisten with rich gold hand tooling inlaid on thick leather, still supple in spite of its age. Several of the Books lay flat, the thickwise view revealing the covers as planks or slabs, the leaves thick parchment whose edges interwiggle like lasagna noodles.

No one will read these books. They are repositories of used words the way a tomb is the receptacle of exhausted flesh. Their words are the accumulated doings of those with power. Some works chronicle the turnings of the universe. Others are merely a residue, kept only to remove them from the realm of life.

Whatever their intent, something of it leaks with time and taints the air. It may be the Books themselves as much as the words they contain. More than anything else, yes, it is definitely the Books. They fill the study with its turgid amber heaviness, more thickly towards the floor in a graduation that implies its weight. It oozes from the Books, smells of Book.

They do not leak much, these Books, but in so long a time the leak has become nearly tangible. The murk is not vile, mind you. It is the color of good bourbon and supports an aroma that suggests great wisdom. It is, however, murk.

Thick sheaves and twine-tied stacks of curly-edged manuscripts lie neatly about the floor and on a worktable, some in obvious review and some in simple storage. The hands that built the bookcases also left their unmistakable impression upon the table, and on some other obvious pieces of furniture set about the Library. The table stands there, against the far wall between the windows. A few of the leaves are sewn into folios, the work only partly done. Others, rolled into ribboned tubes, protrude from a bank of rune-ordered pigeonholes. The manuscripts sport a meticulous hand, illuminated casually but firmly and with conviction. Such obvious care is curious because the very act of drafting and illuminating these pages is the embalming of their thoughts, the bookshelves their tomb. Perhaps the studied attention to detail more perfectly fixed those thoughts to the medium, or maybe the scribe wished only to pay a final respect to them. Whichever, the table displays work dropped suddenly, unfinished.

The Library is oversize but proportioned so perfectly by its furniture and trappings that it seems much smaller. The architectural style is benevolently cobby; every surface of every beam and casing drips of the builder's attention, sculpted to a degree just shy of Baroque, but country in flavor. The artist's technology seems limited to the ax, although a very sharp and skilled ax, while the subject matter displays a distinctly gargoylean bent.

Case-hardened blue-green foiled paper covers the walls from cove to wainscot, paper the color of those steely blue mallard feathers and some dragonflies. Wonderfully lush landscapes, littered with temple ruins and randy satyrs, cover one wall entirely, each with magnificently ornate frames. Leather and parchment maps cover another wall, richly illustrated maps of breathtaking lands and sparkling worlds out there somewhere.

The Library has not breathed since the day of its assembly. The air is close, oppressive in spite of the room's great size, and seems fit only for breathless beings. Brownian dust from that first day still hangs in the air, catching window light and fuzzing vision a little. The atmosphere feels laden, as in an iron foundry, but without the clang.

The window, while clearly transparent, admits nothing beyond, not even the light source. It may be simply another wall hanging, the light springing from the pane itself. The Library has no door, as there is probably no outside.

Where there are no manuscripts there are things; instruments of hand battle, things meant to convenience life and things meant to end it, things to simply hold and enjoy, and things of no apparent purpose. These objects, in contrast to the massy bookcases, are finely wrought, some of delicate woods and brilliant brass, others of richly veined marble with silver or leather trim.

Each one of them is perfect, at once the best of its genre and one of a kind, as though its maker, knowing the work to be perfect, felt unwarranted the risk of an inadequate sequel. Each differs from the others in subtler ways, ways suggesting mutually alien minds that perceive the essence of tooliness in skewed patterns. Each artifact displays a fundamentally right look and feel and balance that hints wealth. In fact, the whole room springs from wealth beyond imagining, wealth against which planetfulls fade, wealth subtending absolute unquestioned mindless control and power. These objects are hints only, however; the wealth is not here.

There must have been no constraint on the construction of the Library other than that it be perfect. There are no flaws; the walls are plumb, the wood is clear, joints join. That's quite a lot.

A fragile crust of dust lightly blankets three large and black Watchers. They are gaunt angular things that move no more than the room moves, things whose only task is vigil. One, clearly an airborne predator, clutches the mantel like prey, nearly blending with the darkened oak woodwork. Only one eye watches, the other long since gouged and scarred over. Two other critters, just as clearly beasts of the soil, crouch in opposite corners, hunched as though weary of their task and wary of each other, but determined to hold. Perhaps these black-hearted devils are dogs; certainly they are powerful swift and sharp-edged.

The first, the air thing, is simply evil. The other two are killers. All are alive, in a way. All are mean.

The carpet is plush, of course, but untested even by the black Watchers; they had come with the woodwork and moved as much. The pattern is a mosaic starburst centering on the room itself, pieced of deep golds at the center, radiating through burnished bronze and alizarin into blue-green and rust at the corners.

About the starburst is a concentric assortment of stuffed sofas and settees. Candyapple wine leather upholstery seems most popular, the color of polished near-overripe crabapples. One davenport sports an awful but expensive broadleaf flowered velour, the kind that binds you up in the tail of your coat when you sit down and you can't slide back up.

A heavy-posted high back chair sits to the side of the fireplace facing into the array. It has no cushion, in stark contrast to the other posh furniture, and uncomfortable in spite of its quality. The furniture array focuses on this chair.

There is a ripping good fire in the place, but it is cold and noiseless, lacking a homey spit and crackle. The fire ignited the last day of construction and has burned ever since, awaiting the return of the Scribe. It is no more a fire, really, than the pictures on the walls are their depictions, or the maps dirt. The fireplace and its display are no more than that; clever and attractive displays. There is no need for light or heat in this room.

There is no soul in the Library and there has never been one. The Watchers would know if there were, for that is their only talent. Their charge is to kill. They have yet to kill and grow impatient for it. Watchers, you must understand, do not kill living things, for living things cannot be here in this place. Souls can be here and souls can be killed. Watchers do kill souls.

The Books, in their serenity, husband wisdom and anchor life against the ablative blast of time in the way that deep-rooted rock shoals stand proof against insinuating surf. Because of that, the Library is the only unmoving place anywhere; every elsewhere reckons from it. Like the shoal, the Books will lose out in the end, of course; time always wins. But that end will not occur in a time with any meaning to those whose lives reside in these books.

Our story is here in the Library, scattered among these Books. Entries registered as they suit the Scribe, in the order of flow rather than of time, and in the Books of Greater Impact rather than in the more conventional Books of Lives. That is because every entry in every Book here links to every other entry, like a spider's web. The story you might trace for yourself is not the story another would find. The story I am about to trace for you has not happened yet, in the same way that you have not read it yet. The parts of this story are here because the Books are here, have probably always been here. In all the cosmos this Library is the only place where now *is* now; the past is only a Book not yet read, the future merely a bottle of ink unopened.

My task is to guide us through this Library, and let you make of the result what story you will. You may come along if you wish, or not. I offer you no warranty other than this: I expect to enjoy myself thoroughly.

Are you ready? You may leave your things here; we will return. Please be careful not to touch anything.

CHAPTER 2

A Furry Fungus Fad

If not for the long winter this spring, East Eard would have been in real trouble. As is, the Eards were only in artificial trouble due to the artificial light produced by the artificial generators. The generators themselves are significant only because they subtend a sole proprietorship run by a clan of Phroggs who are not above taking a profit. Nor below it for that matter. Let's just say they are profitable. The generators that is, not the Phroggs. Phroggs are only profitable in the late fall.

The problem is, East Eards are bald by nature but not by preference. The only practical source of hair is a fungus. This is not your ordinary creeping crud, mind you, but a particularly temperamental strain that will symbiotically adorn the belly of selected Eards only for a special consideration. That special consideration nearly spelled the end of East Eard. At least those parts of Eard underlying this story.

A thick even belly of glossy hair requires a massive dose of orange light, a peculiar shade of orange that produces the complementary color in the hair . . . blue. Come spring, aspiring and perspiring Eards fry themselves in the sun, soaking up that stridently orange light from the hinter of Eard's two suns.

Eard's axis of rotation tilts severely to its ecliptic. This fact, coupled with the steep eccentricity of its orbit, lends it a singular sequence of sunny seasons. A deep, oxygen-depleted blood-red sun during the long dulling winter precedes a three-day spring filled with that glorious orange sun. An intense hot white summer sun graciously apologizes for the winter.

In winter, the meager red sunshine is not strong enough to interest the admittedly fussy fungus. Besides, the weather is just too cold for any self-respecting fungus to ply its multicellular little trade. Often as not, the hair also turns purple, a color closely associated with a fiercely obscene joke concerning a piano tuner and an itinerant but nonetheless footloose magpie. Likely this is the original off-color joke and the off-color was purple. The ultimate insult is to call an adversary a Purple Eard, while the only honorable rejoinder to this affront is "Oh yeah?"

At any rate, purple is definitely out and the highly desirable fuchsia almost impossible, requiring an exposure to the broiling summer sun that often as not put an unreal kink in the fungus. Well, the kink was real enough and the trick daunting, the optimum exposure being 1/50 of a second at f8. Anything less produces a cringing coif of limp straw, more results in turf like double-ought steel wool. The odds are against you, the mistakes embarrassing, and the silly hair permanent. The only out is a shave, putting you simply nowhere with United Fungi.

To get a fine pelt of blue belly grass, East Eards bask for hours in the orange light, brazing the fungus cultures mercilessly to grow the summer social season's status symbol. Only this year there was no spring, no orange light, and no blue pelts.

This is where the frogs-er-Phroggs come in.

CHAPTER 3

The Butter Pecan Connection

There is no practical way to get through this without telling you about the Phroggs. So, here is their story according to the Phroggs themselves, or rather according to their second-rate scribe, Joe Anonymous. Due to a peculiarity in their genetic makeup resulting from a bitter civil war a few weeks back, the Phroggs have no first-rate scribes. Or first-rate anything, but do not say that to a Phrogg.

Joe Anonymous was an inveterate peddler who could sell you anything you wanted and a few things you didn't. He was famous for his line of hardware, old jokes and ice cream. Particularly ice cream. You might not think there are many ice cream flavors that appeal to Phroggs. You are right. In fact, there is only one flavor that a Phrogg can even taste. That one flavor is illegal due to the current coalition government made up of Liberals, Losers and Leakers.

Liberals (if you can imagine a liberal Phrogg) and Losers (easy, if you have ever really talked to a Phrogg) are philosophically divided on the issue of issue. Progeny is a perennial problem among the prolific Phroggs, particularly in these days of progressively repressive zoning laws. Meanwhile, Leakers fight a lopsided battle on the side of the Lops, disenfranchised amphibians who until recently enjoyed the protection of the Losers. You see, Losers were not always Losers. Before that, they were Also-Rans.

As such, they were a privileged class, privileged to protect the Lops. That has all changed now. Lops are a luxury the Losers can no longer afford, and nobody else wants. It's a tragic story, not unlike the Godzillas and the King Kongs of the world.

Anyway, according to Joe Anonymous, the consensus among the fractured factions is that Phroggdom can taste but one flavor. That flavor is Butter Pecan and Phroggs are monumentally bored with Butter Pecan. In addition, Butter Pecan ice cream is an aphrodisiac, seriously compounding the issue issue. The warring factions could not agree on which new flavor to add, of course, and none of the elder MPs would forsake the restorative effects of Butter Pecan. They needed to accomplish *something* in this election year. On the premise that forbidden fruit is more delicious, they (you guessed it) outlawed Butter Pecan.

This act precipitated ice cream orgies you would not believe unless you were familiar with the typically low Phroggy threshold for virtually anything forbidden. Butter Pecan cartels inevitably followed, and with them a Butter Pecan criminal underground. Joe was a dealer in contraband ice cream; a pusher if you will but it was good ice cream by any standards. As you have probably worked out for yourself, Phroggy standards are all but nonexistent.

Joe, as a second-rate (you see!) pusher, had connections with the ice cream underground, and through them to the ice cream cartels. The Butter Pecan moguls first noticed Joe because of the volume of ice cream he moved, a fact publicly attributed to the quality of the product he pedaled. In fact, it was due to the efforts of Old Platypus down in the Flats who manufactured ice cream for Joe in return for a brace of adolescent tadpoles each week. Joe never asked what the old marsupial wanted with them and preferred not to think about it. Old Platypus laced the ice cream with old lace, a process known to her only under self-induced hypnosis. It was this ingredient that produced the high.

Events came to a head when the Family made pointed inquiries into profits Joe failed to return. When that old hag Old Platypus upped protection to two brace per week, Joe's instinctive move was the Lateral Arabesque. This step endeared Joe to the aging though senile hereditary High Phrogg, a monarch of absolute discretionary powers and practically no discretion. In his grace, Joe would be immune to the law and the lawless alike.

The plan was simple. The High Phrogg lacked progeny of any consequence and was anxious to preserve something of his regime for posterity. Consequently, he commissioned Joe to write the complete history of all Phroggdom. Joe delivered it that same afternoon, to the delight of the monarch, and split with his commission before the suspicious cabinet discovered it was lifted *in toto* from an old Mary Worth serial Joe had saved for just such an emergency. However, after reflecting on the total lack of any real Phrogg history, the king decided to make history by adopting Joe's as authentic. Were it not for this otherwise dumb decision, you would never hear the tale I am about to relate.

Long ago, when times were simpler and moved more slowly, Phroggs were spelled just frogs. Do not think they aren't proud of that Ph. It was a long crusade to earn that respect of society. Considering the original frogs started out in a drainage ditch on the edge of a used car lot, making it at all is nothing short of dull.

Well, boring would be something short of dull. The frogs certainly thought it was boring, sitting there all night with hubcaps and cans floating by, making contented deep-throated croakings for the background of adolescent B movie love scenes. Woof! All this to help the Chamber of Commerce promote South Sop as a rest haven catering exclusively to the socially elite of Southeast Sop.

Now there is no Society in Southeast Sop, at least none to which anyone admits. There is also little in Southeast Sop you can describe as elite, except possibly the old rusty Elite Kumquat Peeler in back of the stables. The nameplate is affixed yet and you can still read the specifications. In fact, that's what they do for merriment when things get dull in Southeast Sop.

The merriment derives from a story that, by the way, is totally unknown in Southeast Sop. It relates the origin of the peeler and its place of honor on the dung heap. The brand-new machine was never used and performed only marginally anyway. When the incipient father-in-law learned that Kumquats in Southeast Sop have no skins, he called off the wedding. This was probably the best thing that could have happened to the groom. His relief knowing no bounds, he bounded off into the sunset and did not return until suppertime.

The peeler served as a boat anchor for a while, then as a threat to incorrigible little Sops. It was finally thrown on the dung heap that borders South Sop in response to complaints that dung was blowing into South Sop during the stormy seasons. This gesture did not satisfy the Sops at all, but since their dung always blew back in the off season, they let it go at that.

Now, let's get back to the frogs who croaked for a living in South Sop. You can imagine there is little prospect for a tourist rush from an impoverished state, whose people sit about reading kumquat peelers, to an equally impoverished state that thinks croaking frogs are a tourist attraction. Their contract terminated after several decades. The frogs' lot, as opposed to the used car lot that did only poorly, became dismal.

The frogs, in their struggle for a national identity, eventually found their way into base industries, in jobs so essential that civilization cannot survive in their absence.

I am speaking, of course, about refuse disposal. Forget that garbage, if you will excuse the expression, about industrial revolutions, political awakenings, medical advances, technical discoveries and exploration. Only one factor holds back the advance of civilization and that is garbage.

Look, people just naturally like to get together to read old rusty machines or what have you. Unfortunately, people stink mostly, and their debris stinks even more. Eventually the stink overcomes social instinct. Eventually one will suggest to the other, usually not so subtly, that they clean themselves up and be more respectable. The suggestees take umbrage and we have the basis of all conflict; others are oppressive to you so you must move on or fight. Ultimately fight. Enter sanitation.

The frogs did not realize this in the beginning, or even in the middle, but in the end they sure did. By the time we get to this story, the frogs simply ran all of civilized Sop behind the scenes. Or rather behind a garbage truck.

There were years of struggle competing with the Sops themselves, certainly. There were street wars, killings, extortions and all the other concomitants to civilizing a nation but in the end the frogs won by default. Sops really did not care for that kind of work. They finally ceded complete control of their destiny to the frogs in return for the benefits of civilization. It sure beat croaking for a living in a drainage ditch.

Now do not get it wrong. The Sops knew the situation exactly and liked it that way. The frogs, or now the Phroggs, ran a tight ship and stayed out of the way. You would never see a Phrogg wielding power or anything else fancier than a trash can. They ran things and everyone knew it. In normal times, they liked it. However, by now you have gathered that these are not normal times.

When it came to pass, the Phroggs never did. Pass that is. In the eternal game of turning a profit, passing an opportunity to turn an Eardmark was to pass up your last breath or heartbeat. Here is how they worked. The phenomenally prolific Phroggs built a substantial community estate by willing their bodies to their own rendering, processing and fertilizing industries, then cut their prices. They then bought up the defunct competition, squoze exorbitant profits from the processing plants and ultimately liquidated them as well.

In another, they cornered the market in used Popsicle sticks by cornering the old man in an alley. This ploy brought the kindergartens of a nation to their pedagogical knees by completely disrupting their artsy-craftsy program. It finally gained a profitable concession from the frustrated Boards of Education. In all fairness, the kindergartens fought back brilliantly, if futility, with an extensive curriculum revision centered on papier-mâché. It was to no avail. The Phroggs had long since monopolized the scrap paper industry through the aforementioned garbage collection service. In short, and Phroggs are nothing if not short, they had you six ways from Sunday and Eard has six Sundays every week.

Now you understand the attraction the current furry fungus fad held for the Phroggs. It was an open invitation, virtually an appeal for Phroggy intervention. This next part may be a little hard to swallow, but it may help to keep in mind that Joe did not buy a bit of it either.

Recall the artificial trouble due to the artificial orange light produced by the artificial generators? You may well ask what is the difference between an artificial generator and a real one. That's a fair question that deserves a fair answer. However, you will have to be satisfied with this one.

Generators, as you surely realize, are not really generators. They are actually contrivances designed to convert one form of energy into another form of energy. For instance, they convert waterpower into torque, steam pressure into electricity, chemical reactions into heat, and other noisy processes that appeal to people with greasy elbows. There is an inevitable loss of energy in each step of the process, and so they are not really energy generators at all, but rather energy users. Each device must first use some form of energy to produce less energy in another form. A true generator, on the other hand, produces power with no input. Or at least produces more output than input. The economic advantages of a true generator are obvious and immense, as any fool can see. The Phroggs are anything but fools while the Eards are nothing but, particularly concerning economics.

You need to know that nobody in Eard has any money to speak of. (They all have a great deal they do not speak of but that is invested mostly in script, if not worse.) To an Eard, what little money he might come across has but one purpose, spending, preferably as outlandishly as possible. It was precisely this foolish fiscal outlook that spawned such fads as paper cup rhythm bands (which were more than disappointing to most), solar-powered flashlights, and the current fungus fur fad.

In heating a house, say, or propelling a vehicle, there is no practical substitute for genuine energy. However, when it comes to growing orange light-induced fungus on the belly of an Eard, all sorts of opportunities arise. This pertinent arousal was a hybrid culture of fungus that had abandoned itself to the local Phrogg local. The note on the basket outlined a daring scheme that would raise hair on the back of your neck and, with a little luck, on the bellies of the Eards.

The basic plot: a wildcat colony of disgruntled fungi was fed up with the establishment price support policy restricting operations to the Spring Orange Season. They proposed to open a string of franchised hothouses, staffed by their own who were not too proud to grow year round. For the right price. They came to the Phroggs for financial backing and the technical know-how to produce the particular shade of orange light that turned them on. The bargain was sealed, the chain of spas opened, the lights lit, and the Eards came in herds. And they were moderately successful. Nothing great, you understand, but they justified the investment.

Then the fungi blew it. A Phrogg overheard two drunken fronds discussing how they had fooled the Phroggs. It seems this outlaw band of fungus escaped from an experimental lab in which they had been developed to grow year round, under any color of light. The Powers decided to neutralize the strain to preserve their industry. Learning of this, the hybrid strain hotfooted it out of town and abandoned itself on the doorstep of the Phrogg local. Now that the Phroggs financed the chain of furriers, the fungi absorbed the extra rich orange light of the real generators, multiplied at a phenomenal rate, and set aside enough surplus fungi for a coup d'etat. They had not yet decided just who it was they were going to coup, but it would most certainly be d'etat.

Siphoning off the paramilitary fungi, coupled with the stiff expense to generate the orange light, accounted for the disappointing profit picture. To boost profits and prevent any takeover plot, the Phroggs surreptitiously replaced the generators with facsimiles made of balsa. To compound the ruse, they painted the light bulbs orange. Completing the maneuver, the Phroggs kept the fungus permanently soused with a cheap brew known locally as "Outside Annie's Socks." The fungus never knew the difference.

As we shall see, the Eards did.

CHAPTER 4

Gus, Grapft and Farpl

Now let's take a close look at one special Phrogg, Generalissimo Ultissimo Schwartz. That was his name, not his title. His title is Groundskeeper, J.G.

Gus, as he is known to everyone of higher rank, is a certified Partyhack with Chevron, a designation earned with distinction. He started his career with a low-paying but grungy position in sanitation and worked his way to the surface. Finally reaching a job above ground, he felt a need to enhance his social position as well and joined Phroggs Local No. 1. They put him right back to work in Sanitation.

You see, the Phroggs run all of Eard through a counterculture organization that anywhere else is the Underground. In Eard, it's Overboard.

In any society, political power arises from the ability to grant good things to those who behave a certain way. It is not particularly important which way that is, just so they behave. Benefits trickle down and behavior bubbles up, usually as work. Around and around.

In a circular system like that, one can jump in almost anywhere and pretend to have started the whole thing. The Phroggs jumped into Eard at the point where work starts to bubble up, in the sewers. By garnering control of essentially dirty industries such as garbage collection and used cars, they extorted their way into control of all Eard.

In such a system, money always flows in the opposite direction and Eard is no exception. The Eards pay the Phroggs handsomely for the privilege of turning their political lives over to the Phroggs, retaining only their nominal sinecures. Everyone likes it that way, neat and Overboard.

The key to the whole system is Grapht, money flowing in the same direction as the work, rather than in opposition. Unlikely as it may seem, the Eards pay the Phroggs once to secure a job with the government, and then again to have the Phroggs do it for them. Admittedly the Eards do not make much money that way, but then they do not work much either. They actively court the favor of the Phroggs, scrambling to get on the merry-go-round.

It was that uncounterflow of cash that absorbed Gus in his work for the party as Sanitarian, laundering money. He took Grapht flowing to the Overboard and converted it to taxable income. That way money is taxed every time it moves around the monetary cycle. It is then possible to generate more tax revenue by simply turning the money over faster and faster, taking a tax cut each time around. The faster money revolves, the less money needed. Eventually, in theory anyway, the tax money itself is the only money circulating, generating its own taxes. The Eards squander the rest of the money with impunity.

That was Gus' job, churning tax at piece rate. Initially, he only collected Grapht at the Phrogg local and delivered it cross-town to the Department of Tax. Back and forth; pick it up here and deliver it there.

All that trucking and backtracking got to be a drag. He recommended to his immediate superiors that the Phrogg office be moved to the ground floor of the Department of Tax. This simplified matters considerably.

Gus, not having much to do but walk up and down stairs, began to read the numbers on the bills to pass the time. Then he began to memorize them. Then he noticed that the same bills would pass through his hands regularly. Then he noticed that often as not, a given bill beat him back downstairs!

It did not take long to find the back stairs, and soon thereafter, the clerk who carried the money back down again. Her name was Farpl, and she was a knockout.

In fact, she was light heavyweight champ for this side of the mountain and free-lanced in meat tenderizing to supplement her income. She acquired her position in Tax as a favor from a promoter who also occasionally promoted boxing matches. Gus had to find out just what was going on in Tax and how they were each involved. Farpl and Gus made an unusual pair, he being a Phrogg and she an Eard, so it was not convenient appear together socially. They agreed to meet in the ring.

The details of the fight are not important to the story. Farpl won, of course. Eards always beat Phroggs in a fair fight. That's why the Phroggs originally resorted to their devious occupations. While exchanging blows, Gus and Farpl exchanged details of their careers. Not only did they carry the same money up and down the stairs, they also placed it in each other's OUT box! When Gus grasped the significance, he dropped his guard and took an uppercut that put him in the first row of seating.

If they both put cash in each other's OUT box, then nobody else was involved! Nobody checked the money! They just rang up the tax revenue without bothering to count it or bank it. Since the Tax Guy simply printed currency to cover a congenitally lax accounting system, it was a small step to print the tax revenue as well. The lack of real income was more than offset by administrative savings.

The next step was obvious, at least to Gus. Farpl was a little slow in the subtle techniques of fiscal obfuscation, but understood clearly enough when her piece of the action rolled in. They found they could substitute almost anything in the moneybags. Then by speeding up pickup and delivery they siphoned off vast quantities of money and increased Eard's tax revenues as well. Gus and Farpl should have retired undefeated.

Their supervisors knew what was going on, of course. They thought of doing it themselves but lacked the nerve. They were happy to let someone else try it and it worked so well everyone was promoted regularly. Their security seemed assured.

In no time at all Eard was bankrupt but no one knew it. No one, that is, except Gus who had by this time memorized every cereal number of every treasury note in the land. This is a more formidable task than you might at first suppose. Eard's currency is mostly used breakfast flakes proof of purchase box tops.

He knew they were going bankrupt when he saw Eard was running out of numbers. You see, there are only so many numbers in the Eardian number system that relies heavily on pictograms of fingers and toes. When they are all used, there are no more.

Gus saw that coming and planned to make his move. Having diverted nearly half the currency of Eard to his personal use, Gus found he had to spend a certain amount just to keep things running smoothly. It did not seem to make a great deal of difference how he spent the money. Mostly he spent it in the stock market buying up all the depressed military stock he could find.

Since there was very little military manufacturing anymore, Gus soon found himself in control of the military-industrial complex by default. Most of the military capacity of Eard went to toys and small appliances of late. The industry was doing poorly at that as Eard had yet to discover Christmas. Even so, his buying spree did wonders for market prices.

Manipulation can inflate the market only so far, however. Gus quickly reached that limit since he was the only buyer on the floor. Eventually, he found himself facing either total collapse of his financial empire or going into real profit-making enterprise. Finding poverty wanting, Gus opted for profit.

Gus' path to profits was conventional enough. Find a few legislators who rent by the hour, pass a defense appropriation bill or two and let bids on military supplies whose specs Gus wrote. Then, of course, deliver the goods.

The catch was in delivering the military materiel. You see, Eard was not at war, unless you count that fracas with South Sop about the dung heap. In very short order all military installations, supply depots and docks wallowed in canteens, bedrolls, pup tents and miscellaneous olive drab stuff. New deliveries piled upon old. Eventually, to alleviate the congestion, deliveries were rejected outright and tagged for return. Inevitably, these returns went back to the factories from whence they came.

Read that last line again. Does that plot look familiar? It sure did to Gus who, as you recall, got where he was by recycling tax revenues. The philosophical leap from churning tax revenues to churning pup tents was downhill, ethically as well as geographically. As soon as his plants filled the tubes, new production shut down altogether. Most Eards felt this was a good thing in the end; they did not like working much, and most of the supplies were either defective, dangerous or the wrong size anyway. In all fairness, though, it was the Eards that came in wrong sizes.

Upon hearing of the layoff, everyone gave a cheer and headed for the beach. Work was all right for some, went the general feeling, but enough was enough. After all, what were the Phroggs getting paid to do?

A few still worked hauling all that junk back and forth but it was only a matter of time. Someone, probably Gus, observed that since the same army stuff simply went round and round, why not skip the actual trucking and do it all on paper? Finding no serious opposition to the idea, Gus sold his trucks and headed for the beach too. Henceforward, three secretaries handled affairs nicely.

There was one serious flaw with the scheme; the problem with soldiers. Soldiers, you see, are not manufactured. They come from outside the military complex, from cozy warm homes like yours and mine. When their tour of duty is over, they tend to go back home. Therein lies the rub; there was no war. At least there was no war big enough to warrant the massive outlay Gus needed to produce the profits he extracted from his acquisitions.

For a while things went smoothly enough. Gus sent soldiers off to far-flung outposts and rotated them about a bit. Then he brought them back with great fanfare about their success in defending the nation's borders. But now things were getting out of hand. The Armee was up to its epaulets in surplus. Gus could justify more production only on the premise that the war front was expanding more and more. It would soon become clear to returning veterans that there was no war and the jig would be, as it were, up.

Gus had to find a way to dispose of the excess soldiers. In other words, he had to generate massive battle casualties without the mess and cost of an actual battle. Regular battles cost a ton of money, you understand, while Gus' style did not cost a dime. On the contrary, they made money. The advantages of a fake war were obvious even to Farpl who was still mystified about everything except writing checks.

Inevitably, Gus did the only thing he could. Not the honorable thing, or the prudent thing, or even the only possible thing, but the only thing he could think of in his state of mind. Gus had this knack, you see. In a word, survival was the knack and Gus specialized in it above all others. If you asked Gus what his knack was, he would not say survival. He would probably say it was the harmonica, which he did play well if breathlessly. Nonetheless, Gus was a survivor, the way a cork on a pond is a survivor. Gus could not sink.

CHAPTER 5

One

Everyone owes Gus. Gus memorized the cereal number of every treasury note in all Eard and owned half of them in fee simple. The opportunities to grant favors and extract corresponding obligations are more than unlimited, they are obligatory. So, everybody in Eard owes Gus. Everyone, that is, except One.

One is not an Eard, nor is One a Phrogg. One had not come to Eard; One has always been there. One is probably the first Eard. That is why tradition has it that One is called One. One, however, does not go by that name because One does not go, in the usual sense of the word. Names account for people, but One accounts to no one. Names identify us to ourselves, and to others when the issue is in doubt, but there is no doubt about One.

One walks Eard inscrutably; perhaps observing, perhaps not. It is hard to tell with One because no one sees One, or hears One. One's presence imposes on the vicinity a palpable deja vu that is thickly pervasive and deeply permeating. Everyone within vu loses complete control of their time orientation. They do not just feel as though they had experienced an event previously. They actually relive it without the accompanying awareness of the fact. However, when One releases, things slip back to the present with a jolt, like a channel change or a badly spliced movie. Everyone avoids One. Everyone, that is, except Gus.

Ordinarily Gus is not the sort that, given the choice, would cavort with One, and by unanimous choice, One is a loner. However, Gus had a problem and One has a knack for problems. Some even say that One causes problems, but they do not say it too loudly. Whatever, they are never far apart. Problems and One, that is.

Gus' problem concerned the write-off he was taking on Armee materiel he supposedly shipped to the war. Part A was there was no war. Part B was you could write off war materiel that does not exist but very live soldiers do not go away so easily. Soldiers have a way of coming back home, and when they came back home, they tell all about their adventures. Even the Eards, who dearly love both adventures and shaggy dog stories, wondered about the point of it all. Gus had to get rid of the soldiers somehow. He needed something neat and not too expensive that would just make them go away.

Enter One. Well, not really enter, as One does not come and go as you and I. One moment Gus pondered his predicament alone in his penthouse, and the next he felt the goose-bumpy flesh that fable foretold as the presence of One. They say, they being the purveyors of Eardian fables, that you do not know when you slip out of your own time with One. Only when you pop back. They are right.

Gus found himself. He was inside his own head, looking out through his own eyes at a familiar world he had never seen before. Deja vu is like that; ill conceived. He could watch what happened, listen to himself say what he knew he was going to say, do what he knew he was going to do. But he was just a spectator along for the ride. These things had never happened before, but he knew with certain clarity they would happen. The frustrating part was if he had a choice, he would not say what he was going to say. He saw it coming, but he could not stop it. At the precisely wrong time, when all creation cried out to him to thwart fate in her madcap compulsion to uproot all that is sane and right in the world by simply saying no, Generalissimo Ultissimo Schwartz would say yes. He saw that ill-advised yes coming, knew he would say it, knew it was wrong to say it. But he would say it.

Looking out through his own eyes, Gus beheld One. He, Gus, winced but his body did not. One was certainly one to evoke a wince, varicose veins and all. However, he, One, did not seem to notice. Or care. One clinked a drink he swished in one hand, scratched backhandedly at the small of his back, adjusted his toga, and smiled. He stood at pot-bellied Rodinesque ease, as one who has it made. Really *made*.

"Tell me about it," said One.

"I have a problem. I have to dispose of a few bodies. Live bodies," said the shell of Gus while the real Gus listened, appalled. "I have to have battle casualties to justify my war machine. And I need them quick! People are getting suspicious."

"Why not start a real war. Just shoot them up," observed One.

"What! And blow up my profits with them?" Gus heard himself say. "Wars are expensive!"

"I like you," said One. "What do you want from me?"

"Well, first I have to get rid of these leeches that call themselves Eards," said Gus. He listened to himself admit, without hesitation or reservation, what he had never dared confide to anyone but himself.

"Thousands of them, millions of them. This fake war is just the start, but it got out of hand before I was ready to make my big move. I own that pesthole, pestle to pistol, but I still need the vermin to keep the place running. Eventually I'll get rid of every last one of them. I'd shove them all off the edge of the planet if I could, but for now, I just need to dispose of a few thousand. Anytime this week would be fine." To himself Gus sounded as though that was a very reasonable request.

Gus was, however, shocked. Not at the words, they were true enough. Gus was shocked that he actually said them to one who might use them to advantage. He sure did not feel a need for this blatant up-frontedness and he had long since outgrown any need for adolescent catharsis. Gus' body was totally out of control. He was looking out of a body that went its own way so he could not have been at more of a disadvantage.

One strolled casually over to the bar, mixed a double Old Fashioned, and eased himself into a deep cushioned, wine-colored leather chair. The toga fell gracefully about his portly figure, settling becomingly as though expecting company. The intense blue material was a plush, delicately highlighted cloth with no weave to it. He set the drink on a finely carved gold and granite table Gus had not noticed and considered Gus thoughtfully as he drew easily on a lightly veined cigar. The cigar was very good. One kicked off his leather slippers and plowed his feet luxuriantly through the deep pile of a warm ivory carpet that melted inconspicuously into the crushed rock on which Gus was standing.

Picking up the ten-to-one martini, One motioned to his right, in the direction of the obelisk. It was monolithic rather than masonry. Gus could not see the pinnacle but he could see his name engraved randomly about the seamless marble. There were other names, though none that he recognized, and markings like intertangled felt fibers or a nest of snakes. Gus understood the fibers as time.

Turning to apprehend the breadth of the monument, Gus found it was now a wall that did not end within seeing, but instead returned behind him. The effect was a corridor extending endlessly in both directions with neither a ceiling nor, Gus saw with a rush of vertigo, a floor. Reaching instinctively for One's hand, Gus dropped to his knees, eyes tightly closed. One's reassuring grip calmed him instantly and he opened his eyes to find one wall was now a floor, the other a ceiling. One's three-piece pinstriped suit creased perfectly at the elbow as he raised his iced tea to sip. Gus found that fact intimidating. One looked down.

Gus read the word NOW on the floor, at the tip of One's wingtips, and understood before him lay his destiny, behind his past. A crevasse, a sharp and ominous fissure, crept knowingly through the maze of markings on the floor. It looked for Gus. Its progress was intermittent but inexorable. In the distance beyond, Gus could see massive portions of the monolithic floor drop away into who knows where. Or when. One did not seem to care as he munched a Swiss cheese on rye with some relish. Another slab of the floor fell away.

"What is it worth to you?" asked One after washing down the sandwich with a frosty mug of beer.

"What's it worth?" repeated Gus stupidly, acutely aware of his own parch.

"You have a problem. I can help. I don't work free."

That was clear enough. Gus studied One narrowly, sizing up his tennis whites, the casual ease with which he swung the racquet, and the impending crevasse. Particularly the crevasse that leapt forward with the release of yet another chunk into the abyss. He could feel the squirm of the plane as it adjusted for the strain.

"Well, how about fifty percent the first year, and . . ."

Gus had slipped easily into his pat opener but stopped with a grunt when One side-armed the beer mug at him. Gus did not hear the mug hit the floor but he did feel through his feet that another massive berg had snapped free. The appearance of a second crack from the opposite direction underscored the urgency of the negotiation.

"Can that!" said One with calmly forceful impatience. "What do I need with box tops! What can you *do* for me?"

It was clear that One knew what he wanted but Gus had not a clue. The crunch of the advancing crevassi, now in stereo, suggested to Gus that a more direct approach might be profitable.

"Do not play games," said Gus disdainfully. "You know what you want. You would not have brought me here if I could not provide it. What do you want?"

"I like you," smiled One. "And you are right. I know what I want. You can help me."

"Well?" asked Gus impatiently, between crunches.

"I want Mentor," said One directly. "I have a score to settle."

"What kind of score?" Gus was not sure he really wanted to know.

"That's my business!" said One irritably. Crunch. CRUNCH!!

"Okay, Okay. But how will I be able to do that? I'm no match for Mentor," said Gus honestly enough.

Mentor had an early warning system that was transcendental, renowned for both the havoc it could wreak and its impartiality. Gus violated Mentor's sphere of influence only once and regretted it.

"When the time comes, you will know what to do. Will you do it?" Behind One appeared the splay-toothed grin of a clawed stump with one arm on its forehead.

Gus, spectator that he was, lurched for the controls, yanking knobs and pulling levers in his panic to stop the word he knew was coming.

"Where's the goddam hold button!" he swore to himself. "Don't do it! Don't do it!" he yelled. "He's just baiting the hook! Don't do it!" Gus froze, along with all time, as the body that was Gus finally tripped into destiny.

"Yes," said Gus.

In no more time than it took the sibilance to dissipate, Gus was back in his penthouse, looking up Mentor's zip code.

CHAPTER 6

A Thud Poach

Franklin Crow hardly noticed when the Thud emerged from the ground but his interest was drawn to the scaly creature when it replaced the divot. Franklin would not have noticed it, even then, but for the easy backhand with which the sod was smoothed to its former irregularity. Thuds rarely used the backhand, and then only clumsily. These days the countryside was pockmarked with the open acne of the Thud. It was a rare one indeed that bothered to attempt repair for it seemed they were usually eaten before they half finished. Perhaps that is the reason for the practiced backhand.

At any rate, these thoughts did not interrupt Franklin's concentration; they did not even occur to him. The unusual motion of the backhand swipe, however, did catch his eye. That moment's activity to conceal its birth provided one with the opportunity to pounce on a fresh Thud. It also tipped you off that this was a particularly leisurely and therefore tender young Thud.

So, Franklin's expert eye was drawn to this little brown fellow. While he gathered his wits enough to decide whether to hold his frozen guard over the promising bulge at his feet or dive after this other fastidious but reckless Thud, the Thud winked at him!

It winked again! Then it directed a long world-class raspberry in Franklin's general direction. The racket sent the almost ripe Thud at his feet scrambling back whence it came. Franklin's blood pressure shot high enough to again pass under the belt he cinched up to cut off the circulation to his feet. To finish the performance, the Thud did a remarkably good job of thumbing his nose, considering that he hadn't much of a thumb or a nose to speak of. Or with, for that matter.

Now that was just going too far! Blazes! He could not have cared less when the Thuds began to talk. He was only mildly annoyed when they learned to run. The air or light or something made them go sour so fast every second counted when you had to chase them. Franklin was Regional Champ and was not really handicapped by their mobility, but last week they started demonstrating against the Draft. Before that they wanted voting rights, and before that it was representation on the Rules and Games Commission, and before that . . . Well blazes, he didn't know what. It was a damned nuisance asking one of those little twerps' permission before eating them. How would you like Mandatory Arbitration with a carrot?

The patronizing attitude they took when they submitted was enough to make you repudiate your Immunity! Blazes! That's why he was here in the first place, no Immunity! An Executive out in the woods hunting Thuds! If only they didn't turn sour so fast.

"Well, come on, dum-dum. What's it going to be, him or me?"

Franklin sputtered a broken "Huh?"

Franklin was never particularly fast on the draw but now his righteous indignation at the arrogant Thud gave way to a very unExecutive burst of adrenaline. Franklin was allergic to adrenaline.

"Make up your mind. Are you going to attack or not? I've got an appointment."

The Thud shifted his weight and slouched insolently, an impatient and patronizing expression on his knees.

That did it! Franklin could not stand impatient knees, much less patronizing knees. Elbows maybe, but not knees! He pounced grandly, albeit belly-floppy, on the Thud, just clipping the intonation trailing "It's about time."

He lost interest in the Thud almost immediately, however, just after cracking two ribs on the lumpy ground. Franklin was also allergic to cracked ribs.

The Performance Judge penalized him two points for losing the first Thud, five for squashing the second in what must have been an all-time low in Thudsmanship, and one more for the unbelievably bad form of the belly-flop itself. His dreams of a high point standing, as well as his ribs, were shattered.

Franklin recovered nicely in a few weeks. He set out once again for the woods to recapture the exquisite experience of absolutely devouring the newborn Thud in an almost uncontrollable panic of self-indulgence. During his enforced abstinence in the city, he developed a ferocious and totally distracting need for the little delicacy. Now that he was able to get back to the Thud fields, he was determined to have his satisfaction. It would be a glorious, gluttonous ravaging, unchecked until he lost conscious control and fell into the sated stupor he experienced only once before on his introduction to the delights and mysteries of the Thud.

He stood here again over another slightly undulating mound, desperately trying to maintain control over the increasingly fragile state of his composure. He had to physically overpower his concentration and apply it to the task. He had to maintain perfect quiet while the little Thudlet or Thudy or whatever it was, matured or gestated or whatever it did down there, and finally came into the world on its own. Then the supreme moment. That instant when the Thud acknowledges capture. The ritualistically polite request for Permission to Consume (to satisfy the Law of the Courts). The excitement of the concession. Then the feast!

"Watch it now! You're not being careful. Watch it!" he mouthed ferociously.

"That's better. That's better. Orson said they could sometimes feel your heartbeat or smell your sweat right through the ground," he thought to himself. "He's a little heavy sometimes, but don't take chances anyway. You've waited a long time to get even with that smart Thud with the insolent knees. Take it easy now, here it comes. Easy. Easy."

It might be difficult to imagine Franklin's reaction when the Thud emerged from Mother Earth decked out in bandoleers festooned with hand grenades. In fact, Franklin himself found it difficult to formulate a cohesive course of action. The matter resolved itself quickly enough when the Thud pulled the pin on a grenade. It handed the grenade casually to Franklin and waited curiously for his reaction. This time Franklin had no problem making up his mind. He threw up.

The Performance Judge was a bright and helpful young apprentice who had nonetheless been on probation for overzealousness. He should be commended for reprimanding the Thud (for the disallowed tactic) and Franklin (for defacing public property and/or littering), all while coolly calculating the probability the grenade would go off before the mandatory thirteen-second nonintervention period.

The grenade did go off, to everyone's consternation, at about the fifth "whereas." Only this time, instead of spraying the party with Hawaiian Punch as expected (by the judge and the Thud, but certainly not by Franklin), the party was sprayed all over Hawaii. The Thud's lack of an endoskeleton uniquely qualified it for this effect.

The Performance Judge General Council was not at all happy the Thud had destroyed itself, Franklin Crow, and one promising apprentice judge with a hand grenade. The anxiety subsided, however, when an investigating committee decided the Thud could not possibly have had a grenade. The report must have been an exaggerated misinterpretation of a recurring incident involving an amateur porpoise trainer and an irate husband. This was clearly out of the jurisdiction of the Park Service, so that was about all they could do about it. At least no one *did* anything about it. No one, that is, but Weston Mast. He got himself blown apart too, the same way. In all fairness, though, Weston was hunting mushrooms. Or rather poaching them. And he *had* the Immunity!

We are no longer concerned with wishy-washy Franklin. Or with the grenades for that matter, since they were later ruled a legal tactic on odd numbered days after the Thud went on strike.

CHAPTER 7

Rubb. Just Rubb

Lorga was not particularly happy about the progress of the invasion, but he held his peace while Mollen expanded on the military virtues of his policy of appeasement. His policy so far cost the Pride nearly two hundred thousand of its finest.

The logic behind an attack based on appeasement was beyond him. Moreover, his insistent questioning only revealed publicly his admitted lack of sophistication in military matters. After all, how much is the Minister of Finance supposed to know about war? As Secretary of the Interior, Lorga could not answer that one either.

Considering it took him three days after his election to determine there was no Interior, Lorga, while a bit disgruntled about the whole affair, was not in the least surprised. At least he wasn't up before the Council trying to explain why, in spite of massive outlays in personnel and time, we were winning.

That was a very good question; "What was wrong with winning?" Perhaps the question should have been, "Are we trying to lose?" Or even, "Does it just look like we are winning?" Or, "Am I the only one who thinks we are winning?" Whatever, Lorga was becoming uneasy about the implications of the answers he was hearing.

The matter of Lorga was mooted, however, before these questions were fairly unleashed to seek their answers. Lorga fell asleep at his desk and was swept away by the cleaning lady per the terms of the Domestic Help Act was enacted cheerfully enough while Lorga slept.

By this time it had become obvious that Mollen was not long for his job either. The total collapse of his campaign into an utter peace. The complete demoralization of the opposition's forces. The continued success of the war in spite of every effort. It was just too much! Mollen had to go, and his clutch of advisors with him. All they accomplished in their tenure was to eat the Imperial Hoards and advise their replenishment.

The situation called for action. When you say action, you mean Zerp, a name that has stood for swift decisive action for generations. A name that meant salvation in so many perilous times. A name that strikes fear and awe in the enemies of Eard. A name that means instant retribution to the invader, annihilation to the heretic, justice to the wronged, and a balance of payments surplus. Zerp!

Zerp is not exactly a fully certified household word. The only hard reference to Zerp in anyone's memory was the inaugural invocation that had survived since before Eards counted days; "Remember the Zerp!"

This traditional appeal to the Zerp had always been invoked in a time of crisis but more as a euphemism for "Can the bum!" than as an appeal for intervention by any divinely sentient operative.

This *was* a time of national emergency after all, so the form, if not the actual attempt, must be exercised at once. Although no one seriously believed it had ever happened, the longer the delay, the greater the chance of victory. There was no real debate on the efficacy of the appeal to the Zerp; the point was raised after closing time and the Loyal Opposition was on vacation anyway.

It was thus decided in the wee hours of the second sunrise on the first of Mudge in Grand Assembly of the Entire Elite of East Eard, during the almost holy and certainly rare ceremony of Bull and Barbecue.

Bull referred to the enabling legislation needed to declare a state of Unusual Emergency (as opposed to the Usual Emergency wherein the second course is Prime Minister). Barbecue referred to the face-saving option offered to the cabinet responsible for the emergency. Mollen and his cabinet of relatives and cronies all hailed from the district of Fridiger whose primary export commodity, cronies, were renowned for their barbecueability. This fact explained the Fridigian's typically meteoric rise to power as well as the inevitable declaration of emergency by the legislature.

All the cabinet exercised the option and provided the fare for one of the truly memorable transfers of power in recent history. That is not really saying much since by decree East Eard had nothing but recent history. Mollen himself, however, being the Supreme Commander of all the Eards, felt it beneath his position to submit to the pit, so according to law he was French-fried.

Next in line was a dwarf who practiced witchcraft during half times at athletic events and who was now unemployed after losing his license for malediction. You may have noticed the characters in the story so far tend to be short-lived. Pay close attention to this one. The dwarf's name was Rubb, from Middle Eard.

Rubb received notification of his accession by registered mail. Being generally ignorant of the political situation, and in need of a job, he accepted. This was truly a stroke of good fortune for all Eard. The Middle Eards were very salty and dwarfs were notoriously tough, so a long reign was practically assured. In fact, upon hearing of the attributes of the new Supreme Commander, a movement started among some disgruntled Representatives to impeach the janitorial staff. It failed only because of the domestic help shortage.

Rubb's first duty as East Eard's highest lotteried official was to contact the Zerp.

"What's a Zerp?" was Rubb's first official utterance.

"You're the boss. You're supposed to know these things. Hop to it," he was informed, most respectfully.

Now Rubb was as easygoing a dwarf as you will find these days. He does not get excited much but after many days spent in vain trying to find his office, the executive washroom, or even his own phone number, Rubb was a little put out by the put offs. He was getting the uneasy feeling he was not expected to find the seat of his authority. He was obviously misinformed, diverted, stymied and generally prevented from doing anything at all. Since he hadn't the foggiest what to do anyway, his frustration was complete. The only clue to his duties was the ominous reference in the swearing-in telegram, " . . . and remember the Zerp."

He had long since checked out the telephone directory. No Zerps. He tried asking for Zerps at a tobacconist's shop and at a tavern. No Zerps. It wasn't a patent remedy and it wasn't a disease.

Now in the normal course of events, Rubb was neither normal nor an event. On this occasion, for whatever vagary of the Fates, Rubb became quite unwittingly both an event and, unfortunately, normal.

An event might be the occlusion of a star or the snapping of a twig. In a larger historical context, you might consider the Renaissance an event, or even the current Ice Age. Rubb's ascendancy initiated an event that, in its profound all-encompassing pervasiveness, went entirely unnoticed. Unnoticed as such, you understand, the way the moon's phases subliminally influence the breeding habits of oysters, or residual gravitational waves from the galaxy's origin subtly pervert planetary motions through the stressed ether. Something like that.

The normal part of the whole business was that Rubb, usually the most easy-going of dwarves, reacted in a perfectly normal way. He muttered a formal "What the hell" and did what any easy-going dwarf would do. He would have to talk to Baanquer so he would have to Punt.

You need help to punt. You do not move on Baanquer without covering your proverbial posterior. A confrontation with Baanquer required the composure of a fanatic facing a firing squad, the ethereal logistics of the crossing of the Alps, an awesome expenditure of raw Vaudevillian moxie, and fortuity. Particularly the fortuity.

There was only one man, or whatever, who had ever dealt with Baanquer on even terms face-to-face, or whatever, and survived to tell the tale. That whatever was Rubb's old mentor, Sam Mentor. Sam was a grizzly old wizard who retired from politics in disgust when Rubb, his most promising protégé, decided to go into show business with a traveling ballet troupe and pickpocket ring.

That was more than a century ago and Rubb earnestly hoped the shriveled old hank of horsehide mellowed a bit since. He still winced at the memory of the bolt Mentor leveled on him when he expressed his interest in the stage. Only Rubb's quick reflexes, countering instinctively with a double Exira, saved him from baldness. As it was, his pelt had not lost its kink for nearly three months. Mentor had this thing about going commercial.

So after a hundred years, Rubb was going back to Sam Mentor for help. After all those years on the road with his franchised light show, Rubb was a bit rusty on creative ritual. He needed several days of concerted research and calisthenics to be certain he called up no more than Mentor. One had to be careful not to disturb one of those nightmare things lurking in the limbo repository of the Unworld. These abominations were the result of vendettas, love affairs and more likely than not the novice ineptitude so prevalent today.

Lately he worked almost exclusively in special effects, charms, rainmaking and the like, and he was rather out of practice at conjuring. He was particularly good at special effects and was quite a draw at public events such as festivals and funerals. He was, that is, until being stripped of his ticket. It seems he was involved in a vice/versa ring. Upon being exposed prematurely at an intramural Person Put, he vaporized the referee into a purple cloud. Because of the nice hand he got for the trick, the mandatory sentence of neutralization was commuted to a simple suspension. In any event, the referee had called a poor game and in all likelihood would not have survived the evening.

One had to be careful at conjuring. Rubb had once gotten a bushel of goose down while trying to whip up a steak dinner. Actually, that was due to Rubb's chronic inability to remember zip codes. Another time it was a batch of pre-packaged herbs provided at a discount by old shyster Miim over in South Sop. It turned out Miim had adulterated them, with adults, and what should have been a spectacular implosion at the Standing Pole Vault Finals fizzled like a second hand flashbulb.

After locating Mentor on the charts, preparing the proper rituals and paying up his E and O insurance, Rubb set out for Sam Mentor. This was a greater problem than you might at first suppose. First of all, the federales have been cracking down on the unauthorized use of the frequencies involved. Secondly, Sam Mentor was a congenitally suspicious scoundrel who could sense these things coming before they happened and take evasive action.

Pinning Mentor down was like threading a needle with a cooked spaghettini by giving instructions by semaphore to a hamster with a specific learning disability. The time lapse was fierce; they were in different time confluences and effectively timelining on skew curves. Unless Rubb could compose a massive Chaughtgunne conjurction and sustain it for hours, the venture would likely be a waste of time. But then, Rubb had found, so are pushups.

Forever is a reasonably long time, but to those for whom the word has practical significance it is no time at all. Quite literally just so, no time at all. Rubb is one of these few people who can play hopscotch with eternity and land on their feet, so to speak. Rubb's feet are characteristically large and even more characteristically flat, so that he tends to rebound to an upright position like an inflated punching dummy. That causes problems you cannot imagine. Well, maybe *you* could imagine them.

Rubb had mastered, with Mentor's unwitting help, the unenvied ability to pop out of that property of matter popularly misnomered space-time and into the void from which matter originally leaped.

Unenvied because there is no end to the people who will ask unabashedly for free shows, bilocations, and travel advice with no thought of paying. It was very aggravating to a wizard like Rubb who has more trouble than most maintaining a professional stance.

According to virtually all practitioners of the craft, intermatter travel does not occur. While you read that again, consider that an occurrence is a change in some property of matter that involves an identifiable "before" and a distinguishable "after." These manifest themselves in terms of a quality such as topology, time interval, or spatial aspect, changes that are generally interpreted as the event itself.

However, upon completion an intermatter conjurction leaves an altered "before" that is indistinguishable from its corresponding "after," and so has simply not occurred. Think that does not bug the Feds?

Now Rubb knew no more about the wherewithal of intermatter travel than an equestrian might theorize on horsy metabolism. Rubb could manipulate time and space and do it quite profoundly, if exuberantly. Rubb managed to get where he was going much in the manner of a billiard ball ricocheting about the bumper table, although in all honesty Rubb rather preferred it that way. His success as an entertainer was due in no small measure to his flair for the dramatic, the spectacular and the flamboyant.

This trip was nothing if not flamboyant. Without going into detail about the window-shattering shock that rocked the neighborhood when he jurked into the ether, or the barmaid he singed in South Sop by caroming off a mountain top for a slingshot whip into the yet-to-come, or even the jostled stars that started an ophthalmological boom, it is enough to say that Rubb found Sam Mentor. And surprised him.

Getting the drop on Sam Mentor is a feat still sung about when wizards gather around a campfire to reprise old times. Your guess is as good as any as to when that is, or where. One thing is sure; the wizards never tell.

Sam Mentor felt nothing but the vague uneasiness that might presage a minor belch and had not a whit more time to think about it than has a man before a lightning stroke.

Sam was deviling eggs. When Rubb popped into his kitchen, Mentor found himself instantly suspended like a bat by his claws, which had leaped instinctively to the roof of his cave. His first reaction was surprise that the granite ceiling of his lair was not as hard as it should have been.

This moment's surprise was a lifesaver for Rubb as he bungled the job of releasing his safety belt in spite of hours of practice. By the time Mentor dropped to the floor and Rubb freed himself from the drag chute, they were hurling bolts, Frommelts and curses at each other like they were Bolts, Frommelts and Curses.

To the casual onlooker the battle assumed the awesome aspect of a struggle among the gods themselves. However, the flash and fury of the confrontation was little more than a display of virtuosity such as one might see in a formal fencing duel or a minuet.

Oh, it was serious. And dangerous. One slip and either one would have been nothing more than a ripple in the atmospheric pressure, gently but inexorably entroping into insignificance. In fairness, the reader should understand that the action proceeded according to a carefully defined protocol, much like an oriental tea ceremony or professional wrestling.

Between these two master sorcerers, the battle amounted to little more than a vicious ping-pong game. There was actually little more at stake than their respective psychological edges in the debate that would inevitably ensue.

Since Rubb had indeed gotten the drop on Mentor, Sam was understandably intent on regaining the upper hand any tutor should have with his pupil. Rubb, on the other hand, was certain if he lost his advantage at this critical time he would not only fail in his quest for information but would probably also be permanently marked by the garrulous old bear that was the unforgetting and unforgiving Sam Mentor.

"Take that!" shouted Sam.

"Oh yeah? Take that yourself!" rejoined Rubb.

It should be obvious that while Sam Mentor and Rubb the Dwarf were two legendary exponents of the classic sorcery, both lacked something in extemporaneous speaking. Desperately aware of his shortcomings as a stand-up comic, Rubb had once tried to hire away Sam's old gag writer for his half-time show. He now regretted it ruefully as just one more score to settle. Sam was a bastard about that sort of thing.

After about six hours of fireballs and feints, blue blasts and bolts, tractors, torches, curds and cold cobbles, these most formidable of Eard's sorcerers reduced to flinging half-hearted swear words like prepubescent street urchins.

Rubb half spent himself in launching the surprise conjurction and while he was phenomenal in a sprint, he lacked somewhat in a long haul. Mentor, on the other hand, had always been an endurance man. Nonetheless he was now well past your basic old and obviously rusty at contact sports. Sam realized too late just how long it had been since he had seriously confronted a talent such as Rubb's. In fact, the last real test had been Rubb! One more score to settle!

By this time, they were flipping duds having no more effect than a strong hiccup. Rubb noted with renewed interest that Sam's last shot *was* a hiccup. Rubb had been lobbing ineffectual Whouqshaughts at Mentor and largely lost interest until Mentor emitted the involuntary B-flat peep. Sam had long since retreated into a tidy warp that glowed dully at the prodding but was otherwise unscathed. Rubb gathered his strength and cautiously raised his head to look over the heavy stone table that served as his bastion.

His eyes met those of Mentor who slang over the coat tree for support, one branch hooked in his armpit and another through his belt. Sam was out of the game completely. The only discernible movement in the cave was the lingering reverberation of the Sonic Slurp Rubb had dropped down the chimney some time ago. That attack fizzled when Mentor ducked, rather unfairly. The Slurp itself continued its desultory aggression out of loyalty to Rubb.

Rubb surveyed the scene, the way they always do after a battle, and was no better off for his trouble. For the sake of the reader, however, please note that the room was untouched. The overturned table had been upset a century earlier by a disgruntled lady to whom Sam directed the only romantic overtures of his considerable life. She had casually thrown them back upon learning of Sam's unconventional breakfast habits and ran off with a part-time Vast who turned out to be only half the man she thought he was. The table lay there since that day and certainly as long as Rubb had known Sam Mentor. Every morning when Sam stepped out to bring in the doggerel, he ritualistically tripped over the fool thing out of spite.

Noting that after all was said and done nothing had been said but crisp invective bordering on cliché, nothing done but a thorough reshevelment of a half-eon accumulation of dust frosting the low ceiling beams around which Rubb had looped his famed Spirogyro Slider prompting Mentor to retaliate with his proportionately, albeit inversely, obscure Sneeze (which would have been completely ineffective but for foxy old Sam's uncanny awareness of the pollen count), Rubb realized that he was pooed, squared. So he fell asleep. You may not believe that Rubb could fall asleep at this point, but he would not have sought your sanction in any event. He did fall asleep and that's that.

Edward W. Ramsell

Feel free to parse that last paragraph for whatever perverted pleasure it might provide. But be forewarned that it is carefully constructed according to ancient and forbidden formulae handed down for at least three weeks by generations of Weaxs, ministers in an infamous cult in Lower Lubb about which virtually nothing is known. Whatever decision you make about your own course of action, the author accepts no responsibility.

CHAPTER 8

The Confrontation

Rubb awakened with a stop. That is, when sneaky old Sam stuffed a pair of sneakers into Rubb's mouth, his respiration stopped.

Umph!" umphed Rubb.

"Ah!" replied Sam with some satisfaction. "All right, out with it!" Mentor could not help sniggering at the play on words as he imagined Rubb's reaction to that imperative.

"Oogump snerk," was Rubb's obvious and appropriately obscene reply.

"I thought so."

Actually, Sam had not the foggiest, but considering Rubb's uninvited invasion, which had caught him completely by surprise, Sam was certainly within his rights to play an indignant role. He pursued the advantage accordingly.

Sam paced back and fro imperiously, contemplating the fate of the gasping lump in the middle of the parlor. The pair of tennys in Rubb's mouth was custom made for Sam's feet, with open toes to accommodate the claws. That feature allowed Rubb to maintain consciousness, but hyperventilating through crud-encrusted canvas sneakers blistered his tongue, which in turn caused the desperate gasping. The overpowering scent of Sam's foot powder only added olfactory insult to injury.

Sam's absent pacing was beginning to bug Rubb. He walked with a disconcertingly irregular patter, like water dripping from an eaves pipe during light drizzle or even more like a child's wooden block tumbling down a stairwell. There wasn't a single expected step.

"Clipclopticdunkiduptikdop . . ." On and on like that.

Rubb was almost beside himself in a frustrated rage when it occurred to him to do just that, Beside himself. Besiding was an ancient defensive posture of the Id that dislocated the ether and bilocated the provocateur, the cabalistic equivalent of patting your head and rubbing your tummy. The problem for Rubb was this rite involved reciting a litany of two-lettered words that was tedious under the best of circumstances and nearly impossible with sneakers in your mouth, the open toes notwithstanding.

Luckily, Rubb was saved the trouble when Mentor kicked him smartly in the back of the head, dislodging both the shoes and his snap-on bow tie. His relief was immediate and immense, as was the pain.

Rubb flopped across the floor either like a rag doll or a large wad of bread dough. He stopped slupped up against a post with his feet in the air and his shoulders curled about his head, pinning it against the floor. He kicked the air a few times to dislodge himself from this undignified position and slid to his back looking directly up into a glower that made him wince, then cringe.

"Hoowww commmme iss yooouuu HEEEER!!" An impossibly deep thundering basso profundo shook the very marrow of Rubb's bones and loosened two fillings.

Mentor had a voice that came from overhead no matter where he stood, as though from a loudspeaker on a great boom. In fact, Sam once seriously considered a contract from a movie studio as a voice-over for some obscure deity or another. Sam was so insulted by this blatant appeal to commercialize his hyper-attenuated voice he turned the agent into the potted violet that still sits on his windowsill.

The impression stuck, however, and after an appropriate interval to soothe his injured pride, maybe fifteen or twenty minutes, Sam indiscriminately assaulted everyone within earshot. In a remarkably short time, he was simply insufferable. Mentor got over that phase eventually and only pulled the trick out when the occasion called. The occasion had definitely called.

Rubb had prepared for this moment by listening to 78 rpm records played at 33 but he had forgotten just how effective Sam's voice could be. Or he had underestimated just how mad Sam would be. Probably both.

"IIII Sssaaiid . . ." began Sam righteously, his brow furrowed and arched like a grizzly.

"Aww, knock it off Sam," shot back Rubb with a carefully planned expression of pain and exasperation, touched with barely suppressed indignation.

This proved remarkably effective in spite of Rubb's being on his back at the time. Rubb prepared this particular expression as a last ditch defensive move and practiced it hanging by his toes, under water, and while eating Wheaties. He had not tried it on his back.

"Golly Sam! I sure get tired of that echo chamber effect. Haven't you learned any new tricks?!"

Sometimes Rubb did not know when to quit, but he did this time and held his gaze on Sam Mentor, awaiting his fate.

"Gosh Rubb, I didn't . . . Now just a minute! You . . . I . . ."

Sam sputtered to a stop and noted consternatedly that his voice had risen in pitch about three octaves. He took a few moments to shift his vocal cords back into low gear, gather his thoughts, and choose a few pithy remarks. Just for the effect, he gave Rubb a pithy kick in the ribs.

After a bit of thought, Sam's face lit up as he formulated Rubb's premature demise. Mentor pulled himself to his full height, about six inches off the floor, and prepared a Nolte Slobova, a curse guaranteed in writing to wilt any will to resist. Sam did not intend to be bested by this beasty, this sawed-off stump of a man who left him a century ago as a cocky apprentice with theatrical aspirations and who now returned in a flash and a flourish that even Sam had to admire for its audacity if not its finesse.

Sam concentrated his energies, generating the necessary bevatron potential behind his left frontal lobe. Rubb could see the telltale aura arise about his head and realized that he was doomed. His mind raced, his glands oozed, his nerves steeled, his eyes winced and his gulper gulped.

"Zerp!" shouted Rubb, with all his heart.

Sam somersaulted with the recoil of the pulled Slobova, and stood for a dumbfounded hour. Fully an hour. The word Zerp had so jolted Sam that he momentarily relaxed his grip on the ether. The Nolte Slobova, which should have reduced Rubb to a mass of mumbling metabolism, recoiled like a snapped rubber band, rapping Mentor in the Id such a blow!

While Mentor stood stunned, Rubb rejoined the nap that Sam had interrupted with his belch. On awakening, Rubb bathed, pressed his suede pantsuit in the treadle-powered mangle in the corner, and fixed a light lunch for Mentor and himself. Rubb recalled from his years living with Mentor that the best way to get Sam out of bed in the morning was with a big plate of hot tamales. That was the light lunch, genuine East Eardian hot tamales garnished with whoopee peppers.

"You remembered." Sam came to with a silly grin and a whimper. Upon fully regaining his composure, he melted into tears. "You remembered," he blubbered.

"There, there, Sam, I know," consoled Rubb, a barely concealed smirk of merriment on his chin.

The formalities over with, they sat down to the hot tamales and wine. The tang of the tamales loosened Sam's tongue a bit and his spirits rose as he downed the spirits. Warming to the occasion, and to the peppers, Sam ventured a nostalgic comment.

"I often wondered how you had been getting along, Rubb. How have things been?"

"Good, Sam. Good. A few dry spells along the way, heh, heh. I get along." Rubb paused to appreciate Sam's wince, then proceeded.

"When I left a century ago, I had my heart set on the Chautauqua circuit. That did not work out so well. The only job I could get was laying down smoke screens when things got dicey. It got so that dicey was daily. The boss, some banana named Fmafc, pedaled a fermented chard brew during intermissions. I tried a sip once and I could not focus my eyes for three minutes. He sold a pretty good blend the first night, then switched in the rotgut when the Gilbies weren't looking. After the paralysis wore off the usual reaction was vengeance. That's where I came in and we got out.

"That grew old quick, so I set out on my own. Well actually, they set out without me one night after I resurrected a few old friends for a card game and the old cadavers drank up his stock of hard chard. The note said, 'Roses are red, Violets are blue, get lost.'

"I sort of fell into Commercial Artz to pay regular rent. I worked up a pretty good act and syndicated. Outside of losing my ticket a while back, I've done well . . ." Rubb paused thoughtfully, trying to find the best way to break the news to Sam. "Now I'm Prime Minister."

Sam excused himself politely, but quickly, as he fought off the attacking peppers. He spilled them on his leg when Rubb casually dropped that bombshell and was frantically beating them down before they defurred his left leg.

Presently an interested flip of Sam's tail told Rubb the situation was again under control and to continue. Sam smoothed the still smoldering fur on his femur, dumped the aroused peppers into a deeper bowl, and turned his attention to Rubb.

"And I still don't know what the inaugural telegram meant," said Rubb with a scowl. "Remember the Zerp. That's . . ."

Sam was ready and got his leg out of the way in time. The sparks so startled him he upset the table and had the Devil's own time catching the tamales before they scurried down the holes and niches in the walls of the cave. Sam thought he had succeeded in suppressing the pain of the slipped Slobova, and the word that caused it, but he was still edgy. Once setting things aright, Sam tossed back a shot of Pennzoil to calm his nerves, settled himself on the floor in the center of an open area, and looked around for any other hazards.

"Now, tell me Rubb. How is it you know of the Zerp?" he asked very carefully.

Rubb handed him the inaugural wire and waited a moment for Sam to read it.

"Now you know everything I know. I'll bet a whole lot more. I've never seen Slobova whiplash like that. Does it still hurt?"

"No!" snapped Sam. But it hurt and it showed.

"Well anyway, that's all I know. I looked into everything I could think of. All I get is a blank stare or a fierce take like yours but no information. I could not care less about some fool Zerp but as I told you, here I am Prime Minister and I can't even find my own office. I haven't the foggiest about my duties. I'll take that back. I do have the foggiest. I think there is a war somewhere but I don't know where, with who, or over what. I think there is a cabinet. The last I heard about them they attended a banquet and were never seen again. And I guess there is supposed to be a key to the executive rest room. That's it."

"This I was afraid of. They've infiltrated!" muttered Sam angrily. He fingered the telegram figuratively.

"What? Who's infiltrated? And what did they infiltrate? And who's they?" Rubb could not contain himself at the thought of hard information. Sam knows!

"Easy Rubb. One at a time. I do not think I can really answer your questions. I only have a few inklings, glimpses now and then across time and space while experimenting with telekinesis. And I watch the 10:00 p.m. news. There are a few things that have started to form a pattern and I put together a rough working hypothesis. What you tell me fits in perfectly. I do not know anything for sure, only guesses."

"That's more than I have. What can you tell me?" enthused Rubb, inching closer on his stump.

"Well, we *are* at war, but we do not know it. We think we are at war when we are not. That's why things only seem confusing."

"Uh-HUNH," humphed Rubb. "I see." He didn't.

"Put it this way. We are at war, but not with who we think we are. Whom? Who."

Sam rubbed his forehead with the back of his foot and considered his next words carefully as he was cursed by a chronically hostile syntax.

"We are winning the war we think we're waging and we're losing the war we don't know anything about. The problem is it only appears we are winning the known war on the one hand, and we have less than an inkling about the other."

Rubb started to pack his things, beginning with the parachute, mumbling something about senile old curmudgeons and their home brew.

"Thanks for the lunch, Sam. It's been nice talking over old times. Well, I see by the old clock on the wall it's . . ."

"SSSSITTTTT DOOOOOOWWWWWN!!!" rumbled Mentor. Rubb sat.

"Now listen and listen tight."

Sam imposed his best Waynese and paused for a dramatic moment, visibly impressed with himself. Rubb spoiled it all with an inadvertent well-placed smirk. Rubb smirked a lot, given a pomposity to puncture.

"Well, uh, here's the way I see it anyway," continued a muted Mentor, "but it's just speculation. The Phroggs are trying to take over. I think they are trying to establish a military-industrial complex that will dominate and permeate all Eard. Soon they will own all of Eard. All of it."

Rubb only stared.

CHAPTER 9

The Secret Revealed!

Rubb eased back into the corner where he crouched, lowered his chin to his knees and thought. He knew about Phroggs! They had long ago taken control of the Entertainers Protective Association, and protected them out of their pension fund. He didn't see the exact connection but he was all ears. In fact, Rubb had heroic ears.

"It's Phrogg money behind every MP," mumbled Mentor, "and if the Phroggs say we're at war, we're at war. I'm sure Phroggs control the whole military industry from basic resources up to the Minister of Defense. They've been cleaning up."

"I know. I know," concurred Rubb, "but that's not infiltration. That's the way it's always been!"

"Well, that's not the way it is! And not even the Phroggs know it!" Sam started to say something, " . . .", but didn't and settled into a thoughtful scowl.

"Sam, you're talking in circles. Do you know anything or not?" Rubb could sense Mentor's genuine puzzlement, and wanted to believe he really had something. But golly!

"Again Sam, slow."

"Look, let me tell you about some of the pieces I've picked up over the years. See if you can make any more of it than what I've just told you."

He closed his eyes and contemplated the veins of his eyelids from the inside while he formed a big picture of the last two decades.

"I first realized something was wrong when I conjured up a few ancestors for old times' sake and up popped a buck private in the Eardian National Armee. No ancestor of mine, I'll tell you! There's never been an Eard in my escutcheon and I never . . . Aah!"

Sam recalled Rubb was an Eard upon being kicked in the shin, temperately, under the table.

"As I was saying. I don't seem to recall any Eard in the family so I knew this apparition was either a slipped digit in the channel index or interference from some amateur diddling. 'What are you?' I said. He said, 'Never mind, I have an appointment'."

Sam stopped significantly.

"An appointment?"

"That's what he said," muttered Sam. "Now where would an apparition be going? And who could it have an appointment with besides me? Before I could ask, he walked off. Walked off! I watched him until he was a quarter of a mile down the road. He did not vaporize, he didn't fade, and he didn't nothing. He just walked off!"

"He was real?"

"He was real. Solid as this post," said Sam with a desultory left hook to the massive stone column in the center of the room.

The post had been hewn of living stone when Sam carved this cave in one tumultuous day back in his early Numismatic period. It was earlier than Rubb could remember, and whenever that golden day was, the post was as solid now as the day it formed of the chaos of creation.

"But that can't be! Transformations are real, and sometimes permanent. But conjurctions? Never! Uh . . . How did you do it?" said Rubb, a greedy glimmer in his eye.

Even now, Rubb could not help keeping his eyes open for new tricks for his act. Solid real-life conjurctions would be a sensation! He could start a whole new career with that! Just think . . .

A gruff throat clearing shook him from his reveries, however, a rasp Sam had honed to a fine edge.

"Get those ideas out of your head! I cannot tell you how I did it because I did not do it. I checked and double-checked the charts. I tried fresh brews and fermented stews. I tried everything I could think of, everything in the book trying to recreate the same conditions. I even tried an Anomalous Anopheles!

"It never worked again. At least I could never duplicate it again myself. But it did happen again, while I was working on a new spell to fix that old wart hog of a wizard down in the hollow."

"Are you still feuding with him? asked Rubb. "I thought you two had come to a truce long before I . . . ah . . . moved out on my own."

Rubb well remembered the vicious rivalry between these two, back when he was just a tad apprenticed to Sam by his father. Lordy could he remember! Rubb recalled with a shiver the small war that erupted between the White wizards and the Black, a war ending only when revenue from admissions and syndication dried up from media overexposure. Apparently, Mentor and his rival down the road never finished their private battle. Rubb suspected there was a female involved somewhere, something you never brought up with Sam Mentor.

"You say you conjured another private? Accidentally again?"

"No, not another. A regiment!" Sam shook his head. "I don't know what would have happened if I had been working inside."

"A regiment! That's impossible! Why, the mass ratios alone . . . And the volume of space involved would be out of the question!" Rubb hesitated, then brightened.

"What's the gag, Sam. You trying out a new comedy act, or what?"

"All right, all right. That did not happen. Have it your own way," said Sam petulantly. "But there was still another time, same sort of deal. Rank and file they came, rank and file. Hundreds of them. They just kept coming.

"This time they popped into my interface and then popped back out into I don't know where. Pop! Pop! Pop! Like watching a shooting gallery. They came on for half a day, until my interface faded. Then they just stopped, no fade-out or dissipation. One rank popped out and no more followed. I don't know if they were the last, or my brew reached the hardball stage, or what.

"I tried everything I could while they were coming. I could not stop them, start them, speed them up, slow them down, change their color or anything. Their legs didn't move, or their arms. They didn't walk, they just moved like they were standing still and I was moving." Sam ground to a grudging halt.

"I'd like to do that myself. What did you use?" Rubb strongly suspected the Pennzoil Sam had been chugging with some abandon.

"Dammit, Rubb! That is what I keep telling you. I did not do it! I . . . did . . . not . . . do . . . it!" Sam composed himself.

"I was doing a little research into a patron's family tree. You know, raising the dead and the sort. I've done it a thousand times. It's a package, a potboiler. These guys just walked into the picture by themselves. And so help me, they were real!"

Sam finished off a magnum of 10w30, and sulked back into the niche in the wall under the hubcap collection of his youth. If he had a thumb, he would have sucked it then and there, Rubb or no Rubb.

Rubb considered everything Sam said and his conviction in saying it. He finally allowed Sam knew what he was talking about but he could think of nothing better to say than "What about the Zerp?" So he said it.

"What about the . . . ?"

"I know, the Zerp. Well, I'll tell you, I don't know. I don't know anything for sure, just ideas. But let's go back to the Phroggs.

"You know they push the economy any way they want. Sometimes they do it right out in the open, like the time they invaded the grocery stores like a swarm of locusts and ate up all the merchandise to put them out of business. A few got shot, sure, but they got what they wanted, a monopoly on food.

"Other times they move indirectly, like what they did to the paper punch makers. They got control of all the paper works, pre-punched everything in sight, and left the paper punchers with nothing to do. They never knew what hit them until too late. I had a cousin who went down the drain on that one; he put everything he had into confetti.

"That's what the Phroggs are trying to do now, take over and make a killing, but indirectly." Sam paused for emphasis. "They started a war. What's worse, we think we're winning!"

"Started a war?! But only the Prime Minister . . . Oh." Rubb thought hard about that, and came to the only conclusion he could.

"That's why the last Prime Minister disappeared! And that's why I can't find my office. But what happens when we win the war? We'll be right back where we started, won't we?"

"I thought I told you," muttered Sam with unexaggerated exasperation. "We only think we're winning the war. At least the Phroggs are pretending we are winning. There really isn't a war, you know. It's all on paper." Sam knew he would have to wait a minute for Rubb so he folded his arms and let it sink in.

"Now wait a minute! Let's say they start an imitation war, on paper. Why? To sell war stuff to the government?" Sam nodded. "At inflated prices, I presume. How long has all of this been going on?" said Rubb with a suspicious narrowing of the eyes.

"At least twenty years," replied Sam.

"Twenty years!" Rubb gulped. "OK, OK. Now the only way to make money in war is blow up as much as possible as fast as possible and then sell more to replace it. Rubb rose in animation and inflection as his train of thought picked up speed. Right?"

"Right."

"Then where did twenty years' worth of war material go? We'd be up to our noses in the stuff by now. Come to think of it, I haven't seen a soldier since I was a kid. In fact, the last time was when the Armee intervened in your feud with the Black Wizards. Yeah, how about the soldiers, where are they!?" said Rubb in triumph.

"First the war material," began Sam. "That's all on paper. The cabinet approves the budget, the congregation approves the expenditures, the orders are placed with the Phroggs, the raw materials are ordered, the shipments are made, and all on paper of course. The arms are manufactured and delivered, on paper, and the receipts are all duly signed. The trucks and guns are shipped out to the war zones and are consumed or lost in the heat of battle. All on paper.

"In reality, after the first few years when they probably really did manufacture arms, all of the supplies are simply recycled, sold to the government over and over. That's where all the war materials go, round and round."

"I see," said Rubb, who actually did. "And the Phroggs are in all the right places to see that the paperwork is correct."

"I think you've got it," praised Sam.

"But . . . but . . . What about the soldiers? They would sure know what's going on. The Phroggs can't recycle them! Yeah, what about the soldiers!" Rubb was getting a little petulant.

"Think, you . . . you Sop! What are you doing here?" Sam was genuinely ticked. "Why did you come to me in the first place?" he added in an aggressively patronizing tone.

"Well, I have this little problem with this new job. You see, I . . ." Rubb was cut off by an impatient wave of Sam's tail.

"I know. I know. Nobody will tell you anything," said Sam. He began to warm, like a trainer who could see an old dog about to learn a new trick. "Particularly not about the war. Why is that do you suppose?"

"They're all in with the Phroggs!" Rubb was visibly pleased with himself. After a moment he added, "But what about the soldiers?"

Sam just sat and burned a drilling scowl through Rubb. Rubb started to think fast because it started to hurt. Sam had almost decided he did not want a dullard like Rubb around the place after all when Rubb erupted into speech.

"The soldiers in your conjuration!" Rubb felt the release of the slow burn instantly, and flexed a few joints in relief.

"Good, Rubb. Good. The soldiers are simply displaced into the ether and never seen again. Battle casualties."

"But who can do that? So many!" Rubb knew the answer before he even finished these words. "Baanquer?"

"Baanquer."

"Then there really isn't a war?" Rubb asked hopefully.

"Not that one. However, you are at war, Mr. Prime Minister. Even the Phroggs do not know it. And you're losing."

"How's that again?" Rubb thought the matter was settled.

"Where do you suppose those soldiers are going? On a picnic? They have to go somewhere and when they get there what will happen?"

"Don't they sort of, uh, go away?" suggested Rubb.

He had never tried a real discharge before. Transformations, yes. Those are real crowd pleasers, but any hack could imitate a discharge with mirrors so there was no market for it. Besides, Rubb really did not like to think about what happened to someone who was discharged. It did not sit right with him.

"The ones I saw were real. Everything must be somewhere."

"You mean all of those soldiers are actually, really in true-life in some real place?" He guessed that summed it up pretty well. How else do you ask such a question?

"That pretty well sums it up," replied Sam. "They really are somewhere."

"Where?"

Sam brushed his mustache against the grain, then back again. "I don't know," he said, "but somebody is sure mad as Hell about it."

"They're fighting back?"

"We're losing."

"How do you know we're losing?" asked Rubb, honestly.

"You tell me how we can win a war we don't even know about," said Sam, irrefutably, trailing off into thoughtful reflection.

"I don't know," said Rubb much later, and very quietly.

"Well Mr. Prime Minister," said Sam after a mutual hour spent watching the embers in the wrought iron embrasure reduce themselves to a hot, red, ashy mass. "What are we going to do about it?"

"We?"

"There are only two people in the world who know," said Sam quietly, noting the cornered expression on Rubb's face. "We."

"Do you have an idea where to start? Baanquer?" Rubb seemed resigned to his fate.

"Baanquer. And?" coached Sam.

"And the Zerp!" brightened Rubb. "Say, what in the ever lovin' three-toed world is a Zerp anyway. Dag bung it, Sam, you never did tell me." Rubb didn't need any more blanks.

"They are the ones who are winning," pronounced Sam.

"That was the right answer," thought Rubb.

CHAPTER 10

The Die Is Cast

"That's what I came for." Rubb resumed the conversation in a confident mood in spite of his feelings. "To find out about the Zerp. I figured if you didn't know, you could make connections with Baanquer for me."

"You came here looking for Baanquer?!" Sam could only stare, and did. "You were looking for Baanquer?" he repeated.

Sam regained control, telling himself that it was one thing to be redundant, quite another to repeat yourself. He gave voice to his standard SOB countenance.

"You poor son . . ."

"OK, OK. Knock it off. You said yourself that Baanquer is flying that Armee. And you are the only one alive who has ever dealt with Baanquer. What else can I do?" Rubb was impressed with the conclusiveness of his argument and avoided belaboring the point only with some difficulty.

"Did you try quitting?" replied Sam. "Or maybe just pretending it isn't there?"

Sam really had little to do with the world of the flesh and viewed it with an unbounded indifference. This last remark was offered to Rubb as a valid alternate course of action rather than as a cop-out. Rubb knew it was meant as a genuinely helpful suggestion but the lingering SOB on Sam's face left an abrasive aftertaste.

"No, I didn't try quitting! Would you?"

"Yes."

It was a matter of honor with Sam to quit an untenable situation, gracefully or otherwise, preferably before the tenables ran out.

"Well, I'll quit when I'm ready. When I'm good and ready," said Rubb violently. "But golly whiz Sam, I haven't even started yet. If I don't do something, who will? And if I cannot do anything with your help, what can I do without it? And what could someone else do that I can't?

"Someone's up to something, we both know that. So whatever is going to happen will happen unless we do something. At least we ought to find out whether whatever is going to happen is good or bad, and for who. Whom? Who. Besides, if someone is messing up your business you have a stake in this too. And one more . . ."

Sam largely lost interest in the one-sided conversation until that last point jerked a string.

"That's true. True. It hasn't interfered much, but if this is just the beginning . . ." Sam knew that it was, and pondered the consequences, nodding agreement.

"What now?" asked Rubb. It was one of those questions that come to mind when you are not sure exactly what to do next.

Rubb frequently felt at a loss for words but could usually fake it with sleight of hand or a pratfall. Neither seemed appropriate, partly because of the lack of audience and partly because Mentor had already seen most of his ace razzle.

He had, in fact, taught much of it to Rubb as a last-ditch measure when all else failed. Rubb used it intemperately, of course, along with everything else in his repertory. He did not want to alienate Mentor unnecessarily by displaying his betrayal of a sacred trust through a polished technique that could only come from years of indiscriminate indulgence. Rubb had a developed a terrific pratfall that was completely disarming and wanted a chance to try it out on Sam. But until now, he had consoled himself knowing that the time would come, the time would come.

"How the Hell should I know?" fired back Sam with a wisp of smoke curling from beneath his toenails.

SPLAT!!!

The time had come, and Rubb hit the deck with an unbelievably authentic three-point belly flop that completely disarmed Mentor, put out his toes and visibly rattled him. The rattle sounded more like a giggle.

"I had that coming, Rubb. Nice prat. Didn't that hurt?" Sam knew darn well it hurt and the synthetic sympathy did not fool Rubb a bit.

"I forgot just how clumsy you can be when you try."

Rubb strained to ignore the patronization Sam had thinly veiled in sarcasm and concentrated on not revealing how much it had indeed hurt. In trying to outdo himself, Rubb had outdone himself.

Rubb raised himself to his full short, maintaining all the while a disinterested air of unconcern in spite of the pain, and paused dramatically.

"At the risk of seeming redundant, now what?"

It really was a grand performance and Mentor was really impressed. Really. After making a mental note of the technique and the timing, Sam considered the worth of the question carefully. Knowing his answer's importance to Rubb, Sam resolved to reply in a manner befitting the occasion.

"How the Hell should I know," he uttered softly.

This time it was a well-mannered academic response to a well-reasoned inquiry, without the smoking toes or the flaring nostrils. Sam simply did not know.

"Well, it's not that I don't know, exactly," reconsidered Sam. "The only alternative I can think of has virtually no chance of helping, and will almost certainly destroy us."

Almost certainly sounded disturbingly final. Rubb tried to clarify prospects a bit.

"How almost is almost?" he asked, bracing himself mentally.

"It has never worked before," replied the old wizard irrefutably.

"How often has it been tried?" pursued Rubb.

"It has never been tried," said Sam, as though to a child in a book lesson.

"Never . . . ? Why hasn't it been tried?"

"Because," enunciated Sam carefully, "it will not work." Sam was not getting through to Rubb that he did not intend to destroy himself, a problem he attributed to a chronic cross-species communications dysfunction.

Rubb, despite his lack of sophistication in classical debate, was becoming more than frustrated by his inability to break this circumlocution. He knew the old troll was an archconservative and never bet on anything but a sure thing, relatively speaking. But this run-around had the distinct odor of old chicken about it and Rubb knew the possibility would never have been broached if that hoary hunchback hadn't intended that Rubb try it, however ill-advisedly.

"OK, OK. Skip it. Got any other ideas?" asked Rubb innocently, catching a glimpse of a glaring glance that slipped from Sam unsquelched.

"That was it!" thought Rubb to himself. "He does want me to try it!"

"No!" reacted Sam, a little too quickly and in too high a pitch.

"Rats!" thought Sam Mentor to himself. "He got me."

"All right, Sam. Let's have it. You have some idea and I want to hear it. Whatever it is, it can't hurt to talk about it, can it?"

Rubb knew the answer to that before he finished the question; no, it would not hurt at all.

"Certainly my boy, certainly. You're just too foxy for an old man like me. I can't keep anything from you, can I."

His foxy old leer did not do anything to allay Rubb's suspicion. But no matter. Sam had a built in leer that dated back to the day he walked into a pointy tree branch. He had been momentarily distracted by an otherwise unobtrusive Siren whose only other attribute, by the way, was a badly executed riffle shuffle.

"What I had in mind," continued leering old Sam Mentor, "was a visit to the Zerps!"

Sam smugged smirkly, relishing the reactions displayed in turn across Rubb's stomach: surprise, incomprehension, comprehension, suspicion, fear and finally hay fever.

"Let's go take a good look at them up close."

"When do we start," enthused Rubb with a perfunctory sneeze.

"You mean you want to go?"

"That's why I came to you in the first place, the Zerps."

Now that things were starting to firm up Rubb was genuinely anxious to go, and had completely forgotten the dire consequences Sam intimated would almost certainly occur.

"I'll collect my things."

"Wait a minute. Wait a minute!" Sam paused to collect his own thoughts. "I thought I told you it never worked before. That's pretty stiff odds."

"If it's never been tried before, how are you so certain that it can't be done? Where are the Zerps anyway? What do we have to do to get there?" Rubb was starting to act hurt, like a child who cannot have his own way.

"I don't know, to all three questions. However, I do know we are at war with them and they are winning. Do you want to drop in on a war no one has ever returned from?" That sounded simple enough even for Rubb.

"No one has ever returned from!? Returned from! Then someone has gone there! I thought you said it has never been done before." Rubb was agitated.

"Remember those soldiers that popped in on my conjurction? That must be where they went, to the Zerps as far as I can figure it. But I had no control over it. I tried. Believe me, I tried. Not a single one has ever returned to tell the tale. I have spent years trying to track down any leads, to find out anything at all about them. However, I have never found so much as a rumor. They never come back. Period."

Rubb had to stop and think about that. There was something basically wrong with the logic and that old hank of hair either missed it or was keeping it a secret. Rubb peeled a rock and munched it pensively while Mentor swept up the debris from dinner. Finally Rubb stirred.

"Those soldiers. Where did they come from?"

"They were Eards. I told you that."

Sam went back to knitting a shawl of small purple lizards, apparently unexcited by the question.

"Eards. Eards. Then they came from Eard." Rubb was not too sure what he was saying but that never bothered him much. He pressed on. "East Eard. Right?"

"What? Yes, yes," muttered Mentor, along with a vicious expletive to celebrate a dropped stitch.

"And you didn't do nothing?"

"I couldn't do a thing," corrected Sam. "I've had better luck holding back the tide."

"Then these soldiers were going to the Zerps by themselves?"

It was a good question, and all things considered, deserved an answer.

"No, of course not!"

Sam set aside his task and focused his attention on the dwarf. Rubb seemed about to say something stupid again and Sam did not want to miss it.

" . . ."

Rubb closed his mouth before he opened it, reconsidered, and pressed on.

"Then there *is* someone who can do it. Maybe you can't do it and I can't do it, but someone is doing it."

"You know, you're right."

Sam Mentor, surprised at his own admission and struck in turn by its magnitude, sat slightly ajar.

"And if someone else can send a battalion of soldiers to the Zerps, we ought to be able to send ourselves!"

Rubb was positively elated at the idea, and began sorting mentally through his most likely recipes.

"Now where is that old tome that used to be up here, the one with the appendix on inorganic biology?"

Sam grabbed Rubb by the scruff of the neck and jerked him down off the bass fiddle he was climbing to reach the top shelf of the library. While Rubb slowed to a gentle swing at the end of Sam's arm, Sam carefully explained the situation.

"Getting there is only half the problem. It seems that it can be done after all. However, no one has ever returned, do not forget that. We do not know what happens there. We do not know why those soldiers never came back. We do not know what a Zerp even looks like, much less what it might do to us. And we are at war with them."

For emphasis, Sam let Rubb drop to the floor like a damp rag.

"Then you won't help," sighed Rubb resignedly.

"Of course I'll help, you sawed-off toad."

"You'll go? But I thought . . ."

Rubb was cut off by an impatient flip of Sam's tail, which commanded surprising authority for a tail.

"Who said anything about *my* going?"

Some questions inspire answers, others discourage them. Rubb was not inspired.

"Unh, I get it. I go alone. I take all the chances and you get the credit for writing it up in one of those cabalistic journals you're always reading." Rubb, feeling justifiably betrayed, blurted out, "Well then I'll go alone, dammit! You hear? Alone!" Rubb stood tall and folded his arms in defiance of the fates.

"You're on!" piped Sam, a bit too quickly for good taste.

Rubb did not know the meaning of the word intrepid, along with many other perfectly unreasonable words. If he had known, he would have been the first to admit he was not intrepid. Stupid is what he would say, or maybe dunder-headed, but definitely not intrepid. However, being largely ignorant of the real hazards involved and lacking the imagination to fabricate a prudent supply of alternates, Rubb resolved to go on alone simply to save face.

"Nobody can say Rubb is chicken. No sir! When I return, I'll put together an act no one will ever top! It'll be worth that." Rubb thought to himself for a moment, then added, "But you'll help?" Rubb knew that he would, if for no other reason than to see Rubb get his.

"I will, on one condition."

Sam selected a vintage non-detergent, poured a saucerful, and offered another to Rubb.

"And that condition is that if we come through this with our Psyches, you'll return to your old position here and take over the trade."

Rubb accepted the saucer, deftly slipped the lubricant to a potted octopus that had been making overtures to him all evening, and assented with a desultory shrug.

"Do I have a choice?" The plaintive quaver in his voice was particularly effective, and embarrassed both of them.

"When do we start?" said Rubb in renewed high spirits.

"We already have," replied Sam Mentor with a suspicious study of the dwarf who had just undertaken to save the world.

Sam smiled. In fact, Sam grinned a grin that welled from his solar plexus, a grin that smothered Rubb with a stifling impression of demoniacal collusion, mixed with a little checkmate. The grin persisted through the dinner of charcoal briquettes and AFT aperitif.

Rubb noticed it was still on Sam's face when he awoke before Sam to let out the Fuzzie-Wuzzies.

CHAPTER 11

Final Countdown

One day they began, inauspiciously, and certainly cautiously. Which day is not important and no one knows its date anyway. There was a day when they found themselves at work on their task, a day following one when they were not.

It was not until after Sam and Rubb had tied on one monumental rip-roaring drunk. Impending anathema has an hypnotic quality about it that revels in the raw exhilaration found only in the knowing defiance of Fate. But Sam and Rubb cared nothing for that; they were scared so they got drunk, and felt much better for it.

That done, the work simply began one morning while the sun was on its way uphill towards dawn, while even the nocturnal beasties were sated and through for the night. Crickets had long since given up prospects of whatever they chirp for, or else had got it. Small birds rustled a bit but did not wake. And the glistening dew, reflecting in myriad the sharp pointy crescent of the new moon, made Rubb's feet wetter than Hell when he went out to relieve himself.

Unable to sleep with wet feet, Rubb began reading by the warm fire and slowly organized his thought around the immediate problem. Baanquer. Who is he, where is he, is it even a he? Maybe it is an it! How do we get to him/her/it?

The references were tantalizingly few. A word here, a phrase there. Rubb had seen them before. This time he read and reread them, paying particular attention to the context. For example, Rubb found this line in an ancient leather bound tablature Mentor received in gratitude from a senile old wizard who had lived out his last centuries with Sam;

> *"But behold! A terrible good that is not.*
> *The fire of no light. The light that feeds but itself."*

The reference was clearly to that most powerful of all Daemons, one whose evocation might raise such upheaval even the formulation of its name was an unjustifiable risk. The words were written so that another might use them someday but no further clue was offered the reader. One with the power to make use of words such as these had no real need for them.

> *"Shake the universe; harness the echo."*

Another tidbit culled from the bottom of a vase that had been stolen from a monastery on the third floor of the Financial Center. It was at once an opened door and a wall.

As Rubb read, Mentor sorted his rickrack and bodkins, preparing the laboratory for their ultimate effort. The room was first cleared of the stumps that had taken root. Then the floor was spread with a layer of lasagna pasta covered in turn with a lush bed of virgin dandelion greens picked at midnight (DST) while chanting an old and thoroughly obscene limerick.

The limerick, by the way, once won an award as the "Gawdawfulest Worst" at the National Sorcerer's Exposition of ought-135, after making everyone ill. Sam had been convinced of its efficacy ever since and indeed secured some remarkable results with it. The Limerick, unfortunately, has been lost to Posterity who stole it from under Sam's nose and went on the nightclub circuit with it.

Next Sam laid out a geometric pattern on the floor, a circle within a star within a pentagram within a circle. At each tine of the star was the Rune of those five spirits of power who might be most helpful; Cisly of light and fire, Bookend of energy and might, Cyd of speed, Rheostat of prudence and wisdom, and Thumduk of good fortune.

The symbols of their special powers were prepared and purified according to the prescriptions dictated by their counterparts.

The fire of Cisly was visited in the form of burning flowers of sulfur ignited by lightning drawn from a cumulo-nimbus gathered atop Winesap Mountain at dawn.

The power of Bookend was manifested in a raw egg wrapped in horsehide soaked in apple beer so that it would shrink and explode the egg upon drying, precisely at the point of evocation.

The speed of Cyd was reflected in the movement of a bead of quicksilver dancing in a porcelain bowl cemented to the back of a turtle tethered to a rosewood peg carved of new growth.

The prudence of Rheostat was represented by a raw oyster on the half shell.

The luck of Thumduk was displayed as a floral centerpiece of forget-me-nots woven (using the thumbs and pinkies only) in the form of a modest binomial probability distribution.

This done, Mentor prepared himself by bathing in his mineral spring and anointing himself with Johnson and Johnson's. He dressed from the outside in. Outermost was his purple velvet robe trimmed in gold damascened mail with epaulets, followed by a light tunic of cream silk set off by blood-red piping. Then came stretch-knit tights that were completely uncalled for (but which set off his bony knees nicely) and a pair of aircraft cable suspenders that were completely uncomfortable.

Finally, the countdown began with the recital of all permutations of the letters in the name Baanquer, taken three at a time, while standing with one foot on ice and the other on marbles. His invocation was memorized, his staff within reach, the "Do not disturb" sign on the door.

Rubb, meanwhile, had chanted himself into a trance, isolating himself from his world, draining himself of the cares and distractions of the sensory world. In this elimination of energy-absorbing synapses, Rubb was able to accumulate and focus all of his considerable psychic moxie into the palms of his hands, into a glowing nebulosity that throbbed with the multiplying energy of almost living raw power.

Sitting in the center of the pentagram, Rubb watched, eyes akimbo, as the globe radiated light and life in time with his heartbeat, trying to synchronize that heartbeat with the rhythm of Mentor's trinary recitation. His concentration fed on itself, gathering momentum with each syllable, with each heartbeat.

They swayed together with the lilt of the litany, slowly stepping the pace, slowly building about them the tangible field that would disrupt the ether and call attention to their interference in the nether world, as well as protect them from that same attention.

The fabric of the field wove itself with each muttered monosyllable, with each oscillation of the orb in Rubb's hands. The threads of the pentagram glowed in sympathetic light, then the star and the circles in turn.

Within the inner circle, iridescent tracings arose from the floor, dancing and weaving together in time with the chant, leaving a gossamer network that sparkled in the golden light like infinitesimal beads of dew on the strands of a spider web at dawn. The beads then took on a radiance of their own, a life of their own. This dome of light rose with the quickening tempo, the focusing concentration of Rubb and Sam, working in unison, until it finally closed above them.

"Uuq, Uqu, Quu," chanted Mentor.

The permutation drew to its climax. Sam struggled for the correct pronunciation of the final syllables. These had to be right, absolutely, for there was no second chance. They had gone too far. The demons knew someone was banging on their doors and a slip would reveal to them their adversary's ineptness, leaving Sam and Rubb completely vulnerable to their avenging mercilessness.

"Qqu, Quq, Uqq."

He must maintain the tempo, must not skip a sound, must pronounce it correctly, must not pass Go. This final word would tie the knot, would open the door and send them irrevocably on their way.

"QQQ!"

Sam verily shouted the last word, both in relief and anxiety, for though they were now safe within the net for the time being, they did not know what to expect for their trouble.

Sam's chant stopped but Rubb's heart pumped still, drumming out a steady Dump-thump, Dump-thump, Dump-thump. The golden orb still glowed brightly throbbing with Rubb's heart.

Nothing happened.

Rubb and Sam peered out through the tracery, squinting against the dark. Sam first noticed the turtle was still. Not dead, but the quicksilver was not moving at all. The sulfur was consumed, the oyster gone. As one, Sam and Rubb turned to the egg just as it erupted from the squeeze of the horsehide. The spurt never hit the ground.

"Now!" spat Rubb. "Now!"

"Demons of Hell! Hear Mentor, he who has called you from your rest. Hear me!"

Sam had slipped easily into his basso profundo for the occasion, and looked good in it.

"I invoke and conjure thee, O spirits. Fortified by the power of the Supreme, I command thee by Imholt, Bald, Pauchie, Seded and the most potent prince Cashew. Appear to me! Come now to this place that I have set for thee. Come with speed and in good spirit. Come in human form, not as an ogre. I seek thee in fairness, not in animosity. Appear to me now!"

Mentor raised his staff majestically, paused momentarily, and thumped it thrice. Considering the lasagna and dandelion greens on the floor, it made a terribly jarring, subsonic reverberation, like the sound of two large stones colliding under water or an iron maul on a stump.

With the third blow all Hell broke loose. Icy shrieking winds ripped at the room, distorting the passage of light and filling their ears with the whistling tear of sound catching up with itself. A thunderous shuddering of the very rock from which Sam had hewn his cave rose through the bones of their feet, unsettling their equilibrium like a bobbing ice floe in a storm.

Sam and Rubb knew that this was their test. They must hold their ground and do it with style or be lost. These effects were illusory but tremendously disconcerting. A moment's slip in their grasp upon their senses and they would break their own spell, losing the protection of the golden dome. The collapsing ether and the resultant implosion would literally smear them across the earth like insects under a boot. They held.

Crackling lightning blinded their eyes and raised the hair on their necks. Goose bumps rippled down their arms and legs. Screams, cries, shouts of the most forlorn desperate souls tore at their minds, raising fear in their stomachs and irresolution in their eyes.

Sam and Rubb held. Held their poise and pose. Held their steady glance and steeled gaze. Held their breaths. As they surveyed their ethereal vicinity, Rubb with his back to Sam's in a stance carefully designed to appear not too defensive, they saw the undulating forms gradually materializing at the points of the pentagram.

The first to present a stable manifestation was Cyd, who took the form of a woman. She was tall and dark-haired with a slim body bespeaking an athlete. Her eyes were very large and brown. She gazed steadily at Rubb. She wore contact lenses.

Bookend appeared as a bookend.

Thumduk gathered his strength as a slashing sabre, a blade that whistled near the golden dome of glistening web without tearing it. The blade slowly grew a muscular arm black with sweaty work, which in turn developed a complete body reminding Rubb for all the world of a butcher. Thumduk had a head but no face.

On Mentor's side, Rheostat had long since embodied himself as a red candle in a Chianti bottle. The bottle read 20% by volume, giving Sam pause.

Cisly, demon of speed and light, was last to stabilize as a chrome hood ornament in the form of a semi-nude woman with headdress leaning into the wind which, by the way, still howled.

"May I help you?" said Cisly.

"Speak!" spoke Bookend.

"Mmmmm," hummed Cyd.

"Slash!!!" slashed Thumduk.

Rheostat said nothing.

Sam cleared his throat unobtrusively in an opening first syllable that did not fool Rubb at all. He began with the standard tribute.

"Howdee. Glad y'all could make it."

Rubb elbowed Sam fiercely, pointing out under his breath and through his teeth that aplomb was one thing, foolhardiness something else again.

"Baanquer," stated Sam, figuring to catch them off balance. "Baanquer. I want to see him!"

On reflection, thinking that wasn't pompous enough, Sam added, "All-powerful demons, mightiest of the mighty, most gloriest of the lordly, grant me this, I beseech you!"

Rubb nodded his approval, not knowing anything better to do, and raised his eyebrows in innocent expectation. The speech sure sounded grand to him but he wasn't a devil.

"Thank you," said Cisly.

"What? What?" thundered Bookend.

"Mmmmmm," said Cyd. "Mmmmmm."

"Slish! Slash! Slosh!" responded Thumduk. Then with a giggle, "Slush."

Sam and Rubb turned as one at the giggle. They had not come here to be ridiculed. Even from a devil, or perhaps in spite of it, that giggle was quite unnerving. Considering that devils had little else but devilment to keep them busy, theirs was a perfectly reasonable request and deserved a fair hearing.

Rheostat said nothing. Cisly could not retain a Snurk and let it slip under the golden web to creep up on our fearless friends, leaving a trail of goose bumps as it wiggled up their backs. Bookend simply sniggered, as opposed to a Snurk, and did it quite well for a bookend. In fact, a ripple of giggles seemed to come from all sides now and it was more than out of hand.

"Mmmmmm, snickle. Mmmmmm. Snurkle snurf." That was Cyd.

Eventually the merriment rose to a peal of maniacal laughter that left Sam genuinely concerted and Rubb genuinely ticked. The cacophony multiplied itself like singing in a tiled bathroom. Sam lifted his staff to end the preposterous affair when Rheostat spoke.

There was no signal. The Chianti bottle did not move perceptibly but the uproar stopped with a suddenness that left the impression the laughter was canned. Chianti, er, Rheostat, spoke first with a mild voice that commanded attention. The other visages turned to the red bottle with the wicker base.

"This insult will stop!" proclaimed the bottle.

Rheostat's flame flittered with each syllable and changed from blue to purple to orange with each word.

"This intrusion will not pass with impunity. Mortals who violate this realm with their petty prattling and silly demands will pay dearly for their sport. Therefore, their wish will be granted."

The flame went out with a "pfft."

Sam looked about quickly, only to find the room had returned as it was before their machinations. The pentagram was still on the floor, although now branded into the now limp greens. Aside from the distinct aroma of oregano, little remained of their encounter with Hell.

"What do we do now?" asked Sam after a moment of silent wit gathering. "Did we win or loose?"

Sam scratched at the floor with a scowl that was sincerely rueful and bitter. He was worried.

"I think we made a mistake, Rubb. But there is only one way out now . . . Only one. Rubb?"

There was no Rubb to answer, only two grease spots where he had stood.

A single, insane, compulsive and obscene laugh arose from some ephemeral belly and gathered to itself the idiotic glee of a thousand fools, overwhelmed at the prospect of witnessing the tragic spectacle unfolding. A thousand voices set the stone to ringing with their carillon, imbuing the granite itself with a cynical life that echoed the scorn of Hell for days.

When it was done, Sam observed simply, solemnly, "I'm glad that's over."

CHAPTER 12

The Point is Set

Buried within the bowels of a black hole, the inverted collapse of magnificent Lakkor, lies the essential One. Drawing life from the death of a sun, and fed on the frustrated efforts of elemental energy expanding eternally against its own weight, One lived his obscene life sideways. Sideways is the only way out.

In the oscillating linearity of the ultimate compression of sonular mass, raw intellect alone can sustain self-awareness. All else slows to the turgid wallow that is unitary matter. A mind that is a people, a mind that is a thought at one with the ambiguousness of the terminal inversion can function within the terrible pressure of incredibly heavy light by simply relaxing with the flow of time and nudging the universe with a well-timed burst of synchronous thought, unbalancing the oscillations of the nonexistent hole for a nanosecond or so. One chose to exercise this option only once in real time and all Hell broke loose, in an unobtrusive sort of way.

One is not; at least not in the usual sense of the word. One is a volition, and One is a sequencing thought pattern. However, he is not, a statement that fairly expects elaboration.

Once in a great while a star, by virtue of its advanced entropy, finds itself embarrassingly unable to support its own weight. Lakkor once was a star such as this, a star with a history of brilliance and honor. A star that had husbanded and harbored a race of minds that gloried in its collective lack of accomplishment. Such minds as these! In the universe, there were no other peoples who had so successfully lived out their allotted span, giving nothing to progress and taking nothing but life. The sole reason for their existence was the taking of the life of Lakkor. Theirs was a communal career of pragmatism, a pragmatism as pure and simple as the immaculate radiation of Lakkor itself. Their name was Legion.

Pragmatism can be defined only in terms of ultimate goals, for if it is true that what is right is what works, then it necessarily follows that the goal that is to be achieved determines the nature of what works.

Legion had no goals other than knowledge, so the pragmatic solution was search. Nevertheless, knowledge is not technology, and the search for knowledge is not technological experimentation. Where there is no technological experimentation, there is no discernible socio-economic progress. However, that is not to say there is no knowledge.

The knowledge of Legion extended beyond the sensory world, and the interaction of the mind of Legion touched even their sun Lakkor that nursed them from the vaguest glimmerings of sentience into intellects that could perceive essentials directly, bypassing completely the limiting body granted temporarily by Lakkor.

Lakkor was an old friend to the Legion, a friend that knew intimately every nuance and quirk of their thought. A friend that could keep nothing from them, even their own destruction, their destruction at the hand of Lakkor.

Lakkor told them, told the Legion. He told them a million years or so before the fact. A lesser race than the Legion would have taken no heed; and indeed, there really was little that Lakkor could do to warn them. It is easy to understand why no other race had managed to survive the nova of their star, as the hint is no more than an insignificant red shift in the faithful radiation; a shift that occurs only once, then not again until it is too late. But Lakkor had to warn them, and they were attuned to him when the message of doom came. Lakkor heaved a monumental sigh that they had heard him; the Legion thanked him as one. And as one the Legion survived, melded into a single thought that dived into the inferno in a final act of faith that meant the end of their existence as a people, as individuals and as a reality. In the final collapse of the exhausted Lakkor into the non-existent hole in space, the Legion found its final survival as the ultimate recipient. The awareness that was the black hole drew to itself the holographic vibrations of a universe, considered them, and could only know, for nothing leaves the mind of One, or the hole of Lakkor.

Unlikely as it seems, and certainly no more unlikely than the rest of this business, an eddy in the swirling iridescent fields of manifold thought converged on the black lair of One, and tweaked his interest. Just a tweak. In an infinitesimal lapse of synchronization, the accumulated focus of the wisdom that was One released itself on the node of precisely the one oscillation of the spinning nothingness that would effect an intent. In an instant it was done. No, not an instant, as time is a property of real matter in space-time, and One is not. However, it was done; there was a time when it was not done, but afterwards it had always been so, precisely so. Having emitted his celestial hiccup, One rested and watched.

CHAPTER 13

Pentecost

Pentecost Watts never liked the name he was given. It started out as Pentecost Darn. He changed it to Watts, which has little to do with the story except his name moved from the beginning of the alphabet to the end. Even that would not have affected events if he had gone about it in the proper way, all legal and through the courts.

One day Pentecost Darn-Watts just up and decided he would change his name. The closest he came to any legal procedure was parboiling his old Card. He got a new one, of course. Everyone got a new Card every time the Administration changed. He always parboiled them. Twenty-seven of them so far.

This one time, however, the Administration changed and he did not receive his new Card. Then no more Christmas cards, junk mail or books of the month. Not even insurance premium notices or magazine subscriptions. He was careful to breathe regularly after he came to the realization that he was dead.

When he decided to change his name, he went Cold Cash. He stopped using the credit cards, the checkbooks, even the library card. All Cash. That was it, apparently. They think he is dead. He mentally corrected himself. It calculated he was dead. It must be that fool computer they call the Administration that figured he was dead. Every time that thing gets overheated it declares bankruptcy and issues new Cards. With conditions the way they are, it seems to overheat every other paycheck. It even gave itself an occupational deferment.

Going Cash is no Thudfest either. Some clerks today have never seen a beef certificate! One was compelled to wash her hands after touching his cash. Other establishments have sterilizers to process the folding green.

On top of that, it is nearly impossible to get your paycheck cashed without your Card. Everyone simply uses a Card draft. The only way you can get Cash legally is at the Ateyem, with your Card, of course.

There are other ways. There are always other ways. Bookies only handle Cash. Madams only handle Cash. Auto mechanics only handle Cash. They can always find Cash, for a slight service charge.

Pentecost was dead, so when the check arrived each afternoon, he always dropped in at the local pub, wet his whistle, greased some palms and walked out with a rough approximation of the check's purchasing power in nice crisp counterfeit.

Rough was right! With the explosionary wage-price spiral the way it was, if you didn't spend it yesterday, it would not buy anything today. Well, maybe not that bad, but his Status-Differential Compensation check doubled last year and already doubled again this. Pentecost always converted it to Cash.

Pentecost always spent Cash, in spite of all the trouble he had to go through. Only a certain type of person walks around with Cash in his pocket these days. First of all, you have to be prepared to defend yourself. Cash attracts the honest element like a Thud attracts poachers and a man had to be able to defend himself against Sales and other of society's fringe elements.

When he pulled out that roll of Counterfeit, subtle and often evil glances flashed into dark corners and menacing eyes. (The sort of establishment that deals in Cash always made a point of having dark corners and menacing eyes about. Part of the Sell Our Exciting City campaign by the Chamber of Commerce.) Hick tourists would stare pop-eyed at what must certainly be an industrial spy, or maybe even a real doctor. Sometimes during rush hour Pentecost would stroll into a discount store, step up to the bar and casually pay for a drink with a Thou just to enjoy the awe and oohs and ahhs that bathed a Spender.

For all practical purposes, Pentecost Darn was dead. When the Department of Social Equalization finally learned of his death, they cut off his Status-Differential checks. Of course, that put his status simply nowhere. Of course, he applied again for Status-Differential Compensation. And, of course, that bean-head computer signed him up. Having no previous record of him, it naturally assumed that he was newborn, granted him an even bigger Comp check, and sent him to school. That is why Pentecost Watts survived the first Thud attack.

Starting out in kindergarten at the age of thirty-three is one of those things for which the average high school graduate is not properly prepared. Neither was Pentecost, who was far from being an average high school graduate. As a matter of fact, he was about two years short of it. That was due to some incident involving a ring of used auto parts suppliers, and the law too.

In all fairness, Pentecost actually only sold protection to the ring. The Army school officials failed, however, to see the distinction between breaking the law and blackmailing the lawbreakers, so the lot was let loose. From the school, that is, not from the process of settling accounts with society known as doing time.

By the time the dust settled Pentecost had also settled somewhat and fell into the respectable routine of the status check. As a certified social problem, Pentecost was even eligible for back pay from the Department of Social Equalization for the time in the tank. He promptly blew it all on a weekend in Grinnell.

After turning Cash, being pronounced dead by the currently reigning computer, and being reborn by changing his surname from Darn to Watts, Pentecost went back to school. To kindergarten. Considering his age, he did quite well. That is, until one Show and Tell time when the item he chose to show caused the recruiter to cut him off much before he really had a fair chance to tell about it. Pentecost and the school psychologist had gone round and round about that sort of thing and he suspected she secretly enjoyed it.

This time was different. All recruiters had been very carefully briefed about this particular type of deviant behavior as a matter of national security.

Now before you get things all wrong, perhaps I should explain the incident leading to Pentecost's demise as a promising kindergartner and his initiation into the rarefied strata of the Defense Department. Before I can do that, however, I will have to go back a few years to the Emergence.

CHAPTER 14

Stump

It was the day of the first Thud. Nobody knew it at the time, not even the first Thud who thought he was getting off at the municipal zoo. In those days war meant killing and peace meant not killing. The Thud was to change all of that, as we shall see, but for now it is enough to simply set the time.

Wendall Valve was a biochemist of practically no note. He had yet to take his first degree, but he had cleared one of the most revolutionary high hurdles in scientific thought since the discovery of the Thud itself. Actually, Wendall's discovery predated that of the Thud. The essence of Wendall's theory was simple: there are foods that are either good or bad for you in the right or wrong amounts, vitamins and trace elements that might similarly help or hurt depending on the concentration, and chemical agents that cure or kill as circumstances dictated. It seemed only fair to Wendall there also be viruses that could produce beneficial as well as ill side effects. Perhaps with a bit of luck, there might even be a completely goody-goody virus that did the human race nothing but good.

Now this was a fine theory, but that was all it was or ever would be if it had been left to Wendall. Unfortunately, his career was cut short by a paternity suit. Wendall spent the rest of his days operating a car wash concession and did well at it. He never gave another thought to the virus theory, which is just as well, because he was wrong. Mostly wrong, anyway.

The seed of the theory had been sown in the fertile mind of one of the truly legitimate characters of this story, while Wendall was still an undergraduate and spent hours discussing his fuzzy ideas with other sophist students. In fact, the fuzziness of their ideas was exceeded only by the persistence with which they refused to pursue them.

The man who picked up the germ of the idea from Wendall gave full credit to his source. He never mentioned, however, that the idea was passed to him during a late-night drinking tournament to settle a matter of honor between members of rival intramural ping-pong teams, or that the idea was essentially wrong.

Basically, Wendall envisioned the beneficent and as yet hypothetical virus as one that might be discovered or developed from existing sources and administered to individuals as a treatment for various ailments.

The man who saw the essential truth in this was called Stump by his friends. Stump had no enemies yet.

Stump saw almost immediately the basic element he needed to pull his own ideas together. Stump had spent years in his assistantship research trying to piece together the puzzle of intelligence. Everything about intelligence, its distribution, nature, and development, defied scientific analysis. Oh sure, you could assign numbers on a scale to work men did as a result of what was called intelligence, but that was like reading the speedometer on an automobile. It told you what the current output of the machine was in terms of landmarks but said nothing at all about why the fool thing worked.

The way Stump saw it, there was just something wrong about all current approaches to the study of intelligence. Someone had noticed slight variations in the chemical composition of the brains of intelligent people and concluded that intelligence was caused by the presence of certain chemicals in the body. Administering doses of these chemicals, however, produced nothing but contradictory results and some really monumental hangovers.

Some others associated intelligence, or rather the lack of it, to heredity, environment, upbringing, and just about everything else from the strength of the grip to the molecular structure of the genes and chromosomes themselves. Try as they might, they were unable to find the secret of intelligence so that they might cure the lack of it, and perhaps add a bit to their own. Stump could not do it either.

All of these approaches were wrong. Just plain wrong-headed. However, Stump had been unable to put his finger on exactly the reason why. Many of the factors of intelligence had been investigated with some success because they were indeed factors in the nurturing and development of intelligence. They were all wrong in essence and doomed to failure because they all were based on the same homocentric fallacy, that intelligence was native to man.

Stump's studies began in the statistical analysis of standardized intelligence tests administered throughout the country each year by the Recruiters. He moved on later to psychology and in turn to medicine, biochemistry, and virology. Each of these led him to tantalizing threads of evidence that had a devilish way of evaporating before his inquiry. Statistics led him to associate intelligence successively with climatic conditions, geographical areas, and on one occasion the bumper crops in a stridently tropical country, studied under marginal but nonetheless limited conditions.

Psychology pointed out the distribution of intelligence among populations, particularly genius, followed definite patterns. These patterns could be described by mathematical expressions, but of a complexity that could be manipulated only by super computers. These patterns had no counterpart in any other known biophysical attribute.

That was when Stump took up biochemistry to find the correlation that had so far eluded him. This work led him to the same conclusion to which many other researchers had come: if nothing else, catching a virus would almost invariably result in a weakening of intelligence. If not permanently, then certainly temporarily. If not at advanced age, then nearly always in childhood. But what good was that information? A good virus infection would do the same to many other strengths. His research merely reiterated viruses should be avoided. Stump did not need to study for eighteen years to figure that out.

That was the state of affairs as Stump saw them when he encountered Wendall Valve. That encounter, wherein Wendall espoused his fundamentally wrong theses, pulled together eighteen of Stump's studious years, and led ultimately to the identification of the Immunity.

Valve thought it odd there were no good viruses, that none of them did humankind any good. Why would it not be possible, he asked, to develop a virus that would help? There was the twist of thought that Stump needed. We did not have to develop a benign virus because humankind already owed its most valuable asset to a virus. In short, intelligence was a disease!

Of course, it all fit! The distribution of genius followed the same oddball patterns of epidemics. That was why those equations had no counterparts in psychology. A selectively slow, ponderous epidemic made geniuses, an all-encompassing one the rest of the populace. On the other hand, perhaps the same virus infected all, while the geniuses were most susceptible.

The . . . uh . . . challenged in mind and spirit?

They are Immune.

CHAPTER 15

Foster Pokorni

You have nearly forgotten about Pentecost Darn-Watts. So has the rest of the world, which is one of the great injustices played by history. Considering that nobody has ever accused history of fairness, Pentecost really does not have a complaint coming. Pentecost played a crucial part in the history of his people and deserves the blame for it.

When we left Pentecost during his kindergarten show and tell time, you were about to jump to perfectly reasonable conclusions about the nature of the item he had chosen to show. You are wrong, of course; misdirection is a standard literary technique. If it is any consolation to you, Pentecost had seriously considered that particular subject for a future S/T, possibly a private preview for the sake of Ms. Machd, the instructor. We are not concerned about his prospects in that direction, so fantasize about them as you will.

The subject of Pentecost's exposition this day was a Thud, a small one. This Thud was a very friendly fellow and very talkative. Pentecost presented it to the class quite dramatically by pulling it out of a grocery sack accompanied by a Sevi fanfare for popping corks and kazoo. After a soft-shoe number and a few slight-of-hand songs, the Thud fell to reminiscing about his homeland and history, spiced with a tall tale or two. All of this simply enraptured the kindergartners.

Meanwhile, Ms. Machd saw her chance to slip away unobtrusively to notify the Office of Opportunity, Peace and Security. In her anxiety, she tripped over the old upright piano that had stood in the corner for an eon, or perhaps even an epoch. Whichever, it had not been played well or otherwise, during any lifetime herein addressed.

The commotion of Ms. Machd bowling over the display of sea shells, after careening off the piano in an E-flat minor chord, distracted neither the students who were quite used to this sort of thing, nor the Thud who took it as a compliment.

Thuds were masters of aplomb, not to mention true fighting élan. The Thud nicely worked in the clatter of the bamboo mobile Ms. Machd managed to pull down when she fell over the rack of paint cans. He was spinning a quick-paced narration of the Charge of the Eards, a battle with no historical significance other than it being the occasion of the first practical application of safety pins to modern warfare.

She did manage to notify the authorities eventually, and they stopped by a few weeks later to see about it.

The inspector, a lean but short fellow of either 38 or 64, presented himself with rather a lot of dignity, though certainly the bureaucratic sort. His hairline receded to a point directly above his ears. This feature, coupled with his chin, which receded to a point directly below his ears, produced a powerful impression of some pliable but lumpy desert thrown sharply into a stiff breeze. In fact, he seemed to lean into an omnidirectional wind with a casual perseverance that defied meteorology. He had a quick bandy rooster gait that annoyed friend and foe alike and was given to abrupt changes of direction. That trick served him well in his otherwise undistinguished tennis game but it made extended conversation all but impossible. His suit was invariably a light yellow-brown pinstripe. His name was Foster Pokorni.

"Pokorni, ma'am. Foster."

Foster tended to talk like a government form, last name first, first name last, but he really did not look like one.

"Yes Mr. Foster, what . . ."

Ms. Machd was cut off by Foster's This-message-is-recorded voice accompanied by an intense stare at the bridge of Ms. Machd's nose. The effect was disquieting.

"Pokorni, ma'am, Foster. You notified O.O.P.S. about a possible deviate under Article 279.5?"

"Ah . . . Yes. Yes, I did."

Ms. Machd mentally shook herself free of the disquieting feeling that suddenly came over her and shifted her weight to one side to align at least one of her eyes with at least one of his. Foster, in turn, parried with a very unbecoming slouch that left Ms. Machd's eyes focused on his hairline. When her eyes found his again, they found them crossed. In desperation, she popped out her right contact lens, effectively putting Foster at the disadvantage. The lens dropped expertly into a smock pocket.

"Yes, I did. Come in. Come in. I really did not expect you at all. No one has ever come to see about my reports before."

There was a distinct tinge of hurt in her voice, along with a clumsy little sarcasm.

"Yes, ma'am. We have quite a file of your reports. Checked them all. Checked them all." Instantly, Foster's quick turn left Ms. Machd looking at Foster's ear. "Why are the curtains blue?" he demanded.

"All of the curtains in this building are blue," she replied, incontrovertibly.

"I see, I see."

He was clearly not looking at the curtains. His eyes darted from the half-eaten corn on the cob, which showed the telltale impressions of Ms. Machd's widely spaced incisors, to the load of wet laundry in the half-opened refrigerator.

"His name is Pentecost Watts?"

"Yes, that's right. I thought it strange that . . ."

"He had a real live Thud with him." It was a statement, not a question.

"Yes, that's right. I thought you people would . . ."

"They seemed to be good friends." It was a statement again. Foster saved his questions for those occasions when he didn't know the answer.

"Well, I really didn't have a chance to . . ."

"Blue doesn't look good in this room. Did you try yellow?"

"I like blue," she pronounced very quickly, determined that she would finish at least one answer, no matter what. She waited for a full minute for his reaction. Getting none, she ventured:

"I thought of trying a different . . ."

"Do you keep this Watts kid well fed?" This time it was a question, and Ms. Machd noticed it immediately, in spite of her frustration.

"Well fed?"

"Try yellow." He turned to leave, stopped, turned slowly to Ms. Machd and added, "I think I love you."

"I think I love you, Foster."

"Good-bye."

"Foster, I . . ."

Her thought was cut off by a tender slam of the door. He was gone. After a moment to reflect on the depth and meaning of their relationship, she returned to her cob.

CHAPTER 16

Zerp!

"Say, mister. Ah, how's the war going?" Rubb approached the man sitting on the park bench from a rear quarter. "Any news?"

"Hmm? War? What war?"

The man was apparently older than most of those he had seen so far. He was graying and wore heavy glasses that required him to hold the paper close to his face, even in the direct sunlight. The sport coat was contemporary Salvation Army, the pants very loose about the belt. He needed a haircut and looked as though he was in the habit of doing it himself with two rocks. He finished reading the sentence and looked up.

"War? How's that? Ain't no war."

He peered over his glasses at Rubb, trying to refocus and dilate at the same time.

"Ain't no war."

"Well, could you tell me where I might find one? It's rather important." Rubb considered a moment, and added, "Sir."

The old man finally drew a bead on Rubb, and was clearly having trouble accepting what he saw. Before leaving Pentecost's flat, Rubb had prepared for this expedition by perming his entire body, then waxing his scaly legs. The ringlets fluffed out his head and arms around the tight fitting T-shirt Pentecost had given him, making him look remarkably like a poodle. The back of the bright red shirt was emblazoned "Mel's Car Wash and Grill" and had long since shrunk out of use.

His pants were stretch knit white warm-ups with a green stripe down the side of each leg and a loop under the sole of the foot. His shoes were rough-out tennys to which he had added spikes on the heels. They were very uncomfortable but Rubb found he could stop on a dime. Around his waist was an emergency belt equipped with pouches of assorted occult paraphernalia. A large gold chain slung around one shoulder held his lunch box.

"You betcha, Sonny, I'll show you a war."

Mild surprise, then disbelief, gave way to leering greed as the old man realized this was a Thud, standing right here in front of him, talking to him like people!

"Just you come with me! Come along."

"Ah, well, don't bother to get up. Just tell me how to get there."

Rubb could not help noticing the inordinate interest the old man exuded, and the low bent-knee crouch was unmistakable. When the old man's hands raised in a grappler's stance and his teeth bared inadvertently under a broad grin, Rubb split.

Scurrying zig-zaggedly about the park in his pre-planned defensive pattern, Rubb left the old man in the center of the maneuver rotating as though he were flying a model airplane. Rubb finally tired of that and absent-mindedly came to a stop directly in front of the old man, who by this time was more than dizzy.

"Oops," thought Rubb. "There he is again. He's a lot faster than he looks."

"Gotcha!" shouted the old man, leaping to the attack.

Rubb was off in a flash of red and gold with the old man right behind him, hightailing it like there was no tomorrow. If he caught that Thud there would be! Boy, would there be a tomorrow.

"Now!" shouted Rubb to his feet, which occasionally needed encouragement.

Immediately his feet stopped, digging in with those spiked heels and tearing a trough in the turf that looked as though someone had stopped very suddenly while wearing spiked shoes.

"Whump!"

The old man's stomach slammed into Rubb's back. The dwarf's center of gravity, which was considerably lower than the old man's, catapulted the curmudgeon into an awkward somersault. The two were momentarily face to upside-down face, a look of pain on Rubb, embarrassment on the old man.

"Waaaahooooaaaa!" yelped the old man, just before slamming to the ground on his back. The old man did not move, stunned.

"Hey, I'm sorry mister, really. But what the . . ."

Rubb stood guardedly over the immobile form of the old man who had a wheezing old time trying to speak coherently.

"You win, you win. I'll never . . . I just wanted one more."

The old man was in tears, not only from the pain but also from the loss of this little creature that had come so close. So close!

"But why? What did I do to you?"

Rubb was regaining his wind and had enough time to become genuinely perplexed.

"Why did you attack?"

"I would have been rich. Rich! I could have sold you for a fortune! And one more trip. Rich." The old man was convulsed in anguish.

"Sold me!? For what?"

Rubb did not like the sound of this at all but he came for information and he meant to get it.

"Slavery? A pet? What?"

"Slavery? That's good, good."

A rueful, deep-throated chuckle blurped from the old man. He was trying to roll himself over but the depression he had pounded into the ground made it an uphill proposition in all directions. His landing left a dent in the sod that looked like an angel made by a kid in the first snow of winter. He was having the devil's own time getting out of it. To make sure he did not, Rubb strolled nonchalantly around the old man, occasionally pushing him back in with a forked stick.

"Speak! Why did you attack?" Rubb was enjoying the advantage.

"Don't tell me you don't know. You damned Thuds always know what's coming. I don't know how, but you always do. I wanted to eat you, that's what!" The old man was getting his salt back and putting up quite a struggle.

"Eat me!?" Rubb dropped the stick for a moment, and gave the old man the break he needed.

"Eat me? What for? Why? Wait a minute . . . Why?" This last was shouted back over his shoulder as he made his strategic retreat. The old man, considerably slower than before, lurched after Rubb, one hand on his back and the other grasping out to Rubb.

"Because you're a Thud, you Thud. Aargghh!"

The old man howled in pain and frustration at the little morsel that was easily out-distancing him.

"I'll get you yet! I'll get you!"

Rubb stopped to look back at the old man who now stood wheezing against the statue of some municipal benefactor for whom the birds apparently held little respect. Rubb had little time to reflect on the incident as the commotion had drawn a small crowd. Some were displaying the same battle crouch and leering grin of the old man.

"Get lost," said Rubb to himself. His feet needed little encouragement this time.

Rubb hid himself in the men's rest room for the day and under a pile of windswept oak leaves for most of the night. The chill finally got to him and he ventured out at dawn to loosen the kinks. The clamor had died down gradually over the hours. Rubb hadn't heard a thing but giggly kids for half a night.

Moving carefully along the edge of the park, Rubb surveyed the immediate city and tried to formulate a plan of action. Across the street in front of him was a row of small stores; shoe repair, jewelry, liquor store and war surplus. To his left was a parking lot, with a department store beyond that. On the right . . . War surplus?

Rubb did a take that rattled his chain as his attention jerked back to the shoddy pink and green sign that spelled out Mort's Surplus Supply and Loan Co., Inc. in intermittent neon lights.

In the window hung cameras, coats, binoculars, guitars and an accordion. Rubb recognized everything but the accordion, which he mistook for an instrument of torture. The windows themselves were dirty. The paint about the door was chipped and peeling, as was Mort who was leaning against the jamb sucking on a toothpick. The display of merchandise looked like someone had kicked it over eight or ten years ago and for good measure emptied a vacuum sweeper bag over it all. Mort's eyes followed a particularly undistinguished female down the street until his neck would no longer turn, then turned and receded into the shop.

Rubb had to get to the war surplus store, but he was understandably reluctant to attract the kind of attention he drew yesterday. Feeling perhaps his costume was a giveaway, Rubb took off his tennis shoes and hung them by their laces about his neck.

Rubb fell in unobtrusively with a small pack of dogs who were chasing thither and yon, and had to scamper thither quite a while before they yonned and dropped him off at Mort's.

Panting heavily, Rubb skipped into the shop without missing a stride but spoiled his entrance when his chain caught on the doorknob. It yanked him up in a blinding pirouette that was noteworthy only for its sudden finish, which left him dangling from the doorknob rewound like a yo-yo.

Mort could only stare and did. Rubb wriggled himself loose, straightened his shirt, which had twisted completely front to back, and put his shoes back on. That done, Rubb casually clickity-clicked across the tiled floor to the caged-in counter, determined to display what dignity he had left.

"Whaddaya want?" growled Mort. "Cops after ya or what?"

"Cops?" Rubb was uncertain about his meaning. "Er, no cops. I mean, no one is after me. I just came in to see about a war. You handle war materiel I understand."

"War material! You mean war surplus? Army surplus? Sure, I got everything." Mort chuckled unknowingly to himself. "I got anything you want. Whaddaya want?"

Rubb looked about the store, turning slowly in place. His eyes followed the varnish-stained counter to the wall. The counter made a peculiar angle with the wall, as though it had been taken from some other establishment and installed without benefit of carpenter. On the counter were display cards of fingernail clippers, chapstick and auto fresheners. The glassed-in counter front was filled with cigars, old cameras, pocket knives, waterproof match cases, pipe reamers, a small box of nondescript junk, and a few old blank pistols.

The window was still filled with the same merchandise he had seen from the park, but it was decidedly dirtier from this side. One clothes rack stood along the wall opposite the window, holding a snowmobile suit, six heavy insulated blue hooded jackets with orange linings, an overcoat and two dresses. The shelves behind the counter were stacked in a kiltered sort of order with toasters, electric fans, an ivory-colored radio, cigar boxes containing costume jewelry, watches, cuff links, old coins and cigarette lighters. Overhead, on a rack made from the hooves of a deer, hung a single-barreled shotgun.

"Well, I didn't really need to make a purchase at this time, although I can see that your Army must certainly be well-equipped. I just wanted to ask . . ."

"My Army!" Mort was not sure what to make of that, then took up the gag. "Oh yeah, MY Army. Yeah, nothing but the best for them. We treat them boys right. Now, what can I do you for?"

Mort was leaning over to Rubb for a closer look, one elbow on the end of the counter and one hand on his hip. As Mort had a rather ill defined hip, that hand held its own by hooking its thumb through a belt loop.

"I understand there is a war. Can you tell me how to get there?" Rubb was all wide-eyes and innocence, which usually worked for him.

"You're putting me on," replied Mort after a moment. "Ain't no war. Hasn't been for I don't know how long. Where you been, sonny?"

Mort still was not certain exactly what to make of all this, and hand-over-handed his way back behind the counter to get his glasses. Amid the shuffling of papers, a few muffled thumps and a small cloud of dust, Rubb heard a sharp stage whisper.

"Langly, get up here! Get up here!"

Rubb stood in the center of the floor, hands interlocked behind his back, whistling through his teeth and scratching a design in the floor with his spiked shoes. He looked up to see Mort's face rising like a full moon from behind the counter, complete with horn-rimmed glasses. Shortly thereafter arose Langly, immediately preceded by a tufted cowlick secured by a green plastic visor. Langly looked at Mort and Mort looked back with assent.

Langly began a sideways slither that reminded Rubb of a cobra circling its prey. In fact, Langly wore a double-breasted plaid sport coat with wide lapels over a tight-fitting pair of corduroy pants, the effect definitely reptilian. His eyes fixed unwaveringly on Rubb as he sideslipped his way to cut off Rubb's escape. Mort, meanwhile, picked up a length of pepperoni and held it cradled across his left palm in the manner of a bludgeon.

"A war, you say. Tell me about this war. What do you need a war for? Tell me."

Mort simply oozed fellowship and good cheer as he rounded the counter and assumed the giveaway crouch. Langly, meanwhile, had all but overtaken the door. Rubb was in the proverbial pickle.

"Well, if you folks are busy, I'll just move along. Thanks for the chat. See you now."

Rubb shifted his weight in the direction of the door and saw it instantly reflected by Langly's lurch.

"Don't be hurrying off, now. How would you like to stay for dinner? Heh, heh. Yeah, how would you like to stay for dinner?"

Mort grinned at Langly without taking his eyes off Rubb. While Rubb tried to figure out how he did that, Langly took one giant step in Rubb's direction.

Instantly, Rubb bounded to the corner, knocked over the fingernail files and put one foot in the tray of after-dinner mints. Another spring put him on the top shelf from whence he swung by a deer hoof to the clothes rack, eluding Langly's leap.

Skillfully, Rubb slipped the Bat rope from its pouch on his belt, whipped it about his head like a bolo, and let it fly out the transom. It wound tight around a telephone pole, the little bat thingy imbedded in the wood.

Rubb tightroped the line towards the door while Langly, who grasped strategic situations pretty well, ran outside to intercept him.

"Get him. Don't let him get outside," yelled Mort, who did not grasp strategic situations nearly so well.

Langly changed direction twice in the doorway, like a bear in an arcade shooting gallery, trying to decide what to do.

Mort swung the pepperoni overhead, severing the line and knocking down the shotgun. Mort hot-potatoed the gun for a few seconds, afraid it would go off. Rubb, hanging desperately to the line, swung down and slammed into Langly who had just turned around for the third time. Rubb's tuck position concentrated the shock in Langly's belly, ending his effectiveness as a strategic force.

In his rage, Mort threw the gun after Rubb with a boomerang spin that would probably not have returned it to its master even if it had not gone through the plate glass window. The gun bounced twice, skittered across the street and finally did go off, setting it spinning anew ineffectually.

Rubb was gone. Mort surveyed the damage, assessed the loss of the Thud, sat down on the curb, and cried. Langly was ill.

Rubb scampered down the street and around a corner, paused to catch his breath with his back against a wire mesh trash receptacle, then nonchalantly climbed a telephone pole. He scampered up a feeder line to a rooftop and surveyed the neighborhood.

To his right, across the street and around the corner a bit was the park where he had spent the night. He could still hear the commotion in that general direction, probably because of the shotgun blast that peppered a passing fruit truck. Occasionally one or two folk would chase off into the park or down the street below him, running in a strange, crouchy Groucho Marx sort of scoot, looking sideways into every curve and cubby for something.

It did not take Rubb long to figure out they were looking for him but he still was not certain why. The old man said he wanted to eat him, but Mort and Langly seemed intent on something else. His gold chain? Maybe. Clearly, they were after him.

Some were, but not all, Rubb recalled. Pentecost had spent days with him and they had a grand time. Grand, but not too informative, as Pentecost appeared to be most interested in demonstrating his capacity for fermented grain and his repertory of curious tales about the other type of folk he saw here in about equal numbers. These stories seemed to amuse Pentecost no end but their significance escaped Rubb entirely.

"Whatcha doing up here?"

It was a demand, but couched in a high-pitched voice with none of the gruff raspiness of those people he had encountered so far. Rubb turned to see one of the other types of folk, smaller than the big models by nearly half. Pentecost had consistently referred to them as broads but this one did not seem to fit his description at all.

"Ah . . . just looking around. There seems to be a disturbance around the corner. I just wanted to see what was happening," Rubb formulated circumspectly.

"Oh? Where? Was it an accident? Is anyone hurt?"

The broad was agitated but it seemed more like enthusiasm than concern.

"No, no one was hurt," muttered Rubb thankfully. "Who are you?"

"I'm Penny. Penelope really, but I like Penny. Who are you?"

"Rubb. Just Rubb," replied Rubb.

He hesitated, feeling that he was expected to say more. But not knowing what, he repeated, "Just Rubb."

"That's a funny name," giggled Penny. "What's your first name?"

"They used to call me Wart, but that was a century ago," he responded, translating first timewise.

"What!? A century? Come on, you ain't no hunnert years," challenged Penny, fixing him with a look that was surprisingly fixative.

"Er, well, no. Just kidding. Ah . . . How old would you guess I am anyway?" asked Rubb deviously. Century sure was the wrong thing to say around here.

"You're not a day over fifteen, maybe sixteen," pronounced Penny after a moment's careful scrutiny. "But it's hard to tell. You're not from around here, are you?"

"No, not from here at all," understated Rubb politely, and then by way of diversion, "Say, you wouldn't know where I could get a bit to eat, would you? I'm quite hungry and I can . . ."

"Sure. Why don't you come on down to my place. I'll get you something."

Rubb checked Penny out carefully. This person was only a little taller than himself, and smiled a lot. The hair was long, straight and blond over the shoulders. The pants were of the same heavy blue cloth he had seen on everyone, but somewhat more worn. There was a patch on the seat, he noticed later, and the seat was clearly shaped differently than the bigger types. Penny's shirt was white, loose-fitting and hung shirttail out down to the knees. The sleeves were rolled up to the elbows and the collar was unbuttoned twice. This type of person was easily distinguished by the chest structure even at a distance and Rubb tried to see just what the situation was. He was not tall enough to observe much, and Penny seemed to move discouragingly at his attention, so he let it pass.

"All right, thank you. That would be nice." Rubb was genuinely thankful.

Penny led him down the stairs several flights, around a corner, down a yellow-papered hallway, past about thirty closed doors, and finally to one marked 21 in pealing plastic appliqués.

Penny kicked the door really hard, BAM! BAM! BAM, like that, and waited only a moment before screaming in an unnerving contralto:

"Open that goddam door you little soBAM BAM BAMtch!"

Rubb, completely unnerved, was not sure of the adjective form Penny used but it was certainly emphatic. Rubb gathered himself a bit and was about to suggest turning the doorknob when a rattling chain behind the door stopped him.

The door opened to reveal a short dirty round-faced person about Rubb's own size. This type resembled the other two styles he had encountered so far but was clearly neither, being far too short and skinny for a Type I and in no way structurally similar to Penny.

"Go get MA!" Penny said to the little one.

When this produced no response, at least in the sliver of time allowed for it, Penny screamed an encouraging "Get MA!" and gave the fellow a swat on the back of the head that sent him stumbling out the door.

"Have a seat," said Penny, in a voice that had returned to its normal cheerful lightness. I'll get you something. Sandwich and milk okay?"

"Anything's just fine, thank you."

Rubb was not at all sure about that, but he was hungry and did not see a graceful way to examine the food first.

Looking about, Rubb found a plain but pleasant room with white walls, beige carpet, beige curtains, beige davenport and chairs, brown wood tables and large colored rectangles on the walls smeared mostly with intense blue and orange.

The walls were discolored all about by finger marks at about Rubb's shoulder height, and the carpet was stained by various means in a path between the kitchen and a furniture style box-table in the corner with a frosted glass front. Altogether clean and comfortable, if unimaginative. Penny returned with the food, placed it on the coffee table before Rubb.

"Here you are. Take your time. I'll be back in a second."

She left him alone. Rubb found the food satisfying, if tasteless, finished it and sat waiting for Penny to return. After twiddling his thumbs for a rather long time, and whistling virtually all of the music of East Eard, six polkas, Rubb was getting a little embarrassed sitting there by himself. He had already become aware of his own uneasiness when it was replaced by stark terror as all Hell broke loose.

"Get him! Get that little son of a . . ."

Rubb sprang like a startled cat in no particular direction when his autonomic system reacted to the first shriek. He clawed at the air for a bit and decided to come back down fighting. Penny's war cry was smothered when she buried her face in the pillow Rubb sat on when she dived at him like a swooping Harpy. She did not need to finish, however. Rubb got the message.

The huge Penny-type person called MA! was immediately below him, waddling about with outstretched arms that would not stabilize under the tidal effects of the rolls of underslung fat.

"Oh! Oh, my," was all she could manage to say in a sweet but breathless little Mrs. Santa Claus voice.

"Oh my! Oh! Oh!

Rubb landed full on her vast bosom and sprang with the rebounding flesh like an acrobat from a trampoline. He hit the floor in stride and took off full tilt up the wall and around the inside corner like a cyclist in a velodrome. Rubb whipped around the room three times, timing an occasional ricochet off the ceiling or floor to evade Penny and the little Type III who bounded randomly about, throwing lamps, books, dishes and whatever was handy.

The door was open but recessed in a little vestibule. Rubb would have to take a direct shot at it across no man's land. He got his chance when Penny ran full-face into MA!, bringing everything to a ringing halt. Everything except the idiotic screaming whoops of the little Type III who had given up the chase and watched the proceedings from under the coffee table.

Rubb Immilmanned to the davenport, hop-skipped-and-jumped across the debris and popped out the door with a distinct subsonic reverberation like a Champaign cork. He executed the corner down the hallway, skidding awkwardly on the outboard foot, and was gone.

MA! puffed and wheezed a while, pulled her dress back into order, went into the kitchen and ate a pie. Penny sat in the middle of the floor swearing a litany of obscenities that gave her split ends while Type III took notes.

Rubb careened down the hallways, stairwells and lobby of the apartment building like an Olympic bobsled and skipped out into the daylight traffic without so much as a "Pardon me." The walls were punctured by Rubb's spikes, leaving a perforated trail of prudence and fear.

Rubb was observed by otherwise reliable witnesses making appreciative "Brrrummm! Brrrummm!" noises with his arms extended like a Stuka while executing a difficult power slide off the mezzanine custodial closet. Rubb held an abiding playfulness that spanned both peril and fortune, a trait that probably accounted for the generally low esteem with which dwarfed East Eardian magicians were held.

Rubb was two blocks down the street having a whee of a time strafing ducks in the park when it occurred to him he was here on a mission. He wheeled gently to a stop, set his parking brakes, and carefully considered his next move. Then he sat down.

"Why," the only question to come with any authority.

"Why were they after me? They were all after me all right," thought Rubb. "But they were all so friendly. They weren't mad at me or anything. They just wanted to get me like I was a . . . Well, like a big cookie." As an afterthought, "Penny was sorta cute too, and so nice. Why did she go after me so?"

Rubb pondered these questions, trying to suppress a feeling of rejection that crept in on him. He did so want to be liked, and had set out to make such a good impression on these Zerps. He could not see where he had gone wrong.

"The war. The WAAR!!"

It was the voice of Sam Mentor, his inimitable bass rumbling across to him. Dopplered considerably but unmistakably Mentor.

"You idiot!" encouraged Sam. "The war!" he repeated quite necessarily.

Rubb looked overhead reflexively, although the voice came from no "where" in the usual sense of the word. The words were a function of his mnemonic orientation and generated themselves from the inside out, so to speak. What he heard was his own eardrums, but it was Sam.

"I know, I know," said Rubb aloud, startling a sparrow that was dusting itself in the path.

"I've asked everywhere. I can't find it."

"SSSHH!" cautioned Sam. "Listen!"

Rubb listened for a full minute trying to tune in on Sam but got nothing more than a test pattern. He was about to try another channel when Mentor's voice resumed from a subsonic silence like a record picking up speed.

" . . . and you're it! Be careful!" After a moment, "Remember, no funny stuff."

"Great," thought Rubb, "no funny stuff. What does he think I've been doing here, trick-or-treating?"

Rubb kicked the ground disgustedly, catching his heel spikes in the grass, ripping it with a satisfying skrig.

"Well, what have I got," thought Rubb, trying to assess his position and make sense of it all.

"The old man attacked when I asked about the war. Mort attacked when I asked about the war. That's it. Don't ask about the war. They must be very sensitive about it here."

Rubb reflected about that for a moment, sensing that it was wrong, and replied to himself:

"No, that's wrong. Why would they be sensitive about the war they are winning? Besides, Penny attacked too, and I didn't say anything about a war to her."

"That's right," replied Rubb, momentarily losing track of which side of the argument he was taking. "They all attacked without any provocation."

Rubb brooded about that for a while, flipped a few pebbles at the gold carp in the pond before him, and finally lay down to take a nap under a wide low bush that hung out over the water like an awning.

"The climate here is agreeable, although the folk certainly are not. These funny folk, these Zerp."

Rubb watched the pattern of light through the underside of the bush. He stretched, arched his back and put his hands behind his head.

"They're ALL Zerp!" Rubb sat up with a jerk that shoved his face into the bush. "And we're at war with the Zerp! We are at war with all of them, and that means that they are all at war with me. Every one of them!!"

A flash of realization bristled his back, and he dived for the cover of the bush, burrowing under a windfall of dead leaves. Regaining control of his adrenaline, Rubb ventured a peek out of the covering compost, surveyed the immediate area, and decided it was safe to relax for the time being. He emerged carefully, not making a sound, brushed off the leaves, and squatted by the water to consider his plight.

"Every one of them . . . Against me." Rubb was numb with the enormity of the idea and could only repeat, "Every one of them."

"Every one of them?" It was himself again, asking stupid questions.

"Yes, everyone!"

"But what about Pentecost?"

Rubb's eyebrows raised in mild surprise at the simplicity of that perfectly reasonable question. What about Pentecost? He had lived in the same house with Pentecost for several days, and he never attacked. He didn't do a thing that was inhospitable. In fact, Pentecost was just like one of the family, or rather made Rubb feel like it. Why hadn't Pentecost attacked?

Rubb could see Pentecost was the solution to his problem and a safe place to sleep at the same time. He would return to Pentecost and ask him what was going on.

"Why don't you ask Pentecost," he asked himself.

"I will. Thank you self," he replied making it unanimous.

With the first rays of darkness, Rubb set out to retrace his path to the home of Pentecost Darn-Watts, bypassing the scenes of his unfortunate encounters with the Zerp, noting with a tinge of melancholy the light that still burned in Penny's apartment.

CHAPTER 17

Pentecost Tells All!

"Where did you get it?"

Foster winced down his eyelids accusingly, the way they do in the TV shoot-em-ups, sat on the edge of the table, and crushed a cigarette in the ashtray. He didn't notice his coattail lying on top of the ashtray and casually burned a neat hole in it.

Pentecost quaked as he strained to suppress out-loud laughter and finally did manage to maintain his composure. His only giveaway was a pronounced flushing of the face, which Foster Pokorni mistook as guilt. Feeling assured, Foster pursued his advantage.

"We know you have a contraband Thud. How did you get it? Where is it now?"

"Contraband!?" interrobanged Pentecost. "I didn't do nothing illegal. I don't know anything about it. Where's my lawyer?"

Pentecost professed innocence by his words, but the lingering mirth in his system gave way to a smile that Foster further mistook as insolence. That only made Pentecost giggle the harder.

"We know how to handle you wise guys," he tough-guyed. "We have ways of getting the truth out of you. Do you know what it's like to listen to insurance salesmen for seventy-two hours straight?" Foster paused to let that sink in.

"Insurance . . . nah. You wouldn't do that. I have rights. You're just bluffing." Pentecost managed a pretty good "I'll call you" expression and stood pat.

"Then we go to work with a diet of nothing but Cool Whip non-dairy whipped topping." Foster fixed his quarry with his steely "check" gaze, changing the rules of the game in an instant.

"Cool Whip?" Watts' face paled but he gripped himself and held his eyes fixed on Foster.

"My God," Pentecost thought to himself, "that's diabolical. And it won't leave a mark on the body." Still he said nothing to the bureaucrat.

"And if that fails? Tapes of Geraldo! We have a complete file. You will have an unprecedented opportunity to review them in one sitting. No one has survived beyond seven."

"No! No. What is it you want? Anything!"

Pentecost's composure melted completely, his eyes dropped, and an uncontrollable shudder overwhelmed him.

"Geraldo! Geraldo! Geraldo!" Muttered repeatedly to himself.

"Mate," exalted Pokorni.

"How's that?" responded Pentecost brightly.

"Er, nothing."

Pentecost went back to his quiet muttering, while Foster formulated his line of questioning.

"Let's start at the beginning. Where did you get that Thud?"

"I didn't . . . That is, he got me. I was sitting on this park bench trying to catch a pigeon, for a pet. I like the white and black ones the best. Once I had . . ."

"The Thud. What about the Thud?" redirected Foster.

"Oh, yeah. Well, I was sitting there when he walked up to me and said . . ."

"It walked up to you?" Foster was incredulous. "Don't give me that head cheese. Thuds do not walk up to anybody who will eat them. Mike!" he called to a burly sergeant standing foldy-armed in the corner, "Bring in the Cool Whip."

"No! Wait! Really. I wasn't trying to eat him. Who wants to eat a Thud?" Pentecost's sincerity, accentuated by the prospect of the Cool Whip, stayed the sergeant.

"He just walked up to me and said 'Say, I need a Zerp.' And I said, 'Boy, I sure could use one too.' so I took him down to the Dew Drop Inn and bought him a few pitchers."

Watts' wide-eyed plaint seemed to take.

"What the Hell's a Zerp?" asked Pokorni, his hand raised menacingly ready to signal the officer to proceed.

"How do I know? He didn't seem to like the beer, but he sure was polite about it. He sure could hold his liquor for just a little fellow. Why, he sat there and told the darndest stories all night long. Soppin' up the beer and tellin' stories. I'll tell you, he like to drunk me under the table. And he didn't once go to the can."

Pentecost's wonderment was genuine, and seemed to impress Foster, as his hand lowered to the edge of the table where it drummed on the Masonite overlay.

"Go on. When did you eat it?" led Foster.

"Eat it? Eat what?"

"Eat the Thud. Come on, you were just fattening it up, right?" Foster felt suspicion rising within and moved to the offensive.

"Eat the Thud! I would never do that. He was my friend. Why would I want to eat him?" Pentecost paused for a moment.

"You know, a lot of guys sort of hung around looking real interested. They were just listening to his stories, I spozed, but one of them did offer me some money. I guess I was kind of out of it. Come to think of it, he did try to buy that Thud. Is that what he wanted, to eat it?"

"I can't believe this guy. You mean to tell me you've never eaten Thud," asked Pokorni as if to say, "You mean you've never looked after a woman with lust in your heart?"

"No! Why, no."

Pentecost began to feel like he had been the only kid in the class who didn't get a valentine.

"Was I spozed to?"

"Well, no. I guess you're not spozed . . . uh . . . supposed to eat them, but everyone does whenever you can get one. They're a little hard to get, specially this time of year. I remember a few years back when . . ."

A rasping clearing of the throat from Mike-in-the-corner set Foster back on the subject.

"Mike, get me the file on this guy again. Something's wrong."

He eyed Pentecost carefully, trying to decide if this was a put-on, then fired at Pentecost:

"Where is it now?"

"Where's what?"

"The Thud! Where is it?" Foster shifted in agitation.

"I don't know. He's gone somewhere looking for Zerps. He said he had a job to do, and thanks for everything, but he had to get back to work. So he left. I sent along a six-pack for company, but he left it on the front step. Real nice guy."

"How long ago was that?"

"Oh, let's see. About a week ago, I guess. Yeah, a week."

Pentecost had to count back through PE day, Art day, one weekend, and one field trip.

"Here's that file," interrupted Mike. "Anything else?"

Mike's thumbprint was embossed on the manila file folder like a notary's impression.

"No. Wait outside." Then to Pentecost, "Now, let's see here. Name, registration, race, sex, shuby mutt, bliff . . ."

Foster's voice trailed off as he perused the file, searching for details that he might have overlooked. Pentecost began cleaning his fingernails with the edge of a matchbook, which dulled halfway through the first nail.

Pokorni jerked visibly, brought the paper closer to his face, then looked directly at Pentecost.

"How old did you say you were?"

"How old does it say there?" replied Pentecost evasively.

"Seven years old," said Foster, offhandedly.

"Oh, that's about right, more or less." Pentecost was not very convincing.

"Un hunh. You are two meters tall, weigh ninety kilos, and shave. In addition, you are seven years old. How much more or less, twenty-five years?" Foster leaned back coolly.

"Twenty-six," said Pentecost sheepishly.

"Mike. Mike!" Foster's eyes never left Pentecost Watts. Mike entered.

"Get me everything you can find on thirty-three year old people named Pentecost Watts."

"Darn," corrected Watts.

"What?" asked Foster.

"Darn," Darn repeated.

"What's the matter, Watts? Something you want to hide?"

"It's not Watts. It's Darn. Try Darn," Pentecost volunteered. What the Hell, he figured. It's better than Cool Whip, not to mention Geraldo. They had him.

"Tell us all about it, Darn," Foster pronounced with relish. "Tell us all about it."

Pentecost Darn-Watts did. He told about changing his name, going cash, registering as an infant and going to kindergarten. He skipped the affair with the mother of one of his classmates and the extortion ring he had organized in the lower grades to bring in a little tax-free income. Let them dig that out themselves, he figured. But one thing did not quite figure into this.

What was wrong with not eating a Thud?

CHAPTER 18

A Thudfest

Pentecost Watts' first act as Undersecretary to the Second Assistant Superintendent of Rebuttals, Bureau of Accusations and Diatribes, Department of Truth, was to install draught beer in the men's restroom.

After that, nobody seemed to care much what he did, as long as it made money. Rather, as long as he was not caught making money. In fact, the only salary he received was his expense account, and the only way to make it was to pad it. He had to pay rent for his own office and clerical staff out of his official salary as well as contribute to the Second Assistant's personal welfare fund, leaving virtually nothing after taxes.

Tenure in office was a direct function of one's capacity at creative upholstery, and Pentecost found early on that the more outlandish the expenditure, the quicker the promotion.

The draught beer was a good start for a beginner, but it was humored with embarrassed silence mostly, since there was no profit in it. What was the point, he was asked pointedly.

After that, Pentecost wrote up a White Paper proposal to study the potential genetic damage of reciting off-color jokes during pregnancy. The paper itself, a sandwich of a white page of proposal, the last white summary, and conclusions page, and two hundred pages from the yellow pages, was stamped Top Secret and submitted to committee for consideration. After the coffee break it was given approval, and was funded by lunch. Pentecost was on his way. Not bad for the first day on the job.

That afternoon, he submitted a requisition for seventy-two truckloads of oranges, which he had already sold short on the commodities market. That requisition was approved by the Second Assistant who also sold them, but too late. Pentecost moved into the Second Assistant's office by three o'clock in the afternoon.

At 3:05 p.m., he was invited to the daily Thudfest. Each afternoon the Executives gathered in the penthouse office of the Superintendent himself and Pentecost was now a full-time Executive, J.G. Each took his place about the round walnut table in the walnut paneled conference room. Each had a heavy walnut chair upholstered in plush crimson red velvet, his name deeply carved into the left armrest. The carpet was equally crimson, and plusher yet or plushier. Whatever, the place was neato, and Pentecost, being new to this Executive business, was all hicks about it.

He was still gawking at the Van Goghs and the Rembrandts when they brought out the Thud. Pentecost hardly noticed the silence that dropped over the room, as he was momentarily distracted by a rather well executed walnut torso.

He did turn back to the table in time to get in on the last of the Rite of Concession. Only then did he notice the Thud in the center of the table, looking a bit bored by the affair, and munching on used spark plugs.

Pentecost was startled by the presence of his little friend, here in the Executive conference room, and started to wave hello. He stopped in mid-motion, however, just as the chairman finished a hurried " . . . and according to the law do you accede?"

The Thud no more than nodded when he was immediately set upon by the Executives and literally ripped apart like a Thanksgiving turkey. He was gone in an instant; no bones, no hide, nothing.

Pentecost was thoroughly shaken at the sight, and the realization that this was not his friend Rubb failed to settle his nerves. He shook at the thought of what had happened, and long after the others had filed out of the conference room he gulped coffee at the sideboard, trying to forget.

Regaining his composure after relieving a queasy stomach in the Executive restroom, Pentecost approached his immediate superior Varval Coupon.

"Say, Varval," opened Pentecost, uncertain of the pronunciation, "That, ah, Thudfest. Does that always happen? To the Thud, I mean?"

"What? Yes, of course, Did you think we sang Christmas carols?"

Pentecost tried to hold steady eye contact, but Varval did not cooperate at all and eyed him suspiciously, all squint and eyebrows.

"Well, tell me. What did he do to deserve that? That was terrible!"

Pentecost was having difficulty with his stomach again, and tried unsuccessfully to block the all too vivid memory.

"What did he do!? He didn't do nothing! That was a Thud. That is what they are for. Say, what is the matter with you? Where you been? Don't you know what Thuds are?"

Varval's expression varied from blank incredulity to full-faced disbelief as he tried to assess Pentecost's abysmal lack of understanding of the nature of life. Pentecost might as well have asked, "Where do babies come from?"

"Oh sure; sure," Pentecost responded quickly, not wanting to appear any more ignorant than necessary. "I know what they are. In fact, one of my best friends is a Thud."

That sure was the wrong thing to say. Coupon's explosive convulsion sprayed a chocolate and almond donut evenly over the entire wall behind Pentecost. Varval's rising blood pressure tipped Pentecost to the danger and he managed to duck in plenty of time. His experience in drinking contests to settle matters of honor stood him in good stead and he was proud of his defensive skills.

Pentecost found his own way out, thank you, and retreated to his office where he contemplated the afternoon's events. After signing a few credit vouchers for himself, finalizing a reciprocal rip-off with another office in the State Department and instructing his CPA in the intricacies of the deal, Pentecost called in his personal secretary, Mary Lou Wahoo McGee.

"Say, Wa . . . er . . . Mary Lou," began Pentecost, looking down at her warmly, "What can you tell me about these . . . uh . . . Thudfests each afternoon?"

Mary Lou covered her warmly, raised an eyebrow at the naiveté and replied, "Whaddaya mean? They're Thudfests. They're all the same."

"I know, but what about them? I mean, why?"

"Why? I dunno. How should I know anyway? Just the Executives go to them. You're supposed to know all that, Mister Executive."

Mary Lou seemed puzzled at the questions but was enjoying Pentecost's discomfort in having to display his lack of experience at this Executive game. She let a little smug of superiority creep into her otherwise brainless assortment of expressions.

"Okay, okay. Thank you, Miss McGee. That will be all."

Pentecost watched her appreciatively as she left, but she covered that too.

He thought out the problem carefully, and considered his position as a rising star on the Executive horizon. He was reluctant to expose his vulnerability on an issue that was apparently an every day requirement for every Executive. At the same time he was understandably unwilling to witness this horrendous spectacle every day, at least not without good cause. Wishing to endure neither sanction nor ridicule further, he put in a Need/Now to Research, specifying an expert in Socio-economics.

Presently an old man appeared, dressed eloquently in understated Salvation Army, thick glasses and hair that looked as though it had been trimmed with two rocks.

"They sent me up from Research. You need a Sociologist?"

"Yes, I do. I . . ."

Pentecost hesitated, struck by the old man's appearance and by a tinge of recognition. He waited a moment but nothing registered.

"I have a few answers that need questions. First tell me your name?"

"Stump," answered the old man with a wipe of his nose. "Stump?" mused Watts. "Stump. Unusual name but I cannot recall where I've heard it. Anyway, I need a little help. I'm new at this Executive business; there are a few things I do not understand. For instance, what is this Thudfest all about?"

"Thudfest!?"

Old man Stump had been swaying in time to his palpitating heart, and concentrating mostly on breathing regularly when the word yanked him into an intensity that caught Pentecost with his defenses down.

"Thudfest? What is it? Why do you ask that now?"

"Now? Well, I just sorta wondered. You know . . ."

Pentecost stumbled to an ungainly stop, straightened himself and with renewed confidence replied:

"Wait a minute. I am the Asker here and you are the Askee. I asked why the Thudfest every day?"

"You really don't know, do you? Well, I can tell you, but I'll warn you now that you may regret it."

"Regret it?" repeated Pentecost.

"Never mind. What do you want?"

Pentecost watched old man Stump closely while he organized his thoughts.

"All right. At this Thudfest this afternoon they ripped this poor guy apart and ate him. Why was that? What did the Thud do?" Watts squelched a queasy belch at the thought.

"That Thud gave your Executives another day."

The answer was deliberately terse and obtuse, escaping Pentecost entirely.

"Another day? How's that?" Watts responded leadingly.

"Those buffoons you call Executives, they're hooked."

Pentecost had run into these guys before. They have a little knowledge or skill that you needed and they milk it for all it's worth.

"Look. I want to know what's going on around here and you are going to tell me or I will get someone who will. You will be out of this pitiful job that keeps you in wine before the sun sets. Is that clear."

It was most certainly clear, and Stump knew he was had.

"All right now. Why do the Executives need a Thud every day? Let's have the whole story straight." Pentecost settled back a bit, folding his arms.

Stump indicated a chair with an unconscious gesture intended to gain concession, but he did not wait for approval to sit down. He simply creaked into it, showing every one of his years. Watts did not object.

Stump cleared this throat, removed his glasses, and cleaned them meticulously with a grayed handkerchief that could not possibly have done any good. Replacing his glasses with dignity, Stump proceeded to pull up his sock, hitch up his baggy pants, readjust the coattail he was sitting on, and smooth back his hair. He had just reached for the other sock when Pentecost splintered seven pencils in such quick succession that chips and pieces were flying like popcorn. Stump casually watched the debris settle, glanced at Watts long enough to note with satisfaction the fury of frustration in his eyes, and began tutorily:

"The Thudfest is necessary to the survival of the Executives. Without it, they will succumb to Intelligence. The only thing between them and those poor Brains is the Thud and they know it."

Stump paused significantly letting this sink in. When it obviously did not, he added:

"The Thud is a specific for Intelligence."

"What the Hell are you talking about, Stump?" Watts drew a complete blank.

"Intelligence," teethed Stump with some exasperation, "is caused by a virus. Stump's A-Varietal they call it."

"A virus!? You mean some bug makes people smart?" Pentecost did not believe it for a minute.

"Well, not everyone," replied Stump eyeing Pentecost meaningfully. "Only those incredibly intelligent men who can speak directly to computers, who can manipulate sixth degree Fourier functions sideways. These men are the only ones who understand the Administration and deal with it. And they are its slaves."

"Slaves? How can that be? With their brains they could . . ."

"Go elsewhere? And do what? How many Administrations are there?" The question needed no answering but Pentecost tried.

"Well, they could invent things or solve problems. Or something, couldn't they?"

Pentecost was not sure why he was asking since he did not believe this virus business anyway. However, he had heard tales of the Brains.

"Invent things? Who would make them? The industries that are controlled by the Executives, that's who. Sure, if the Executives need something invented, it gets invented by the computers under the direction of the Brains, but the result is exactly what some Executive ordered; no more, no less. The Brains work with the computer exactly the same way that an engineer of old tended a steam locomotive with an oil can. Squirt here, squirt there. Keep it running. Feed it, talk to it, tend it, and baby it. And if you don't you are dumped, blackballed, destroyed."

Stump's bitterness was genuine, and Watts cleared his throat after a few moments to ask:

"You were a Brain?"

Stump could only look up into Pentecost's eyes ruefully.

"What happened?" Pentecost was becoming a believer.

"I wouldn't be a slave to that Thing. That's all. Everything turned on that computer, every decision. Whether it was reallocation of jet streams to water an arid corn crop or just to place an order for toilet paper, that computer had to be consulted. No one made a decision without it. It was just a pile of transistors, no more. The monumental foul-ups I had to straighten out were just too much to take. So I fixed it."

A twinkle of skullduggery wrinkled his crow's feet, then vanished instantly as Stump recalled that he was talking to an Executive. Pentecost let that pass for now, filing it away like a boot pistol.

"What sort of foul-ups?"

"Some were funny. Like the urgent orders it sent out to produce toasters at maximum capacity because the predicted bumper crop of wheat would mean more bread and thus more toast. We built sixteen years' worth of toasters in one year before that computer stopped it, and then only because production was converted to skateboards for exercise to counteract obesity brought on by the increased consumption of toast."

"I don't remember anything like that," challenged Pentecost, "it would have been in the papers, or we'd see toasters all over in the stores."

"Oh, that all happened down there deep in those transistors. The toasters were built, all right, but the rest was spurious static discharges of some sort. Never did figure what. The crime was that while that computer was worrying about fat people and skateboards, other essential jobs never got done."

Stump was warming to his audience, and needed only a nod to continue.

"Other things weren't so harmless. Our computer regulates all life functions for the economy for this continent. Indirectly, it can and does heavily influence those regulating four other continents. Based on a completely groundless assumption about the viability of a competing government, the computer directed economic reprisals that unsettled that government and threw its economy into ruins. Just a twist here, a canceled order there, a bullion market manipulation for good measure, and at least a half million of those poor unsuspecting peons died of starvation, pestilence and civil war before the computer changed its mind and made them an ally!" Stump breathed heavily, shook his head in resignation, and added, "Now they're the fifty-fourth state."

"You did that?"

Watts was not sure what should be his attitude towards this relic who looked nothing like he talked.

"No, I did not do that. That thing they call the Administration did that and a lot of other things like that."

Stump hacked up something and spat into a freestanding ashtray next to the chair. "Too many things."

"Well, anyway. What does all of that have to do with these Thudfests?"

The conversation was getting a little sticky and Pentecost did not like to see grown men cry.

"The Executives own the Administration and everything that goes with it, including the Brains. However, to keep your job as an Executive, you must also have smarts, of one sort or another. But not too much smarts." Stump paused dramatically, fixed Watts' eyes.

"The Thud is a specific against the Stump A-Varietal virus. Without it an Executive will Otis-out beyond smart and become a Brain, a slave to the Administration."

"But . . ." Pentecost could not think of a question, or at least not the appropriate words for one. His perplexity showed, however, and Stump took up the clue.

"But what about you?" Stump was brimming with satisfaction. "You, Pentecost Watts, are Immune."

"Immune? Immune to what? The virus?"

Watts began to have doubts again about this whole cockamamie affair, and made little attempt to conceal his reservations.

"That's a lot of crap, Stump. Period."

"I know, I know. Moreover, you are not an Executive. You did not see a Thudfest today, and you will not see one tomorrow. And there are no such things as Brains and Administrations."

"Sure, all of those things are . . . Well. Yes, they are. But I am not a Brain. No one ever accused me of being smart at anything, much less Executiving.

"What am I doing here in the first place, Stump? All I know is I got picked up for not eating a Thud, arrested and grilled. Next morning I was told to report to this office. My name was on the door, the clothes in the closet fit, the chair in the Superintendent's office even had my name engraved on it. Everyone knew my name; everyone talked like they were old pals.

"I don't know what happened but it sure wasn't because I have any brains. The only virus I've ever had laid me up in bed for days. The only thing I learned from that was to stay away from it."

Pentecost had pretty well wound down and quit rather than finished.

"So what is your conclusion? You don't understand anything so what I've told you is wrong?"

It was a neat angle, and Pentecost resented it in spite of his inability to respond gracefully.

"No, Dammit. I mean yes, you're wrong." Watts fumed for a minute and came out with it, "I don't believe a word of it. Show me."

"Let me tell you a few things about yourself. First, you have no family."

"Why, yes, that's right. How did you know?" Watts suspected his position in Research.

"And you have no record, financial, academic, criminal or otherwise, longer than this last Administration. You're newborn, so to speak."

"Now wait a minute! What did you do, get a report on me before you came up here? I get it. The old mind reading gimmick. You got the dope on me before you came, right?"

"All right," responded the old man patiently. "You've been on the job how long?"

"Today was my first day."

"And how long did it take me to get here after you called down a Need/Now?"

"Well, not more than two minutes, I guess." Watts was listening again.

"And you're on the seventy-third floor. How long does it take that Executive Express elevator to get here? Ninety seconds? How did I get that report, memorize it and get here in that time?"

Stump knew he could have done just that if he wanted, but Watts did not.

"And besides, do you think a sack of bones like me can just pull out anything I want about an Executive's private life anytime I want without authorization?" Stump knew that he could do that too.

"Well, I suppose not." After searching for a challenge for a minute he came up with, "Okay, tell me, how did you know my name when you came in here?"

"It was on the door," answered Stump casually, "but that's not your real name, is it now."

"Er, no," sheepishly. "Go on, what else?"

"You have a monstrous capacity for alcohol."

"What's that to you, you some blue-nose teetotaler or something?"

Actually, Pentecost could not have cared less about society's opinion of his drinking. Alcohol had never had an effect on him whatsoever and he was not even sure what all the fuss was about. All he knew was he could drink any man under the table.

"Only that a complete resistance to the effects of alcohol is one of the symptoms. For instance, you haven't been to a dentist since you were a child." Stump was completely matter-of-fact about it.

"Now doggone it, Stump, how can you know that? I brush my teeth good every day, and I use mouthwash and everything." Watts did not like personal dings like that.

"When you were last there the anesthetics didn't work and the pain was so great that you've never gone back. Small wonder. No painkiller will work on you, Pentecost whatever-your-name-is."

Stump allowed a moment for the stunned reaction, and proceeded.

"And you don't take Recreational Chemicals."

"Naw, that stuff's a lot of baloney. They don't really do anything for you. It's all in your head."

Pentecost realized against his will that his abstinence would be in no report about him, it would only be noted if he did use them.

"And you, Pentecost X, are a natural-born criminal." Stump looked him straight in the eye, and said it in the same tone of voice as if he had complimented his flower garden.

"You have no scruples whatsoever."

"What's a scruple?" asked Watts suspiciously.

"There is nothing you wouldn't do or say for a buck," translated Stump.

"Why, thank you. But what about the Thudfest?"

"I told you. They are a specific against Intelligence," repeated Stump. "There are several strains of virus, some more severe than others.

Everyone is susceptible to them except those who have suffered irreparable brain damage."

"But if I'm immune, why ain't I stupid?" asked Watts reluctantly. "If you're right, and people start out as dumb as cattle, and they only get smart by catching your flu or whatever it is, and I'm immune to it, then I should be stupid. Right?"

"Oh yes," agreed Stump, impressed with Pentecost's sustained chain of logic.

"But you miss the point. You are not immune to the virus. You got that all right, just a mild case but you got your share of intellect. In your perverse sort of way, you will do quite well with it."

Stump paused to gather the full dramatic effect, his fingertips together in the classic spider-on-a-mirror posture.

"You are immune to the Thud."

"Then," said Pentecost deductively, "that's why I don't like to eat Thuds. And I suppose that is why I got arrested."

"Arrested? What for?" asked Stump. "Not eating a Thud?"

"Yes, as far as I can tell," said Pentecost. "That's all they asked me about, this Thud that stayed with me for a while. Great little guy and all, but he left before I was arrested."

"You talked to a Thud!?" Stump's jubilation was exceeded only by his elation. "When? Where was he? What did he look like? What . . ."

"Just a minute, Stump. I've got a few more for you," interjected Pentecost. "There are still a few things I haven't figured out."

"Okay, okay, what is it?" Impatiently.

"Now you said that if the Executives don't eat Thuds, they'll catch the flu and become Brains. If they haven't caught the bug, then they should all be stupid, right?" Watts stopped momentarily to catch his breath and formulate an addendum, allowing Stump to say:

"Wrong."

"But you said they . . ."

"I did not, you did," said Stump condescendingly. "The Executives have all been infected by the most potent form of the Intelligence virus, the Stump A-Varietal. They were, and in a sense still are, Brains."

"Then how . . ."

"Through family ties, money political power, strings. Many reasons. They may have had special talents for Executiveship. Other reasons too. Whatever they are, they must have a Thud to nullify the debilitating effects of being a Brain. You see, the Brains are super intelligent because they live their lives so much faster than everyone else. They can concentrate so much more brainpower in a second. But they burn themselves out in no time at all, a few years at most. There are plenty of replacements so the Executives let them go out like light bulbs. Pfft!" After a moment, "That's another reason I got out."

"You mean that a Thud works like an aspirin and after a while it wears off?" Pentecost seemed to understand this time, and proceeded, "So they have a Thudfest every day to keep the Intelligence away."

"Yes, Pentecost," said Stump patronizingly. "Every day forever."

"But why the ritual? Why the big deal? They could just make some cold meat sandwiches," asked Pentecost.

"Oh, it's a form of displacement or something. They are slaves to the Thud, but that is unthinkable to a man in a position of authority. They have turned the whole thing around so that in their minds the Thudfest is a prerogative of the privileged Executive class. And I guess in a sense it is," explained Stump. "But they are still slaves to the Thud as the Brains are slaves to the Administration."

"One more, then it's your turn," said Watts reasonably. "You said just now that you 'got out.' You were a Brain, but you got out. How?"

"They caught me disobeying orders. Something about a construction project, an Executive country club or something. I would not do it so they put me out on the street. I am a NoOne now. No money, job, home, nothing, not even welfare. This job in Research is illegal, a favor from a few friends. Just enough to keep me alive."

Stump shook himself free of the wistful mist in his eyes and asked unexpectedly, "How old would you say I am?"

"Oh, I don't know. Sixty or seventy, maybe more. Why?"

"I must be slipping," mused Stump; "I'm thirty-nine."

"The virus?" asked Watts sympathetically.

"Yes. Now it is my turn. This Thud of yours, when did you talk to it?"

"Well, I was walking down the street when he just came up to me. I thought he was some deadbeat, gonna hit me for a sawbuck. But he just said 'I need a Zerp.' He didn't know what that was and I didn't either. Never did figure it out. We talked over a few beers, told some stories, you know. He sure told some strange stories about his hometown, funny stories. I mean weird."

"Was he wearing a red tee-shirt?" asked Stump.

"Yes. Well, no. That is, he wasn't when I met him, but I gave him a red shirt. It was an old bowling shirt of mine. How did you know?"

"What did he tell you," pursued Stump with excitement. "What about his home? Where are they from?"

"I'm not rightly sure," answered Watts honestly. "I couldn't place it at all. He called it Eesturd or something like that. Not around here."

"Not around here!" Stump rolled his eyes at the understatement. "Don't you know that they emerge from the ground, like they were digging out of a prison? No one knows how they get there. We have spent billions trying to find their source but they just crop up without notice. Here for a while, then there for a while, at random. You had a chance to find out and you didn't even ask!"

"Well, how should I know. Who cares, anyway? There are a lot of places I do not know about. I don't miss them and they don't miss me. What about you, what's your interest in this anyway?"

Pentecost was a little put off by Stump's implied assault on his good sense, and even more by his reflexive defensive reaction. Stump paused for a moment, looking Pentecost directly in the eyes, then slowly explained:

"Our world is collapsing, Pentecost. Slowly but certainly, it is slipping apart like an ice palace in Hell. I want to help kick it down. I did what I could do and I can do no more. I just want to go out knowing that I was a part of pulling it down, even a board or a shingle. I want a part in the wreck."

Pentecost, who always saw his world as reasonably solid as long as his Status checks came on time, really did not understand the significance of that little speech. Stump's sincerity was genuine enough and in deference to the old man, Pentecost tried to take him seriously.

"I see." It did not fool Stump.

"Sure you do!" exploded Stump. "That is why you spent days with a live Thud and have nothing to show for it! If you had even the foggiest grasp of the significance of your own Immunity, you could be powerful beyond belief. And you let it slip away!"

Pentecost did not like that at all but could think of nothing to say that would not set off another tirade. They sat there glaring at each other for three minutes, cooling off. Finally remembering that he was the Executive here, Pentecost decided to terminate the audience after clearing up one point.

"Okay. So the sky is falling down and the Thuds are our salvation or whatever you want. I'm an idiot too, if you want. You are still a wine-sodden wrinkled old has-been who piddles in daydreams and fairy tales. And you are beginning to bug me. I have one more question, then I want you out of here. Question: how did I get this job?"

"I put you here, if you're the one," responded Stump impertinently.

"You? How?"

Pentecost had not expected that answer, although he had expected impertinence.

"The last thing I did as a Brain was program the Administration to search for a man like you; no history, no ties, no responsibilities, no scruples, and most importantly, complete Immunity.

"The Administration was waiting for you, had put out an AllCall on anybody who demonstrated Immunity. It has been looking for you for years. There is a reward for the lucky man who spotted you. Everyone would think you were a criminal, but when you were apprehended, you were made an Executive. The job was waiting for you. And if you're the right man, you can do no wrong."

Stump smiled for the first time, with obvious satisfaction.

"Good luck, Pentecost. You will be the most despised man who ever lived and there is nothing you can do about it."

With a chuckle of glee, Stump very deliberately closed the door and snapped the bolt with a final tug of the doorknob. Pentecost shook his head in discomfort at the unfortunate scene by the senile old man and picked up the telephone.

"Give me Security," he said coolly into the mouthpiece.

A moment.

"An old man was here just now. He threatened me. I want him stopped. Yes, do whatever you want, but stop him. Thank you."

CHAPTER 19

Up The Corporate Ladder

Rubb sat back in the leather swivel chair, propped his feet up against the edge of the genuine Butternut desk top, puffed luxuriantly on a real tobacco cigar, and contemplated his budding career as an Executive.

"There are clear advantages," thought Rubb, "to being an Executive. And I haven't been attacked once since I moved in here."

He allowed his eyes to linger in turn upon the three phones on his desk, the gold pen and pencil set with his name carved into the base, the appointment pad in the center of the expanse of hardwood desk, and the Executive yo-yo at his right. They were all very fine, but he had yet to use any of them in his first week on the job, except the yo-yo. In fact, he was not certain at all about his duties. Pentecost indicated that Rubb was a consultant of some sort, but he had not been asked for advice and had offered none.

His office door plaque said "Mr. Rubb, Consultant, Resources and Provisions." That sounded adequately grandiose, but when he asked Pentecost what Resources and Provisions meant, he replied with only one word: "Thuds."

Whatever that meant, there appeared to be no problem in securing it for they certainly had not required his help.

Rubb wandered around the office for the first day, looking at the completely unintelligible smears that were framed on the walls by way of decoration, then tried the various beverages that were kept in rather excessive supply. They were laced with a strong chemical flavor that Rubb could not place, but were otherwise not very good.

After a few minutes enjoying the view of the city from his penthouse office at the phenomenal altitude the Zerps seemed to prefer, Rubb started to be bored. He tried scanning the booklets that Pentecost had recommended and enjoyed so much, the ones that focused on the Broads. Aside from satisfying, more or less, his curiosity about the chest structure, they proved unenlightening.

In that regard, Pentecost tried to explain in some detail the two basic flavors of Zerps, and went on at great length about the pleasures involved. However, the fundamental differences between Eard and Zerp precluded any other than a polite acceptance of what for Rubb was a mystifying complication of a basic reality.

Increasingly Rubb found himself prowling the office like a caged beast, and in spite of the incongruously stern warning against it, he tried once to leave for an afternoon airing. That proved a mistake of the first order. The guards at the door, after overcoming considerable surprise at his unannounced appearance, fell all over themselves hustling him back into his office. They were strangely anxious that he not be touched but at the same time quite insistent that he stay in his office.

Actually, they slammed and bolted the door with some enthusiasm after shooing him back with the butts of their rifles. Rubb decided not to try that again, at least not until his plans were better developed. The overriding principle involved was clear; he was a prisoner, reaffirmed by the belated admission that he had walked into this open-eyed.

Rubb sat in the deeply upholstered swivel chair, gently swinging his feet in small arcs and humming a tune, trying to reconcile his foolhardiness to his stupidity, when he felt a stirring in his left parietal lobe.

"Rubb. Rubb." It was the unmistakable rumble of Mentor's voice. The tone was that of a mother to a child who had just spilled the milk.

"Sam!" Rubb sat up straight so quickly that the chair rolled backwards a few inches in recoil. "Sam! Boy, am I glad to hear from you!"

"Quiet! Listen, I cannot do this forever. Where are you? Are you alone?"

"Yes. Well, no," reconsidered Rubb, recalling the two bruisers at the door. "That is, I'm sort of under house arrest, but I can talk."

There was nothing from Sam Mentor for a palpable moment, then, "Aw, Rubb. Aw." Sam was in audible anguish at this turn of events and allowed a bit of it to surface. "You idiot!"

"Now, wait a minute, Sam. I tried my best, and I can still . . ."

"Quiet!"

Sam sounded like he was talking from the other end of a long sewer pipe but still managed to burble with authority.

"Something's happened here. I am not sure what but something has happened! What did you do?"

"Nothing, nothing at all."

Rubb thought fast, reviewing his steps for the last two months looking for anything that made sense on a galactic scale.

"But I did find out something. There is no war here. None at all."

"No war?" A pause, then, "But I've just interfaced another displacement of soldiers. Thousands and thousands of them! They are going to the Zerp, I know they are. More than ever before. Haven't you seen them?"

"No, not a thing." Rubb added the only significant thing that occurred to him, "But one thing is funny. Every Zerp I've run into has attacked me. Everyone except one. He's the one holding me prisoner."

"Attacked you?" came the echo. "Why?"

"I don't know, but they all know something I don't," said Rubb ruefully. "When they see me, they go after me like I was a plate of your tamales. I'd swear they were going to eat me, or something, but they do not seem to be cannibals at all. Just folk."

"?" came the reply without comment, other than the musical "ding" of the return.

"Oh yes," continued Rubb. "They're all pretty nice folk. At least until they see me. Then all Hell breaks loose. I had a few close calls until I figured out to stay clear. This one guy, Pentecost, was my friend, so I went to him. Now I'm sort of under protective custody."

"Have you talked with anyone in authority?"

"No. I've been pretty busy just staying alive. I'm just twiddling my thumbs now. I have a job of some sort. Pretty nice, too, if you don't mind feeling like a sixth toe."

"You have a job!?"

If anything, the distortions of warped space had amplified Sam's tone of disbelief.

"Doing what?"

"I don't know. Nobody told me. I've been sitting here mostly looking at the walls." Rubb paused for a moment to decide just how to tell Sam what he was thinking.

"I think maybe I'm a prisoner of war, like the whole place is full of Zerps and every one of them is at war with me."

There was a distinct click as Sam put the connection on hold. Rubb lit up a length of drapery tie and slowly bellowed smoke rings, one inside another, waiting for Mentor to respond.

"Rubb, I have to leave soon! Get this right the first time. Do whatever they want. Do whatever they want! It's important!"

There was a bit of static, a wisp of the Top Forty, and a last tender word from Sam,

"And don't do anything stupid!"

"Sam! Sam?"

Rubb panicked a bit when he sensed the ether collapsing like water around a dropped pebble, and pleaded for additional information.

"Help!" Then, "Help?"

Sam was gone.

CHAPTER 20

Gabriel

Sam Mentor paused a thoughtful moment, allowing his bile to gather a full head, and then attacked the smoldering pot of incense feet first. Concentrating the full fury of his frustration on the little brass potlet, Sam drove it completely through the low-slung table that served as his staging area. The heavy oak splintered across the grain, sending a shower of wooden shards spinning through the wisps of smoke that still lingered, and splitting the silence of the pre-dawn with a crackling shock that raised dust for two way-the-hells in most directions.

"You idiot!" he raged at the crumpled pot. "You consummate cretin!"

The completely innocent incense pot cringed in fear, and scuttled beneath a fragment of the table only to be blasted by a thick blazing bolt wrought of pure vengeance, guided only by Mentor's overwhelmingly mindless compulsion to destroy. The earth railed at the whollop, rippling liquidly away from the impact only to rebound off the walls of the cave and return the favor at the epicenter of the blast. The floor reverberated a few more times before settling down to a regular roll, only a little more lilting than before.

That done, Sam popped open a beer and sulked to his favorite easy chair on the second story portico overlooking the village.

"My word! What could Rubb have been thinking!" muttered Mentor. "Getting himself into a fix like that without my help."

"Klaatu." he hollered in the general direction of the town. "KLAATU!"

A squat troll roused itself from the debris in the corner behind Sam, yawned luxuriantly from head to toe and wandered loosely in the general direction of Sam's bellowing. Trolls do not wake easily. When they are not awake, they are not alive so Sam's yelling was actually an affectionate infusion of cosmic life force, like jumper cables. That analogy limps a little, but then so did the troll.

"Klaatu, bring me some magic stuff," Sam barked, swirling about the cave. "We have work to do!"

"Do you have anything special in mind," asked Klaatu, understandably uncertain, "or is this just another trip?"

"No. I mean, yes, I do have something in mind. Bring me a Code Red prep," growled Sam as he shoved his double-elbowed arms through the sleeves of his bulletproof vest.

"This may take everything I've got."

Klaatu nodded as far as possible for a no-neck creature and set about the preparations. His motions, though dulled by death, were smooth and practiced as he arranged the paraphernalia. Trolls are never awakened until needed, as they are a foul lot, and given to excesses that revolt even the trolls. As a result, Klaatu had spent virtually his entire waking life assisting Sam's machinations.

Well, there was *one* night. A broken-hearted Sam resurrected Klaatu as a drinking companion after being jilted by a large barmaid who took exception to Sam's habit of downing draughts in one gulp, mug and all. Sam and Klaatu crashed resoundingly that night and Klaatu enjoyed rather more respect from Sam in the eons since.

Klaatu was a professional at his trade and Sam noted with admiration that everything casually assumed its proper place. Klaatu had the

Bric-a-Brac well trained, each piece scrambling into formation with some enthusiasm. The tub of flat diet cola had been filled and occupied the center of attention, administered to by a crew of charcoal briquettes that were busily drawing runes on the staves while Klaatu chopped up a cold pepperoni pizza.

Sam had accumulated a legendary stock of leftover pizza, and was justifiably proud of it. He had even written a monograph about the efficacy of petrified pasta in summoning perfectly dreadful things from One knows where. He still had several thousand copies on hand and Klaatu thoughtfully chopped up a few of them as well.

Around the tub sprang sprigs of asparagus, encouraged by the low-calorie rubber cement Sam sprinkled in a series of whoop-dee-doos around the tub. The asparagus grew to its nominal height under these aspersions, bowed ritualistically to the charcoal briquettes, then entwined each other to spell out an ancient vegetabolic anecdote that Sam had designed initially to ward off mosquitoes.

Sam slipped into a lime green jump suit and jumped over to the sideboard to mix the potion of dried Druid, clam's blood, and fresh sand pickers from a puppydog's tail. This concoction warmed slowly over a flaming lump of brown coal chipped with a silver pick from the wall of a mine whose shaft has no end. After reaching a boil, the slop was set aside to jell.

Next, Sam draped a rusty chain over his right shoulder, across his chest, and down through his belt on the left side. To this he fastened the anchor from his fishing punt to act as a stabilizer in case of a lapse in the luminiferous ether. Over everything else, Mentor put on his ancestral Coat-Of-Many-Baseball-Cards, a heavy greatcoat that virtually dripped of wholesomeness.

Meanwhile, Klaatu rounded up the andirons, a few teak logs purchased from a peddler who looked like a large bear with bare feet (but who drove a hard bargain nonetheless), and the flame of a flint

141

spark touched to a cattail. The tub of cola began to move oily with the convective rhythm of an uneven heat.

Sam circled backwards about the simmering half-barrel of brew, randomly tossing in first the leaves of this plant and then of that book, really getting into it. The shutters on the windows began to clap with Sam's step, syncopating the slap of his feet on the floor with the clink of the chain.

This rhythm was picked up by a piano, bass and drum combo that Mentor had hired some years earlier. He had not had occasion to use them before this but he was certain that their cheerfully persistent lack of practice, coupled with their ineptness, would either enhance the proceeding significantly or commemorate his demise with the Dixieland revelry he had specified in his will. The drummer had only one drum, however, and was capable of only one tempo, which aggravated the drum no end.

Timing this spell would be crucial. The tub of cola was made of wood, and the fire beneath it would eventually burn through, dousing the flames instantly. When that happened, the ethereal bubble being forced upon the cosmos would collapse in an implosion too fast for the eye to see. Certainly too fast for Mentor to save himself. Everything within the asparagus ring would compress beyond, or more likely below, comprehension, only to pop out again Somewhere Else. Somewhere Else, not being on the charts, was a fearful prospect indeed.

Sam did not need to contemplate the consequences of a slip; he had been frizzled more than a few times in his career and had long since abandoned the science of Trial and Error. He was professionally careful as he added the final ingredients, a colony of greedy ants that had unwittingly stormed the cave during Sam's ablutions. Checking the candy thermometer clipped to the side of the tub, Sam found the mash had progressed well past Hard Ball, nearly to Cracked Tooth so he hastened things a bit.

Grabbing the salt cellar on the sideboard, a meat cleaver with a cloven grip, and two nondescript rodents that defied description, Mentor began to juggle with one hand. With the other, he tied a full Windsor knot in an argyle snake that did not cooperate at all. Settling into a comfortable pattern, Mentor soundlessly mouthed an ancient rondo, picking up on the clunk of the stuck key the piano player berated needlessly. The chant's invectives curled the carpet about the edges, and cast a pale haze throughout the cave, rainbow-ringing the candle lights.

Gradually, Sam allowed a sibilant aspiration to render the chant cautiously audible:

Shekinah Sheznumker Shimglimmer Shilt,

Zenithal Zamindar Zinjanthro Znup!

Over and over Sam repeated the chant, steadily quickening the tempo until he could recite it irregularly, once for each belching bubble that rose from the pot. Mentor held that metre while he reached askance for the jellied sandpicker on the sideboard and dropped it, vial and all, into the pottage.

WHAM! That was all there was to it, just one WHAM! There was not a reverberation or an echo. The sound was exactly like a cannonade into a featherbed. The shock felt like a swat in the head with a wicket, although it left him clearheaded.

Thinking momentarily that he had jumped a timing chain, Sam reached automatically for the reference manual that he always kept hanging by its thong from the pillory. It was only after retrieving his empty-handed arm that Sam realized the cave had completely disappeared.

With that, Mentor noticed that the vast completely empty plane on which he stood curved imperceptibly in upon itself an impossible span overhead. He also noticed right away that he was naked and it was extremely cold out. Er, in. Lastly, he could not avoid noticing the gigantic beast standing directly in front of him. It had not been there when he looked up to check out the ceiling, and glancing around Sam could see that there was no place on the featureless plane where it could have hidden.

The creature stood, it seemed, for an hour, motionless on its lone columnar leg. The leg was easily the thickness of two men's chests, and plated with polygonal scales that were not straked so much as stacked, like cobblestones or like corn on a cob. The foot radiated claws that gripped the ground casually in all directions, reminding Mentor of a long-taloned bird holding its prey. This stump of a leg carried an incredible gaping jaw hung with long crystalline tine-like teeth that rang sweetly by some remote agitation, the way a goblet will when rubbed by a wet finger. The upper and lower teeth intermeshed in such a way that it would be impossible to bite anything without opening virtually the entire top of the head.

This problem apparently never arose, since the thing had no identifiable head, only that jaw. Above this jaw extended its only appendage, a smaller structure like the foot but slimmer by half and longer by twice. If the beast had a face, this arm, or whatever, would have been in the spot occupied by the nose. There was no nose, head, eyes or ears, only the grasping flower-clawed arm. Sam succumbed to a playful compulsion to name it Kickstart.

"Uh, hello," said a very tentative Sam Mentor, back-stepping mentally. "You from around here?"

The only reaction Sam got for his trouble was a businesslike tightening of the claw's grip on the floor. Kickstart was impatient about something and Sam's casual approach was sure wrong. The sense of urgency about it increased geometrically moment by moment but Sam was not sure how he knew that.

Being at a distinct social disadvantage, Sam decided to proceed on the premise that this was exactly what he had conjured, although not at all what he had expected. The cave must still exist around him. Klaatu and the Brics as well as the Bracs were close at hand, although that seemed of little comfort right now. This bubble and the one-legged mess in front of him were real.

"But," mumbled Mentor to himself, "why didn't I get the exchange? That spell always gets the exchange."

Sam did not have time to answer that one for himself. A deep rumble of his Id told him that the oaken tub was beginning to burn through and the spell was in jeopardy. He would have time for only a few well-chosen words. There would be no second chance.

"Zerp!" he said as sincerely as possible. Then again if possible with more.

"ZERP!"

Mentor covered his head with his arms, closed his eyes, and wondered ruefully if he would be aware of the moment he was no more.

The jaw smiled. No question about it, the thing was smiling at Sam. The relief he felt passed quickly as that fanged slash of a mouth curled on past a friendly grin, right into an unnerving leer. The crystal teeth splayed awkwardly at the strain, and the overhead arm began to jiggle convulsively, as if laughing at an obscene joke. Mentor was certain that the joke would be on him.

"Yes, yes. Zerps."

Kickstart had not spoken, but Sam heard the words clearly, along with a low undertow of chuckle that bespoke two voices.

"What do you want with Zerps?" The voice was hard as those teeth and cold as Sam's feet.

"I have this friend, Rubb. I'm trying to get him back. You see . . ."

"No! Do not lie to me." The voice was mild, almost femininely conciliatory this time, as a mother to a wayward child.

"I have to go."

The beast lurched as if, in fact, it intended to go, the claws releasing their grip but leaving no mark in the surface. It was not at all obvious where it could go to around here but since Sam had not seen where it came from, he took it at its word.

"Don't go! Don't go! You're right," yelled a very truthful Sam Mentor, mustering a fervor born of his impending doom.

"I lied. I do not care what happens to Rubb, but this is not fair. I do not know who you are! You came to me, you know. What do you want of me?!" Sam's Id trembled again ominously.

"Who said anything about fair."

Kickstart's response was incontrovertible. This time the lispy voice rang of a kazoo submerged in beer, then changed suddenly to a Wagnerian soprano.

"You have been chosen."

Sam was thunderstruck, but a sharp after shock in his Id spurred him to speak out again, quickly.

"Chosen?! For what! What am I supposed to do?"

"You have already done it. Nice work."

The voice was computer generated, and ended with the ring of a cash register. Unmistakably, a cash register.

WHAM!

Sam was sitting in the middle of a puddle of slop from the burned out tub, still smoldering acridly. Klaatu was shaking him and slapping him sharply across the face. Sam slapped him back, rocking the poor troll onto his haunches.

"Hit me again and I'll boil you in the next pot. What's got into you, Klaatu?" barked Sam, rubbing his cheek defensively.

"I thought you were dead. Mercy! When that bolt of lightning hit you I thought you were gone."

Klaatu's concern for Sam's well being was genuine, since only Sam could regenerate life in the faithful troll. When that inevitable day came that Mentor met his match, or his maker, Klaatu would revert into a wisp of dust that had never lived, a point that Sam brought up more often than mere paternal pride might warrant.

"Lightning? When? While I was gone?" asked Sam absently, figuring that accounted for the WHAMs.

"No sir. You were not gone. It happened not half a second ago. You were just getting started on your downhill run. You dropped in the sandpicker jelly as usual and when I handed you the old life insurance policy for the invocation, it hit you. Right out of the tub. Blew the bottom out, and put out the fire like that."

Klaatu attempted to snap his fingers for emphasis but his fur-lined palms muffled the effect anticlimactically.

"Are you sure you're not hurt?"

"No, yes. I don't think so."

Mentor knew that he was not hurt in the least, just wet where he was sitting in the stew. He had to take a moment to think about that episode with Kickstart. It felt as though he had been gone for an hour but Klaatu said he had not been gone at all, that the lightning had struck just now.

"Klaatu. How many bolts of lightning were there?"

"How many? Why, only one, Sam."

Klaatu looked up from his ministrations, satisfied that Sam had suffered no permanent damage, not even a powder burn.

"You look like it missed. There isn't a mark on you."

"That was not lightning, Klaatu," said Sam with a hint of understanding creeping into his voice. "And I don't think that I am Sam Mentor."

Klaatu nodded, packed the first-aid kit into its pigeonhole by the window, and started back to the kitchen when an inadvertent take wrenched him at the realization of what Sam had said. He did a neat sideways somersault, spinning to a stop facing Sam.

"You don't think you're you?" he asked reaching again for the first-aid kit.

"What you see isn't Sam Mentor. At least not the Sam Mentor that was here a moment ago. Something's askew, but I'm not sure what."

Sam Mentor, he realized chagrinedly, the grandest wizard in all Eard, the oldest, richest, vilest, smartest, ugliest, and sneakiest sorcerer ever to brandish a scepter had been had. Had good! Klaatu disengaged himself and retreated backwards into the kitchen to ponder events over a hot basin of dishwater.

Sam mused for a moment about what he had just said, while deliberately twisting a strong drink from a creosoted post selected from his carefully hoarded private stock. Clinking a few cubes into the glass, Sam meandered over to the fire pit and curled up against one of the stumps, an old friend that he had found abandoned so long ago that both had forgotten when. They had grown up together and Sam always felt that he could confide in it.

His eyes glazed over as he stared at the fire, allowing pieces of the problem to congeal out of the smoke from the pit. Mentally, Mentor juggled them, trying to fit them into the Big Picture.

"First," he mumbled to the stump, "there is the matter of Rubb. He's There, in trouble, and that means trouble Here, likely as I am doomed. Then there were all those soldiers going There, too, but Rubb did not find any of them There. They must have come from Here."

Sam could tell by the expression on his own face that none of that made sense yet. Checking back over his shoulder, he could see the stump was stumped as well.

"Okay," Sam continued, "all those soldiers came from the war, and the war started with the Phroggs. That was where Rubb came in."

Mentor scratched the back of his neck to loosen an entrenched flea, and snorted to himself cynically.

"Anything yet?" he called absently to the stump.

The stump was unmoved by the logic of the discussion, but it did offer a gentle snuggle against his back. Sam responded with a pat on the root and resumed counting off the facts on his fingers and toes.

"That beast, Kickstart! How does that fit into this mess," Sam asked the smoke. "I was trying to get back to Rubb to find out what had gone wrong. The ritual was right; I should have gotten the Exchange and they would have put me right through. I have done it a hundred times. What could have happened?"

The smoke's response was to get into Sam's eyes.

"It said I was chosen. That was the word, chosen."

Kicking another chunk of coal into the fire, Sam slipped a bit further down onto his back. The stump shifted its weight to get a bit more comfortable, seeming to show a little more interest. As stumps go, that is quite a lot.

"That abomination Kickstart came for me, I'm certain of it. I had no control. Who was controlling it?" asked Sam loudly enough to startle Klaatu from his dishwashing.

"Who was controlling what, sir?" said Klaatu with an appreciative look at his reflection in the shiny china dish.

"A monster. I saw an incredible monster, during that lightning," said Sam. "Someone sent it to me. It had a mission. Something damned important to go to all that trouble but I don't know what."

"What did it look like?" asked Klaatu, his interest diverted from his household duties.

Leaning loosely on the mop he had been using to clean up the spilled pop, Klaatu began to consider the possibility that Sam had jumped a groove. What with all the talk about being gone for an hour during a stroke of lightning, seeing monsters, and even saying that he wasn't Sam Mentor, Klaatu found himself compelled to certify his stake in the matter.

"Do you want to tell me about it, Sam?"

Sam did, in some detail, the bubble, the double-ended Kickstart, the cold, everything in detail. The conversation with the thing was still alive in his mind, and the pervasive feeling that it was still present in the cave here with them began to creep in on Klaatu, too. Klaatu's eyes widened as the narration progressed, his face paling proportionately.

When Sam finally finished, Klaatu gathered himself, dragged the mop over to the pit alongside Sam, and paused to scratch himself behind the ear.

"Sam, I think I should tell you something. That one-legged mouth, did it walk with an end-over-end flip-flop, like a slinky?"

"Well, I didn't actually see it walk," recalled Sam. "But seeing how it was built, that was the only way."

"Sam . . . Sam, that was my cousin, once removed on my left side." Klaatu watched for any giveaway Sam might provide, and finding none, continued. "We met at a distance on the way here, when I was waking up. I wondered what it was doing in the neighborhood."

Sam's face crinkled and curled, battled with itself for control and lost. It did something it had never done before; it cried.

"Awww," blubbered Sam. "Why did it have to be family?"

CHAPTER 21

The Armee

Rubb noticed the movement out of the corner of his eye, glanced up from the crossword puzzle in the Journal of Waste Disposal, and met eyes very much like his own.

Rubb's eyes returned automatically to 13 down, which called for "A mobile device used to compact non-ferrous refuse." Twelve letters starting with H. He had returned to 13 down at least twice this week alone, and was getting a little frustrated with this particular word.

Actually, it wasn't only this word that bothered him. After a month of work on the puzzle, he had yet to fill in his first blank. This word, of all words, was on the tips of his tongue and he knew it would come. It had to come. If he could only concentrate hard enough, it would come. This word would unravel the whole puzzle somehow, and from that opening would flow the solution to the fix he was in.

He didn't really think everything through in exactly that way. If he did, he would have been embarrassed by the fallacy. His frustration was burbling up to a rumbling rage in his breast, and right now, the focus of his rage was this confounded crossword puzzle and this twelve-letter word starting with H.

Equating that word to his socio-economic predicament was the sort of irrational association in which Rubb specialized, instinctively languishing in indecision when confronted with overwhelming odds. He could reduce the monumental to the manageable only by fixing on a comfortable little task that was eminently copable, equating that to the dirge that was upon him, and checking out. It usually worked. It didn't solve many problems, mind you, but Rubb could generally check out at will. Except this time and except for this exasperating word. Twelve letters starting with H.

The visitor cleared his throat, "Unnka!", like that.

"I'll be right with you," said Rubb with annoyance, "Be right with you."

"Ah, pardon me? Is this where I'm supposed to be?"

The fellow was in some discomfort and the pain in his voice showed. Er, sounded.

Rubb glanced up again and froze. "Who are . . . What did you . . . Where did you come . . ." Rubb stopped, counted on his fingers and continued, "Why are . . . When did . . ." and stopped.

Extricating himself from his emotional involvement with the crossword puzzle, Rubb directed his attention full onto the short (it now seemed) brown-green scaly creature that stood awkwardly at attention in his crisp new uniform. Orange epaulets set off the plaid dress uniform nicely, picking up a glint from the scabbard he held horizontally at arm's length over his head in salute. The scabbard wasn't loaded.

Rubb would have recognized that uniform anywhere else, but was having an uncommon time with it here in his office. Recognition seeped in soon enough, however, just after he read East Eard's national motto emblazoned on the helmet, "Death before dishonor, but can we talk about it?"

Rubb's jaw worked up and down a few times, like a guppy gulping air, but he managed to say no more than might a fish. His eyeballs started to dry out so he blinked once autonomically, then resumed gaping.

"They told us they were going to take a picture and to salute until the flash went off. Did you get the picture yet?"

The little soldier hoped sincerely that Rubb had done so, and lofted his eyes to the scabbard overhead.

"Uh, ease off," said Rubb, overcoming his disbelief.

Not being certain of the proper form of command, and getting no visible results, Rubb tried to pick up on the obvious hint the soldier was mouthing at him.

"Back off. Ease up. Take it easy? At ease!"

"Oh, wow!" said the soldier with a clatter of the scabbard against his spurs. "That sucker's heavy!" He rubbed his left shoulder with his right hand while twisting his head and neck to loosen the kinks.

"Am I in the right place?"

"I'm sure I don't know," said Rubb truthfully enough. "Where are you supposed to be?"

Rubb thought that was a fair question inasmuch as he didn't know what he was doing here himself.

"I hoped you'd know. They only told us we were going to war and that we'd get our swords when we needed them. Felt pretty dumb holding that empty scabbard, I'll tell you."

"You were going to war? Where? Here?"

Rubb's surprise at finding an Eard in his sequestered office gave way to surprise at finding him looking for the same war.

"Well, no, not *here*," answered the soldier, sweeping the plush office with a convincingly swashbuckly swish of his scabbard.

"Probably outside somewhere. Are you a general or something?"

"No," said Rubb, after almost conferring that rank upon himself. "No, I just work here. But who are you, and how did you get here?"

"Slumpblock," said the little soldier.

"I beg your pardon," said Rubb, "I thought you said Slumpblock."

"That's my name, Slumpblock. Grande Armee of East Eard, Upper Malaise Volunteers. Private first class." He paused absently to touch his silk-screened shoulder patch.

"I was volunteered yesterday by my folks in return for a tax break on their victory garden. I went through basic training this morning on the train out of Windbreak. Then they lined us up to take our picture. The next thing I know, here I am. Who are you?"

"Rubb," said Rubb. "Rubb of Middle Eard, District of Almost Anywhere," this last an allusion to his vagabond ways. "I was looking for the war too, but I never found it. At least not the war I came for. But I've been under house arrest for more than a month and I'm beginning to think I'm a prisoner of war."

Slumpblock ducked to a semi-crouch, scanned the ceiling reactively, as if he were expecting an air raid, and raised the scabbard noisily to a two-handed ready position in the manner of the Samurai. The racket was a puzzle to Rubb as the scabbard had no moving parts. While this pose was undoubtedly intended to intimidate, Rubb was at a loss as to what defense the scabbard would offer in an air raid. The plaid uniform spoiled the effect, however. He looked rather more like a lawn tennis dandy squaring away for a backhand. Rubb was impressed anyway and felt a modest surge of pride in the efficiency of the Armee of Eard. This soldier had obviously undergone a rigorous regimen on the train this morning.

"Relax," said Rubb after playing along with the air raid bit for a moment or two. "I think we're safe for the time being."

Rubb rubbed a non-existent speck of something from his left eye with his right middle finger, cleared his throat lightly, and sat down at his desk with an air of importance. This was his turf, for the moment, and he had precious little to account for himself lately, so he let his eyes survey Slumpblock leisurely while he carefully composed his next question.

"Zerp!" shouted Rubb explosively.

"Zerp. Zerp! ZERP!!"

Slumpblock sprang straight up, landed with a thump, and backed off reflexively, feeling behind with one hand for a defensive position and trying to raise the scabbard to the ready position with the other. At the first Zerp! Slumpblock had jammed his finger into the mouth of the scabbard and was flailing it awkwardly about like a badly mishandled jointed threshing stick. He whapped himself in the cheek twice before settling down to relatively complacent apprehension. Rubb made a mental note to reassess his first impression of the Armee of Eard.

"Zerp?" said the soldier with a glance left, right, and up again. "I ain't got no Zerp."

"No? Then why did you jump like that?" countered Rubb.

"Jump?! Eard! I thought you were coming over the desk at me! Hey, look. My nerves are like raw meat. Whaddaya want, Zerps? Okay, you got 'em. Just tell me what it is and you got 'em." Slumpblock actually pouted.

Rubb studied Slumpblock carefully, trying to decide whether this Eard knew anything or not. He sure looked innocent enough, standing here like a frightened little boy in his Sunday best. On the other hand, he *was* standing here, in this office-prison where no one else had passed either in or out in a month. There was much to ponder in that.

Mentor and Rubb had called in more than a few heavy markers in order to punch Rubb through that hole in the ether. A few markers, a lot of careful preparation, and a level of finesse that only derives from decades of practice. In fact, Rubb honestly felt that no one else could have pulled off the conjurction without literally raising the dead in retaliation. But here was this bumpkin standing here like he had just gotten off a bus! He must have had help to get here and whoever helped Slumpblock was the one Rubb wanted to see.

Rubb sat scowling on both the inside and the outside of his face, while Slumpblock poked about restlessly, embarrassingly aware that he was in the wrong place but not in the least certain why. Finally Rubb stirred himself, lifted his chin from his knuckles, and leaned back in his chair.

"Who's they?" said Rubb simply.

"They?" said Slumpblock, if possible even more simply.

"You told me they were sending you to war, and they were going to take your picture, and I don't know what else," explained Rubb patiently. "Who's they?"

"Why, the Phroggs. Who else?"

Slumpblock's surprised innocent look did not seem to strain his faculties unduly, so Rubb took it to be genuine.

"Oh, yeah, right. The Phroggs."

Rubb had himself forgotten about the Phroggs so he allowed as surprised innocence was appropriate, but that really didn't explain anything. Phroggs are many things, but they are not wizards. Magicians, maybe, but they are genetically incapable of real wizardry. That's why Rubb made such a good living performing for them; there were no Phrogg genes for ethereal sensitivity. When it came to spells, they were dyslexic. Phroggs were completely color blind and tone deaf in the nether world, and could no more have projected this Slumpblock into his office from Eard, than Rubb could project himself back to Eard a cappella.

"But how did you get here?" said Rubb. "What did they do to you? They couldn't have done it themselves. Who helped them? Did you see anything strange going on? Or maybe strange people?"

"Wow! What do you want first?"

"Anything, Eard. Anything!" Rubb was working into a low-grade rage again.

"Well, there was this strange looking thing. It sorta flip-flopped around the place end-over-end. It had one big leg with claws all around, and one little leg on the other end. And a grin that . . . !"

" . . . !" was right!

Rubb was bowled out of his chair with a shove that sent him sprawling. Instantly, he was assaulted by the whooping and yelping of a mountain of little soldiers like Slumpblock, all tumbling into his office as though tipped from a basket. Those on top cursed those coming from behind and those on the bottom screeched in pain and outrage. Those who could jumped out of the way and scurried about, swinging their scabbards and taking cover behind the drapes and curtains. A few were trying to organize an attack, while others were digging in for a defensive stand. The racket of the clanging scabbards, jangling spurs, shouted orders, and cries of frustration combined to completely unnerve both Rubb and Slumpblock, who were frozen in their tracks at the spectacle.

By the time the guards in the hallway decided to investigate the commotion there were several hundred soldiers in Rubb's office. Upon opening the doors, the guards also froze in their tracks. In turn, all the little soldiers froze. The whole room was silent for a moment. The two relatively gigantic guards tried desperately to accommodate the sight of hundreds of Thud, while the Eardish soldiers gained an appreciation of just who the real opposition was.

In unison, the Eards looked at their empty scabbards, at each other, at their officers, and took up the cacophony with renewed exuberance. Rubb went for the wet bar behind his desk, and Slumpblock jumped in the dumbwaiter. The two guards panicked from the room, shouting for reinforcements. Encouraged, the Eards charged the doorway, breached it handily, and stormed down the hallway in determined pursuit.

In a few moments, Rubb's office was completely silent again. Behind the bar, Rubb was beginning to appreciate the battery of chemical beverages that these big folk favored, finding that in his past experiments he had simply not infused enough. All that was needed, apparently, was to drink two or three bottles at a toss. Rubb set the third bottle down, wiped his lips on the bar towel, and looked about.

The room was completely demolished, not a piece of woodwork left unhacked by the scabbards. His desk looked like a miniature toothpick factory, the wainscot like the locker room floor in a golf and country club. The carpeting was shredded for camouflage.

Another surge of nationalistic pride welled in Rubb at the efficiency of the Eardian Armee. Having no particular emotional attachment for the office itself, however, Rubb picked up the broken shaft of the clothes tree, whacked out a window or two, and then threw it across the room. It clanged into a wood-grained metal door let into the wall.

"Yelp!" echoed the little door. "I give up! I give up!"

Rubb approached the dumbwaiter door and knocked three times. The door responded with three little clangs. After a moment the little latch turned, and Slumpblock peered out.

"Are they all gone?" asked Slumpblock after sizing up the devastation.

"No," answered Rubb, "You're still here."

Taking that for affirmation, Slumpblock slipped out of the little door onto the floor, brushed himself off, straightened himself and his dignity, and said with grand composure, "I always thought they were a rowdy bunch. Say, I'm sorry about the damage."

"No problem," said Rubb with a gentle wave of his hand to indicate there was no problem. "I've wanted to do that myself more than once. What was that? Your unit?"

"Yep. They come on like a plague of locusts."

Rubb nodded, looking again about the room. He could hear a renewed commotion from the streets below coming up through the broken windows. The Armee must have found its way out of the building. Rubb strolled over to the windows, stepping over the debris unconsciously. He was absorbed in thought, trying to get a handle on the significance of that little war. Looking down, he saw that the situation seemed to have reversed itself and the Zerp were chasing the Eards out of the building. The Eards were scattering like startled grouse, and while he watched they seemed to melt into the neighborhood. Then it was quiet.

That must have been one of those mass conjurctions Sam Mentor had told him about. So this *was* the right place, those big people *are* Zerp, and someone *was* sending big chunks of Eard here. Scratch that; the Phroggs were sending them here, but with help. Whose help? There was that thing Slumpblock said he had seen just before they were interrupted.

"Say, Slumpblock," said Rubb aloud. "What was that thing you were telling me about, the thing with the claws and the big grin?"

"Big grin?" The voice, far too deep for Slumpblock, chilled Rubb to the toes. "How's this?"

Rubb turned to see Pentecost Darn-Watts wearing the biggest, broadest, meanest grin he had ever seen. Well, Rubb had seen such a grin on a few occasions, but all of them were ominous, if not worse.

"Nice work, Rubb," said Pentecost with a chuckle that started in his solar plexus. "Nice work. You don't know how much this means to me."

Rubb knew this to be true.

Pentecost Darn-Watts stood in the doorway, feet spread and shoulders set like Samson between the pillars, about to take on the world. He looked into Rubb's eyes so intently that, taken along with the grin, Rubb could only goosebump profusely.

Pentecost stepped into the room, closed the door gently, and moved to the bar without taking his eyes from Rubb. The grin was beginning to set.

The bar had been largely devastated in the battle, such as it was, and Rubb had himself chugged the best of what survived. Pentecost finally wrested his eyes from Rubb to find a drink, scooped the debris from the bar with a sweep of his arm, and settled reluctantly on a bottle of Annie Green Springs.

Returning his attention to Rubb, he found Rubb attending to paperwork at his desk as though nothing had happened. Rubb shoved a drawer home with a businesslike flair, tapped a sheaf of paper square, and casually looked up to Pentecost, eyebrows raised expectantly and pen poised to take notes.

"Yes, Pentecost. What can I do for you?"

"You have already done it."

If anything, Watts' grin broadened, causing Rubb to tense instinctively as though he were on the business end of an armed rubber band. Rubb expected Pentecost's face to give out shortly and was prepared to take cover at the first sign of structural fatigue.

"You have already exceeded my wildest expectations, my little friend."

"Hey, look, I'm sorry about the mess. We had a little, ah, get together, and it sorta got out of hand."

Rubb was not a practiced prevaricator, and was an even worse liar.

"Don't worry about it, Rubb. You've more than made up for it." Pentecost let his grin fade a little as he kicked his way through the shredded carpet and broken furniture to Rubb's desk. "We'll have this fixed in no time. We're expecting guests."

"Guests?"

"Oh, yes, didn't I tell you? You can expect more company for another of your little, ah, get-togethers," said Pentecost.

"There's more? Coming here? When?"

Rubb knew that another invasion was a bad idea, if for no other reason than Pentecost's thinking it was a good idea. Rubb decided to be coy.

"Good heavens! Tell me more! When?! How? Quick, out with it!"

"Easy, Rubb. You'll know when I do. They will come. They will come."

Rubb sensed that Pentecost knew that Rubb knew something about all of this. In fact, Rubb did know about the massive conjurctions that Sam Mentor had witnessed, but beyond that was a void. What puzzled Rubb was that Pentecost seemed to know a great deal more about the comings and goings of the Eardish Armee than his recent career in Kindergarten would have implied. To think that was only a few months ago!

"Why here?" said Rubb after locking looks with Pentecost, both failing to read the other's thought.

"Because you're here, I think. Is that important?" Pentecost watched Rubb closely for any clue.

"Well, am I here because you knew they were coming, or did they come here because they knew I was here?" Rubb stopped to track that through on his fingers, and added, "I think that's important."

You're right, that is important. But I don't know the answer to that. As far as I'm concerned, it doesn't make much difference either way. What's more important is that it will happen again."

"How are you so sure of that?"

"Thud, of course."

Pentecost watched Rubb even more closely, like a cat intent on a rustle in a bush.

"Thud. That's it? Thud?"

"We haven't seen one for months. Like I say, since you came. There had to be a connection. I don't know what it is, and I don't much care, but something's different from what it was. Thud don't come the way they used to. Now they come in herds. And you were the first." Pentecost paused dramatically, pulled on Annie, and continued, "The way I figure it, you're their leader. They'll come following you. Or maybe they're trying to rescue you. Whatever, they'll come."

"Rescue me!?" echoed Rubb, thoroughly confused. He knew that he had nothing to do with that Eardish infantry, and there was no way they knew about him.

"Rescue me from what? From you?"

On reflection, Rubb noticed how that sounded like an uncommonly good idea.

"From what indeed!" Annie gave her all. "Would you like to see from what?"

Rubb felt his nape hair bristle both in anticipation and apprehension. He nodded dumbly, knowing intuitively that this was exactly what he had come to see.

"Well, come on then, Rubb. Let's take a look at your handiwork."

Pentecost took Rubb paternally by the hand and led him toward the door, clearing the way with a backhand swipe of his right foot.

"By the way, what do they call you back home? High Thud? Thud One?" Rubb broke stride in disbelief.

"Or maybe Your Thudship. Your Thudjesty? Your Thudcellency. That's it! Your Thudcellency."

CHAPTER 22

The Flang

"You have already done it." Mentor mulled that over and under. "That's what it said, that Kickstart. You have already done it."

"What's 'it'?" asked Klaatu.

Klaatu busied himself straightening Mentor's robes for the call on Rubb. He set them out carefully in the order they would be needed, neatly pressed and free of static cling. Klaatu had learned to be particularly fastidious about static buildup when an inadvertent thunderstorm on Mentor's garb diverted him from a quest for a long forgotten beer recipe into a limbo of lost mail that took days to unravel, like backlash on a fishing reel. Klaatu thought his master would never return that time. Mentor did return, but madder than Hell. Having just come from Hell's suburbs, Klaatu knew how mad that to be.

That was a long time ago. At least Klaatu guessed that it was a long time ago; trolls cannot tell time when they are dead. Mentor seemed to have settled down by the next time his services were called for, and so it must have been a long time. That is the stuff of a troll's reckoning.

"I don't know what it is," answered Mentor. "I don't know, but I have to find out soon so I don't do it again. Maybe so I can do it again. I don't even know which." Sam slouched against the icebox, popped another beer, and scowled walleyed into the mop.

"When did you do this alleged it?" asked Klaatu, disturbed at the change that had come over Sam of late.

Of late was a broad term, perhaps as precise as a troll could be timewise. Klaatu was accustomed to being browbeaten and thrived on Mentor's vituperative nature. Each surge of anger was a fresh infusion of vital force, and Klaatu reveled in them. Now that Sam had turned sullen, these life forces had lost their fizz and Klaatu suffered sympathetically. If Klaatu could tell time, he would know that it had been only a day since the encounter with Kickstart.

"I don't know that either, but it must have been either our attempt to contact Baanquer, or when Rubb disappeared. In fact, it must be one of those two things, because we didn't do anything between. Perhaps it was both of those. Either one could have jarred the ether and jerked that thing out of nothingness; both have certainly attracted its attention. But you said Kickstart is a relative of yours, so I didn't create it! It was looking for me, I know it was!"

Sam sloshed down the half magnum of beer, turned to Klaatu with renewed interest.

"Say, Klaatu, you did say this Kickstart or whatchamacallit was related to you, didn't you?"

"Why, yes, I did."

Klaatu felt Sam's dander coursing in his veins again, and perked up like a stepped-on inner tube.

"What can you tell me about him? Or it."

"Her," corrected Klaatu. "That thing you call Kickstart is a her. But that's nominal at best; there is only one."

"Well, what can you tell me?"

"You call her Kickstart. Elsewhere she goes by Gabriel. She's a free-lance gofer." Klaatu caught Sam's puzzlement in his veins before Mentor could verbalize it. "You know, a runner, and errand doer."

"Ah. That helps immeasurably," said Sam with a gleam of satisfaction in his eyes. "And who does our little Miss Kickstart work for now?"

"Your little Miss Kickstart/Gabriel doesn't work for anyone. She pokes into whatever devilment is at hand and takes her own counsel. We don't trust her and we don't admit to knowing her in polite company. She's trouble, plain and simple." Klaatu stirred the hops tea and looked back at Sam.

"But you said she was a gofer; she ran errands?! She must run them for someone."

"Oh, she does. She meddles in others' business. But she runs her own errands."

Klaatu wiped both hands with a downward palms-in swipe at his apron and tasted the barrel of sorghum using his thumb as a dipper. A nod to Sam signaled the prospect of a memorable brew. Over their years together, Sam and Klaatu acquired the habit of settling down to a barrel of Klaatu's home brew at the end of each life together. Each of Klaatu's lives, that is. The brew settled things, let Klaatu slip into the nether world at peace with this one, and bent Sam.

"I see, I see."

Sam didn't really see at all, but taken at face value, Klaatu's words indicated that Gabriel's penchant for treachery commanded respect.

"What do you suppose she wanted with me?"

"I don't know, boss. Unless she meant just what she said."

"How's that?"

"You said she said 'You have already done it. Nice work'?"

Klaatu had a remarkable memory for one who wiped it clean with every death. Perhaps that's why he was such a quick study; he had to start from scratch each awakening.

"Maybe she's just an onlooker this time, saw a nice piece of work, and wanted to stop by to compliment you on it."

"No; I don't think so," much as the idea appealed to Sam. "I felt I was to account to her for something. And that doesn't explain the remark that I had been chosen. Chosen for what, do you suppose?"

"You were chosen to do what you had already done. That's why it was such nice work." Klaatu's logic was impeccable, if circuitous.

"But what did I *do*?!"

Sam shook with the frustration welling within, kicked wildly at a face cord of split hickory by the fire pit, and ripped the top off another can of store-bought beer.

"Can't you hurry, Klaatu! This junk doesn't work any more."

"I have to let it age a little more, Sam."

Little more was another of those trollishly loose time-terms that meant little to Klaatu and less to the beer. Sam and Klaatu would drink it, ready or not, when the time came to drink. Fermentation was not a serious consideration as Klaatu had adjusted the recipe, substituting alcohol for the water. Other than that, aging was mostly a matter of form.

"Well, then, let's get started."

Mentor flipped the coin, shrugged, and gave the thumbs-up sign indicating that there would be but one chance. One chance because Sam had decided to Hotwyre this projection to Rubb and bypass Central, a move that would involve unconscionable risk under any other circumstance. But Gabriel had intercepted his last standard call to Rubb, a feat that was as difficult as dipping out a speck floating on water. It couldn't be done without breaking the surface tension. Apparently Gabriel could do just that, etherically speaking, and slice across the cosmos with a Seeker; a semi-live outburst of hate that now comes hermetically packaged.

He was certain Gabriel couldn't do it alone; the power investment was too vast, the commitment in Obs incredible. It was only used where the payoff was certain in prospect and staggering in scope, the operative confident of immunity from investigation. One who could wield such a tool was in clear violation of the Code, but was also beyond reach of it by virtue of a loophole that had been written in for just such an eventuality. Whoever was bankrolling this job, Gabriel had her resources, resources that Sam had to respect and grudgingly admire.

So, it would have to be a Hotwyre.

HotWiring straddled an underground network that placed the caller at the absolute mercy of virtually everyone else on the network. That was the whole idea, to draw down reinsurance from every wizard between Eard and Hell, but only a little from any one so as to attract no attention.

One wizard will not willingly allow another to dip into his pocket, as industrial espionage is an occupational hazard otherwise roundly discouraged, so there is a price to pay; absolute dependency on the goodwill of everyone on the network. Thousands of them. Every one of them will watch every step, every word, and take notes. Not only would Sam lay bare to any casual onlooker his most secret of secrets, but he would also risk annihilation at the hands of anyone who fancied the end of Mentor. If a step was stilted or a word awry, Mentor would rocket into the Void as his cosmic moxie snapped like a rubber band. As the Void was endless, so would be Sam's demise. However, proof against another intervention by Gabriel could only be secured by dissipating the load, and multiplying the risk, over so many individuals that no Seeker would notice. That was the theory anyway.

Sam tugged into his elbow and kneepads, cinched down the crash helmet, double-knotted his steel-toed shoes, and inflated the Mae West. Klaatu flashed the Ready/Alert by launching a colossal Roman candle up the smoke pipe. The popping of the salutes told Sam that all systems were go.

Sam took up the lilting chant that had no vowel. Vowels would not pass this way, as knots on a thread will not pass a needle.

> *"Pst/nth/pst/Blt,*
> *Tsk/Ms./Tsk/mm.*
> *Pst/bbl/tsk/blvd,*
> *Tsk/shh/pst/zzz!"*

Tension mounted as every wizard in the network drew up the slack at their other ends. Mentor's arms and legs stretched outward into a spread-eagled splay that formed an X, intersecting at Sam's heart.

Mentor picked up the pace of the chant as he felt himself lift free of the floor. Sam's fingers assumed the classic splat configuration, his toes pointed to the right and left, perpendicular to his line of sight. He hung in space, stretched like a pelt on a bow, facing the blank stone wall at the far end of the cave. The wall had been dressed down and polished to a perfect plane for the occasion, and Sam could see his own apprehension reflected in the granite.

Klaatu pulled Sam backward by his belt and released him with a subsonic twang. Mentor's body swung slowly forward, still asplay, and stopped momentarily as the network pulled back against his momentum. Like a pendulum, he accelerated backwards twice as far and again stopped as his weight balanced the tension trying to throw him forward. His chant quickened with the beat of his heart and the whip of the resonating network. Forward, backward, faster and faster, his reflected face flashing closer and closer.

Now the idea is that as the network worked up to escape velocity, Sam would slingshot in a full-face belly flop, flat into the stone wall. If everything worked as planned, Mentor would flash through the wall unscathed, involuting his reflection and blasting directly into Rubb's immediate vicinity, following the traces of Rubb's residual vapor trail. In the trade, this was known as The Flang.

If, on the other hand, things did not go as planned, Klaatu was instructed to paint the wall over and let the cave out as his retirement annuity.

Whichever the result, the situation was replete with sensory feedback.

Mentor reared back for what was to be the final fling, the taut strands of the Network singing with anticipation. His flesh settled itself momentarily as he stopped absolutely in space, drawn to the limit of the Network. In that suspended instant, Mentor shouted with all the gusto he could muster,

"Pull!!" This last very sincerely.

Klaatu, anticipating the injunction, slammed his hands together, popping the paper sack resoundingly. The explosion, multiplied by the double bagging so much in vogue these days, startled Sam in spite of himself.

FLANG!

Mentor was gone, with only the lingering ring of a sonic boomlet to indicate something had happened. A telltale tingle of excitement electrified the air as all over Eard wizards congratulated each other, the Gordian lines abuzz with news of their finally achieving success with the Hotwyre. The excitement faded gradually as they rang off one after another and went to make plans of their own.

Klaatu stood quietly watching himself in the polished stone, shocked at his own appearance, but determined to keep vigil for the virtual glint that signaled Sam's return. He would have only an instant to brace himself as Sam came rumbling through on the rebound. If Klaatu missed the tackle, Mentor would shoot out the front door like a blast out of a shotgun and land somewhere in the next county. So Klaatu watched intently, preened a little surreptitiously, and waited.

Sam waited too, poised in limbo as he traded places with his reflection in a process that he didn't understand but could only assume was proceeding normally. He couldn't move a muscle, nor could he perceive any motion about him. He couldn't see a thing, but it was not black or gray light; his eyes simply didn't work here in the way that red has no up. He remembered hitting the wall, but not that it hurt any. It felt more like he had popped to the surface of a pool of quicksilver, emerging with a little snap as the surface tension of his own world whipped around his body and ejected him. The sensation was even a little pleasant, but then any sensation at all was welcome. Sam was beginning to relax a bit and enjoy the feeling of euphoria that followed an adrenaline high.

FLANG!

Sam ripped through the drapes hanging over the patio window to Rubb's office and blasted around the room twice at full throttle, the drapes snapping and crackling in his slipstream. The crash of the windowpane and the shriek of the rocketing Mentor completely rattled Rubb, who had been sipping an iced tea and contemplating his crossword puzzle. Rubb dived under the desk as Sam swooped overhead, pulled a pretty neat Uey, and blasted out the window again. The room reverberated with the metallic clang of the Flang. Rubb peered over the edge of the desk only to see the office drapes banking into an approach pattern over the city. Rubb sized up the situation quickly and opened the window on the other side of the office. In the meantime, Sam managed to untangle himself from the drapes somewhat, exposing his head but leaving a streamer of billowing brocade trailing like a kite tail. Sam timed his words carefully.

"Rubb!" shouted Sam on the way into the office. "It's me!" on the way out.

Rubb was stupefied with recognition, thinking all along that this was another of those cursed machines in which the Zerp shrieked about their land. He had watched them come and go, sometimes approaching his penthouse so closely that their roar would set the structure ringing.

He wondered when one would hit the building outright, and until this instant assumed that one had.

"Sam!" shouted Rubb to the streak in the stratosphere. "Come back Sam . . . Come back!"

Rubb watched the wizard describe an arc in the sky, bank back towards Rubb, and draw a bead on the office window. Rubb hit the deck.

"Icantstop," shouted Sam over the rush of air and flap of fabric. "I'm HotwyredandIdonthavetimetochat . . . Justlisten!"

Sam made a sound like a thumb pulled from a jug as he walloped through the office and out again over the city; "Thubb," like that. Sam flew belly-floppy and spread-eagled face on to the wind rather than in the classic fist-first Shazam style. While this pose provided a variety of control surfaces, it was not aerodynamically stable and set up a standing shock wave that preceded Sam like a big pillow. Every time he plowed through the office Rubb's ears popped. Anticipating the next transit, Rubb yawned widely and stood clear.

"Bigstumpwithclawsonbothends!" shouted Sam, swooping low to grab a decanter of muscatel from Rubb's desk. "Agrinyouwouldntbelieve! . . . Gabriellll!"

Thubb-Pop. Thubb-Pop.

"Dammit Sam! What are you talking about! Wait! Wait! Get me out of here!" Rubb panicked at the thought of being left behind after coming so close to salvation.

"Youhavetostayhere!" Thubb-Pop. "Itsallgoingtohappen . . . Fast!" Thubb-Pop.

"What's all going to happen!? I don't even know what's going on. What can I do here!"

Rubb was shouting at the wind that whirled papers about the office in Sam's vortex, kicking up a dust devil in the fireplace. Sam was a quarter mile out and didn't hear a word.

Rubb braced for the impact again, wrapping one arm around a plastic potted plant that was bolted to the floor.

Thubb. WHUMPP!

Sam had maneuvered the drapery into a drag chute and pulled the rip cord as he entered. The chute opened sharply, like a shook-out sheet, and bit the air like a sea anchor, yanking Sam to a standstill right over Rubb's desk. Sam's alien reality strained violently against the draw cords as the Hotwyre wrenched at his body. Mentor was out of place in this world, which is one of the drawbacks of the Hotwyre, and he was squirted about the displaced space like two palms on wet soap. Sam, though technically stationary, was being pulled tautly horizontal against the unfurled drapes. Sam casually set the empty decanter back in its place.

"Whatever you did, Rubb, you sure upset things. Nice Work, I think."

"What did I do?!" cried Rubb. "I haven't understood a thing since I got here."

Sam wrestled himself around to a sitting position in the cradle of the drapery draw cords, but sideways to Rubb as the tension of the Hotwyre torqued his body relentlessly. Getting comfortable after a fashion, Sam smiled to Rubb and looked about for another decanter. Finding none at hand, he continued.

"Rubb. I don't completely understand everything either. Things are different! Since you left everything seems so . . . Well, it seems normal!"

Somehow, that sounded anticlimactic to Rubb. Expecting rather more, Rubb pursued the point.

"Normal?" Rubb asked pointedly.

"Yes. That is, I've noticed that the world seems to hum like it hasn't since I was a kid." Sam Mentor actually wisted.

"Ah, could you be a little more specific, Sam. We've got to get out of here you know."

Yes, yes. Well, Rubb, in the week you've been gone I've noticed . . ."

"A week!" cried Rubb. I've been here for months! I don't know how long; six or eight anyway. What do you mean a week!" Rubb tilted his head ninety degrees to square off with Mentor accusingly.

"Months? Months? How can that be! Why, only yesterday Klaatu and I called. But we were cut off!"

"Yesterday? You didn't call yesterday. The last time you called was only a few days after I blew in here. Like I say, months ago. What's kept you?" Rubb stayed in his adversary mode.

"But it was yesterday, Rubb. We were cut off. I tried to warn you about Gabriel, but they got through and cut us off." Sam was as perplexed as Rubb.

"Right after you disappeared, that time we called Hell, I tried to get you back but I was intercepted by this fanged grin with one leg. Klaatu says her name is Gabriel. Nothing but trouble."

Rubb sorted through his experiences darkly, knowing he had heard something about a fanged grin somewhere. It wouldn't come.

"Intercepted! How can that be? That's impossible. I thought it was only an anachronism in the Code."

"So did I, Rubb, but Gabriel did it. Not alone, though. She had help. Big help. I couldn't wait any longer with that much power hanging around. They knew where I was and I suppose they know where you are too."

Rubb jerked at that!

"So that's why I Hotwyred. It worked! It's never been done before, Rubb! With a little bit of luck they weren't watching and they don't know I'm here!"

"They. Who's They?"

"I don't know. I really don't. However, this Gabriel knows. In fact she said I had been chosen."

"Chosen. For what?"

"Who knows! Gabriel isn't the real problem, just the intermediary as far as I can figure it. She knows, but she just does her own thing. I'm not even sure which side she's on. Enough of that. What's going on here? What did you do to change things so?"

"I didn't do anything I can put my finger on, Sam. I was attacked by everybody I talked to, so I fell in with this Pentecost character. He was the only one who never attacked, so I thought I was safe. He brought me here. Some friend! I've been locked up here ever since. The only company I have is Slumpblock. Oh, yes. The Eardish Armee comes through every afternoon at 3:05. Other than that, this place is deadly dull."

"What did you say?! The Eardish Armee?" Sam lurched, lost his balance momentarily and struggled for purchase. "Every day?"

"Oh, yes. Didn't you know? Those mass conjurctions you told me about, they come right through here. We just step aside while they herd them on through. Regular as clockwork."

One knot in the draw cord slipped in astonishment and Sam scrambled to hold it. He was losing.

"How many, Rubb? How many have come through here?" Sam was livid. "Think, Rubb! Think! It's important that I know exactly!"

"Well, there must be hundreds every day, maybe a thousand. They just pile in like a basket of fruit, and they haul them out. They tear the place up every time, and next morning it's been fixed up again. In fact . . ."

"How many!!!"

"Oh. Say, Slumpblock. Slumpblock!" Rubb banged understandingly on the desk drawer where Slumpblock had retreated when Sam first blasted through the window.

"Slumpblock. How many soldiers are there in one of those units of yours that come through here every day?"

"How many?" Slumpblock blinked at the daylight, then at Sam. "Well, for a while at first there were only a few hundred. Now there must be ten thousand. Every day."

Sam was at a loss for words, either regarding the ten thousand soldiers or Slumpblock. "Nearly a million!" That was a good word.

Slumpblock's eyes rolled upwards for a moment. "As of yesterday, that's one million, three hundred fifty thousand and one, counting me."

"That's it! That would account for it!"

"Account for what? What are you talking about?" asked Rubb.

"That's what's changed everything. It's like everybody on a ship crowding on one side to watch a disaster," explained Sam Mentor excitedly. "They cause a disaster they came to see."

The cords that had been heroically restraining Sam went into their inexorable unravel. Sam leaped into action, if one can be said to leap when up is sideways, and prepared to disembark by snugging his goggles about his ears.

"Wait! Don't go yet. I have to get my things."

"Sorry, Rubb. You can't go," said Sam to a shocked Rubb. "If I tried to take you with me, you'd be splattered all over the inside of your reflection."

"What?"

Rubb did not understand at all, so an answer would have been pointless, but Sam was here and in a position to know what he was talking about.

"Never mind. I'll come for you later." Sam saw the slipknots were about to live up to their reputation. "But watch out for Gabriel. Remember, a big grin with claws on both ends. She'll be nothing but trouble."

One knot gave way, letting Sam slip awkwardly with a quick spin. Sam unsheathed his pocketknife and started to cut the other draw cord with the little saw blade thing.

"Wait! Wait! What will I do about the Eards that keep coming? Can't you stop them?" shouted Rubb. "They eat them here! Rip them apart and eat them!"

Mentor stopped sawing and gaped at Rubb. Too late. The last strand snapped and Mentor cannonballed out the window in a screech of torn atmosphere that set Rubb to spinning about the potted plant. Sam had gotten turned around and roared out the patio window backwards, his eyes wide-fixed on Rubb, his arms and legs spread-eagled.

"Don't forget! Don't lend Gabriel any money!" shouted Sam as he receded into the Sunset. "Klaatu sends his love!"

FLANG!!

Klaatu had only an instant to yank the rope and draw up the safety net he had contrived to catch Sam Mentor. He saw in the wall the watery waver of his own reflection and sprang for the rope, grabbing it on the fly.

Sam flashed out of the wall backwards, and hit the net square on his back. Pulling the net to its limits with his momentum, Sam dropped to the floor with a muffled thump into a pile of knotted rope.

"Nice work, Klaatu," said Sam sincerely. "Nice work."

CHAPTER 23

Setting the Trap

Generalissimo Ultissimo Schwartz set the snare carefully. As landlord of Eard, Gus found that setting snares was relatively easy. The hard part was selecting the bait as Mentor had little use for the wares of civilized Eard.

In fact, Mentor was not really Eardish, his mother being a Sop and his fathers both Musicians. Esthetics aside, the extra set of genes Mentor carried in every cell as a result of such bad timing resulted both in his uncanny facility with things superEardian and his almost complete detachment from things just plain Eard.

Almost, however, implied a host of opportunities to Gus, the primary problem being only one of finesse. Mentor was good, damned good, and wary of intrusion. Gus was no match for Mentor on his turf, so Gus would have to lure him out. However, what would be the bait! That was the problem that had obsessed Gus for months as he wove the web that would be the undoing of Sam Mentor.

The brownout turned the trick for Gus. Something happened, something so subtle that for all his intelligence systems, Gus was completely unaware. Nevertheless, Gabriel noticed. It was Gabriel's business to notice things like that, and keep him informed. Over the years, Gus had paid Gabriel a bundle for that service and collected only this once. However, this once was more than enough to justify the investment. Gus had the key to Mentor's weakness and built his trap around it.

Gabriel had left a note on Gus' desk. The message was simple, "Where is Rubb?" The author of the note had to be Gabriel, as the words were hacked into his desktop as though with an ice pick. Where's Rubb indeed! Gus had forgotten all about the Prime Minister!

There really was not much for a Minister to do in Eard these days, prime or not, the Grand Assembly having laid itself off for the summer. The Prime Minister, holding a nominal position at best, had only one responsibility; sign the Articles of Adjournment and head for the beach. If Gus needed any formal legislation, he simply appointed another Assembly, told the clerk what he wanted, and the outfit rubber stamped it without review. The Prime Minister signed and that was that. But something had gone wrong a few Assemblies ago, something that escaped Gus' notice at the time.

Somehow, appointments to the Grand Assembly had been drawn from an old magazine subscription list for the Sleight of Hand Quarterly. The Prime Minister chosen by the old cleric in personnel was a dwarf with a record of minor run-ins with the law. That was why he was chosen to be Prime Minister. The dwarf's name was Rubb. Rubb had never taken the oath of office officially, but that was not unusual as the business of the Assembly was usually over before a full quorum was met. At any rate, Gus had only to forge any necessary signatures and let it go at that. So did everyone else. Everyone, that is, except this dwarf named Rubb.

Rubb's file showed that he did in fact show up to take office, although several months late due to his involvement with a road show. He seems to have made quite a nuisance of himself looking for something to do. Out of work and apparently under the delusion that the Prime Minister was paid a salary, this Rubb person poked his nose into everything for weeks. Then he disappeared. End of file.

After deciphering Gabriel's cryptic message about Rubb's whereabouts, Gus sent out a trace starting with the magazine subscription list. Rubb was seen in and out of his quarters for a time, then nothing. He seemed to disappear from Eard altogether. Then came the brownout, Gabriel's message, and the knock at Gus' door.

"Come in, Sam Mentor," said Gus, oozing congeniality. Gus hardly interrupted his rhythmic stroke as he rubbed the sanding block over his desk. "Come in."

Sam Mentor stepped into the penthouse office as though he were stepping into a rowboat; precisely and with assurance, but with an acute awareness of his center of gravity.

In such a situation, one does not know exactly which way the boat will slide, but one is certain that it will indeed slide unexpectedly. One looks not only at the boat, one looks also at the horizon, and so Sam Mentor looked at Gus with one eye and scanned the room with the other. One does not step gingerly on the boat's gunnels but rather launches one's weight into the center of the boat with authority. So Sam strode to the center of the room without hesitation, planted his feet squarely and opened without taking his eyes from Gus.

"Our business was settled years ago. What is it you want now?" Sam was impatient.

"I can do something for you and you can do something for me."

Gus said that without disturbing the smile on his face. In spite of appearances, Gus did not feel like smiling. From his only experience with Sam Mentor he knew that he would not, so he had set the smile with hair spray. The effect was good, as long as the hair spray held, and Sam was a bit aback at the confident manner of this Phrogg before him.

"I need nothing," said Sam disdainfully. "I draw my sustenance from nothingness and I am accountable to no one."

While that was certainly a grand statement of his philosophical orientation, in point of fact Sam Mentor relied heavily on Klaatu's beer. But Sam quickly qualified his remark.

"I choose what I take from others, but I never need. I may give to others as I am motivated, but I never bargain."

"Bravo! Well spoken, Sam Mentor!" said Gus with a shout of glee. "That was magnificent!"

"Thank you," said Sam uncertainly.

The boat moved unexpectedly but Mentor did not move so much as a twitch. His eyes lingered a bit too long on Gus as he assigned point values to the alternative probabilities that presented themselves.

"Let's get down to business, Sam." Gus cleared his throat a little while he chose his words. "I have a problem and you can help me. A little matter of soldiers that keep disappearing from my Armee."

"Soldiers?" responded Sam with a raised eyebrow. The probability distribution collapsed three orders of magnitude.

"Come, Come, my dear Sam Mentor," said Gus in his most ingratiatingly offensive manner. "You've been monitoring my little sendoffs for months now. Maybe I . . ."

"Years," said Sam evenly. "I knew about them before you did."

"You couldn't . . . !"

Gus abrupted himself, madder than Hell that he had been outfeinted and distracted by the crackling hair spray that started to give way.

"That is, you didn't know where they were going." Damn!!

"Neither did you," said Sam with a sly little curl to his mild-mannered smile. "In fact, I don't believe you knew they were going anywhere."

"Hah!" rejoined Gus.

It wasn't a "Gotcha" kind of Hah. It was more like a juvenile "oh yeah?" Hah. Gus was not at all happy with it either, so he tried again.

"All right, smarty, you tell me where they're going."

Mentor paused for a moment to consider the wisdom of that. He was certain that Gus really did not know where they went, but someone sure did. At least someone ought to know and Sam was determined to find out who that was. What little knowledge he had was his playing hand and he did not want to squander it.

"Later, perhaps," replied Sam. "But I can tell you that I didn't know you were responsible. That is, until you told me just now."

That was a grade-A Gotcha and Gus winced at having given so much away so early in the game. Sam was right; Gus did not know at first that those soldiers were being displaced into another Wherever, and he sure as Sop did not know where Wherever was. Gus and Sam glared at each other for a full minute, Gus steaming in frustration and Sam smiling.

"All right," blurted Gus, nearly shouting. "Who cares where they are! I'm happy to be rid of the little pests! But I brought you here for a reason and I can spell it out for you in one word: Rubb!"

"Rubb!" Sam caught himself, but not before revealing his surprise that Gus knew about Rubb. Frantically, Sam struggled to cover his slip.

"Oh, you mean the Prime Minister. How is the old chap these days?"

"Nice, Sam. Nice," said Gus with real admiration. "But let me rephrase myself." Gus paused as though he actually were trying to rephrase the word Rubb.

"Wherever Rubb is, he's in trouble. I do not know exactly what your stake is in this, Sam, but Rubb's fate is tied up with yours. Right?"

Sam Mentor's face was a wall, both his eyes fixed on Gus' right. Gus' eyes were wide-spaced and moved independently, which was a great asset in his regular noontime game of tag with the household staff on the front lawn, but they were also opposed, making it impossible to fix Sam effectively in return. Resigning himself to a one-eyed duel, Gus proceeded.

"Now that that's settled, I want you to understand that I can help you. Do you understand?"

Sam only stared intently at Gus, waiting for the Phrogg to set the hook.

"I'll take that as a yes. All right then, Sam Mentor, here is my proposition. Wherever Rubb is, you had nothing to do with getting him there. Neither did I. But . . ."

"I know better than . . ."

Sam stopped to reconsider Gus' words. Could it be that he really had nothing to do with Rubb's projection to Zerpland! As much as Sam recoiled at the possibility of his own impotence in the matter, it could explain a few things, not the least of which was his impotence in the matter.

"I'm listening."

"That's better. I see we're going to get along nicely." Pause. "Now, as I was saying, I can help you. Your fate is tied to Rubb's, and I can cut that knot. I can save you, Sam Mentor!"

Sam snorted at the implications, all of them! Did this Phrogg think that he would abandon Rubb? Well, maybe he would at that, but this presumptuous amphibian had no business offering to save Sam Mentor. Sam need only snap his thumbs and Gus would have never been. Maybe he should have done that the last time they clashed.

But no! If it were true that Sam had not projected Rubb, and it was certainly true that Gus got all of his information second-hand after the fact, then the situation today would be no different! Gus or no Gus, Sam decided to attack.

"You have no power to harm me or save me, you egotistical fool!!" spat Sam in a pretty good temper. Drawing a deep breath, Sam warmed two clicks and turned his eyes red at the corners, muttering deeply but distinctly

"You have sealed your doom! Make your peace with whatever you call a god!"

Sam reached into the space at his right, claws outstretched as though to pull a gigantic doorknob. Instantly, a fireball engulfed his fist like a miniature sun, crawling with flaming, writhing, worm-like tentacles that twisted themselves into the white-hot knot. Sam drew his arm back like a kegler. Sam had always been a spot bowler and Gus could see that the spot Sam had selected was his nose, such as it was. Sam's arm started forward.

"No! Wait!!" Sam stopped.

Gus had not expected to come to violence quite so soon. Later perhaps; Sam had a reputation for this sort of thing, and his last encounter with Sam prepared him for the inevitable attack. Still, Sam was being somewhat more than merely dramatic. That fireball looked real enough, and Sam looked positively crazed.

"Hold it just a minute, Sam. Don't go off half-cocked now. We can talk. Set that thing down."

"Is that the way you pray to your god?" said Sam with a one-sided smile. "You have a short memory, Gus. My little pets here have been itching to get another bite out of you. My regards to Hell!"

"Oh, Gabe," sing-songed Gus. He looked past Sam Mentor and gestured as though for the maitre d'. "Can you give me a hand?"

"Don't try that old trick," said Sam, his smile broadening. "Next you'll tell me my shoelaces are untied." Sam adjusted his grip for a hook and released.

"Gabe!"

Pffft!!

In mid-stroke Sam's fireball sputtered to an ineffectual sprinkle of ash that settled noiselessly on Gus' desk.

Sam Mentor knew better than to make any sudden moves and dared not take his eyes off Gus. Behind him tingled the light ring of a crystal goblet being rubbed by a wet finger.

"Gabriel?!" Sam was incredulous.

"That's right, Sam." Gus leaned back in his plush leather swivel chair and smirked broadly in spite of the crumbling hair spray.

"You don't think I'd let you in here without a pet or two of my own?"

Sam did not turn around. There was little point in it. He knew that Gabriel had no face and was inscrutable in consequence. Gus' face, however, was typically Phroggish, with no control whatsoever. Hence the hair spray that crumbled and fell in a light snow in Gus' lap. Whatever chance he had depended on reading that Phroggy face correctly.

"My compliments," said Sam graciously. "Well, if that's settled, I'll be . . ."

"Nothing's settled, Sam Mentor. I have a few thoughts to share with you, then I will dismiss you. Whatever terms we come to, Sam Mentor, I am in control now. Completely in control."

Sam, knowing Phroggs were given to hyperbole, discounted that statement somewhat, but the presence of Gabriel counted more. Gabriel, on the other hand, was free-lancing and probably only here for amusement or at the bid of someone else. Certainly not at Gus' bidding. Someone was managing Gus through Gabriel and only letting on that Gus was in some sort of control because it suited their purposes. Who!??

"All right, Gus," said Sam, relaxing back onto his heels. "Let's hear it."

"That's more like it. Now, the matter of one ex-prime minister by the name of Rubb, also ex-journeyman magician," resumed Gus in a businesslike manner. "Rubb's in trouble. There are only two choices. In a word, it's either you or Rubb."

"How's that?"

"As I said, your fate is tied to Rubb's. Your futile attempt to tempt the fates only kicked up a nest of vipers. You have no idea of the mess you are in, and you are in it together. There are forces at work that even you do not suspect, Sam Mentor, and you have managed in one stroke both to attract their attention and arouse their wrath. The hammer will fall, Sam

Mentor; the question is only whether it will be on you, on Rubb, or on you both."

"That sounds like three alternatives. You said two."

"If you do nothing to cooperate, it will be the doom of you both. That is set and it is your own handiwork. I had nothing to do with that, and you know that is the truth." Gus paused for agreement.

Sam reflected on that truth. Gus did not know what was going on with those soldiers, and apparently still does not know everything, so most of what he's saying is being fed to him. On the other hand, Sam had no reason to believe other than what he said, secondhand or not. Sam and Rubb knew that they had taken a colossal chance in trying to contact Baanquer and this was their reward. Okay, given that they're both in trou . . . Baanquer! Baanquer, of course! Sam felt his blood pulse at the realization, and struggled to conceal it.

"Whatever else you do, don't tip your hand now," Sam reflexed to himself.

"All right," said Sam aloud, "What's your deal?"

"You come to work for me. Let us say something in Public Relations? And forget about Rubb. He's just one more of thousands of battle casualties."

"Work for you! Doing what, might I ask?"

"Yes, you might, but you'll get no answer. At least you will not get an answer until I have something for you to do. However, I will need your guarantee that when that time comes, you will do exactly as I tell you. No more, no less. In the meantime, you just butt out and occupy yourself puddling around with those accursed brews of yours. They're harmless enough."

"And if I don't?" Sam bridled but held.

"If you don't like that idea, your only other alternative is to take Rubb's place, wherever that is and I make Rubb the same offer. He'll suit my purpose every bit as well as you."

Gus studied Sam Mentor carefully, but found little comfort in what he saw, an unblinking expressionless face that had weathered eons of ill wind. Gus knew Sam well enough to fear the machinations of that gnarled mind, and fervently hoped Gabriel had not set him up on this.

That possibility colored all his planning and would have deterred him from taking on Sam Mentor but for the implied promise of a free hand in Eard and wealth and power beyond all reckoning. He had tried Sam Mentor once before, and lost. Gus lost himself recollecting that day.

It was a day like all days in Eard, deadly dull and humid. Gus had yet to make his mark on Eard, unless you count the sitzmark that still commemorates his short stint as a hod carrier. In fact, that job had satisfied his curiosity about work. From that point on, Gus had taken extraordinary measures to avoid it.

One of those measures involved running errands for an old Platypus down in the Flats, an unlikely entrepreneur who sold ice cream, of all things, to a con man known only as Joe for lack of a given name. Gus' job was to pick up a package at the drop and deliver it to the old marsupial. For this he earned his keep and all the ice cream he could eat.

The trouble started when he tried to go into the ice cream business on his own. Knowing that old Sam Mentor could conjure up most anything out of his books, Gus contracted with him to provide ersatz Butter Pecan ice cream and went into direct competition with Joe. Except for one problem, this would have worked out since Joe was on the outs with the Elder Eards anyway.

Gus studied Mentor's habits carefully, noting his coming and going. Satisfied that he would have time to work, Gus slipped into Sam's cave one night when the wizard was on his weekly provender forage and began to conjure his own ice cream using Sam's recipes. There was not much of a trick to it, there being little magic involved in ice cream, and in no time at all, Gus was churning out Butter Pecan like vanilla.

The problem came when Gus had made all he could handle and tried to turn off the spell. No luck. The ice cream just kept piling up in the cave, and pushed out into the valley.

Mentor came back in time to clean up the mess with a snap of his thumbs, more amused with the diddlings of this precocious child than angered. Gus' wits saved him further embarrassment; he offered Sam a piece of the action. A partnership was struck and the money rolled in. However, Gus could not be satisfied with a split. He had to have it all and determined to get it by changing banks for his checking account.

Gus figured that his profit picture would improve dramatically if he didn't have to pay Sam royalties for the ice cream. He was right; he didn't and it did.

He had forgotten, however, to include Sam Mentor's temper in the profit and loss statement. Sam had learned long ago about deadbeats, and wasted no time sharing his wisdom with Gus. Upon the receipt of the third insufficient funds notice, Sam descended on Gus with a wrath and vengeance that marked Gus for months. Mentor knew with an unholy precision that point, short of annihilation, that evoked maximum pain, even with the dull-witted Phroggs. Sam lingered on that point with exquisite relish, leaving Gus a mumbling lump of fear and quiver.

Gus survived, of course. There was no point in firing a warning shot only to smother it with death. Sam had not been crossed in centuries, and if Gus carried his badge of honor publicly, he would not be crossed again. Gus learned his lesson. And he never forgot. Never.

"You okay?" asked Sam with mixed feelings.

"Um! Ah, yes, where were we?" Gus pulled himself back from his reverie with a revitalized sense of retribution.

"If I recall, I just made you an offer, one that I fully expect you to refuse. Well?"

"Let me get this straight. If I agree to . . . uh . . . double-cross my old friend Rubb, you and this thing behind me will let me go peaceably."

Sam watched Gus closely, and caught Gabriel's nod reflected in Gus' glistening eye.

"In return for this, your beneficence, I must sign a blank check payable and due/on demand and be your lackey till then. Is that right?"

"That's right, Sam." Gus grinned knowing Sam would never agree to be his servant.

"And if I don't, you, and again I presume this thing you call your pet, will abandon Rubb and myself to our hard-earned fates. Right?"

"Wrong," responded Gus with a pointy-fingered jab at the air. "If you do not, Rubb will have his opportunity to abandon you to your fate."

"Well, then! I accept!" Sam crossed his arms, smiling with satisfaction, and looked around for the door. "Now that that's settled, I . . ."

"You mean you will do it?! You'll do whatever I tell you?"

Gus glanced quickly beyond Sam Mentor to Gabriel for assurance, but Gabe was gone!!

"Ah. Good! Good!" Rats, thought Gus. What do I do now? "I'm glad you came to your senses."

Something went wrong! Sam was supposed to refuse and that would be the end of Sam Mentor! Where's Gabe!

"That's it? All right, then, keep in touch." Sam moved for the entry.

"Wait! Uh, don't you want to know what will happen to Rubb?"

"Not really," replied Sam. "He's no worse off now than before I walked in the door and he tends to bounce back like a punching dummy. He'll do no better or worse without my help."

"But, but," sputtered Gus, not sure what to do next. Where has that Gabriel got to now? "But what pledge do I have from you?"

"You have the pledge of one who has never done a whit more or less than his word in all things." Sam's eyes fixed Gus two to one. "If that's not good enough, then the deal's off. Is that good enough?"

Gus knew in his belly that something terrible turned on his answer. "Gabriel!" he thought ferociously, "where the Hell is Gabriel?"

She had conveniently neglected to tell Gus this might happen. Sam was supposed to refuse to take any orders from a Phrogg; he has never taken any orders from anyone, never in all remembering. Gabe implied Sam would refuse, Rubb and Sam would trade places, and a thankful Rubb would capitulate. End of Sam Mentor. However, Sam agreed! Now Gus found himself having to accept Sam's terms.

"All right! All right!" shouted Gus. "You're on!"

"Yes, I am," said Sam Mentor quietly. "Yes, I am."

As Sam strode out of the office, Gus was so incensed that he missed a light glassy tingle lingering in the air, a tingle with a chuckle.

CHAPTER 24

Dance

"Klaatu!" bellowed Mentor at the top of his voice, and then, "KLAATU!!!" belying himself.

"Wake up, you shriveled roadkill. I've got work for you!"

Klaatu did not stir, but even as Sam thrashed about his truck, looking for not even Sam knew what, Klaatu's hide softened and swelled with the infusion of Mentor's emotions. The revitalization of a troll like Klaatu was a slow process, partly because Klaatu tended to overload in the brunt of Sam's massive ego and partly because Klaatu's Id was becoming work-hardened.

Sam was usually very patient about reviving Klaatu, and gave him only an occasional paternalistic reminder, such as, "Breathe, dock post slime! Breathe!"

Usually, that is, but this time Sam was in a hurry and not in a paternalistic mood at all. He grabbed the jumper cables, slapped them to Klaatu's forehead, and yanked the starter rope. Klaatu jerked with the electric pulse of the little Otto-cycle generator, inflating like an air mattress. Sam brushed off his sleeves with satisfaction and returned to his search.

"Where in the Six Hells is Rosamunda!" demanded Sam. "She's got to be here somewhere!"

Sam slammed a few things about, chugging up little puffs of Dust from corners of the Workbench. The Dust seemed to have been left undisturbed in all time and resented the intrusion. The Workbench itself had been inherited from Sam's own mentor before Sam was born. The old wizard who left it to Sam was more rock and tree than flesh and blood and had never really died, at least not in the usual sense. The Workbench and all its Dust, particularly the Dust, was left in trust to Sam who used it rarely, and then only for the sake of Nostalgia.

Nostalgia, his mother's sister, had seized unilateral responsibility for Sam's cultural development years ago and insisted on dropping by unexpectedly to see that he was constructively engaged. When she did, Sam would simply step over to the Workbench, whip up a few gold ingots for her out of Marigold blooms or some such, and send her happily on her way. The Workbench was full of neato tricks like that, boilerplate with which Sam no longer trivialed.

The little generator kapukketed to a jiggly stop as Klaatu began to move under his own power, flexing a bit to lubricate his joints. He popped the little rubber suction cups from his forehead and stared at them dully while Sam's sense of urgency warmed his toes and pushed a tingle of excitement through his kinked veins.

"Oh," murmured Klaatu warmly, "That was good!"

"Klaatu! Where have you been? I need you! Now! Hurry!"

Klaatu took a few fumbling steps, stopped to straighten himself up, then meandered over to the Workbench where Sam was furiously disheveling Dust and shoveling debris that had, over the years, ricocheted off the garbage can lid.

"Klaatu, have you seen Rosamunda? I know she was here the last time I saw her."

Sam slammed a stack of heavy manuals to the floor right next to Klaatu who was concentrating on catching the crawly things that scurried for cover before Sam's rampage. Klaatu stood for two or three seconds while his yet sluggish nerves reacted to the startle. "Well dammit, Klaatu. Look for it!"

Klaatu finally jerked at the dropped books, breaking the trance, and began to look about the Workbench as though he knew what it was that Sam wanted. For good measure, he slapped a slat about a few times, blew the Dust off a flask and a pestle, and tried his best to look intent. He had no idea what he was about.

"What did you do with her, Klaatu?!" barked Sam in a smolder. "I know you had her last!"

Sam swept one end of the Workbench clean with a frustrated backhand, splashing alchemistic stuff all over the cave. A heavily riveted brass retort rolled irregularly across the floor, spilling a terminally desiccated potion of unknown design and potency into a drunken trail to the lip of the fire pit. Another projectile, a crystalline object that looked like one of those molded platters for serving slippery deviled eggs, but with shock absorbers, crashed satisfyingly against the granite keystone column. Other pieces of junk went their own ways, generally heading for cover as the thrash and commotion of Sam's search bated.

Klaatu waded through the fallout, kicking this and peering under that, trying different pieces at random for heft and whip. His attention was attracted to a hammer of sorts, a stumpy maul half his height and twice his weight. The head looked like it had once been a segment of an oak tree, now badly splintered and beaten, but it was made of a densely soft ironish metal that would take a thumbnail impression. The handle was hickory and much too large for Klaatu to fist his grip completely. The shaft was fire-hardened and carved to a comfortable two-handed fighting grip with a leather wrist thong. It was not made for the hand of an ordinary man, nor for anything constructive. It had been made to kill. In spite of its appearance, Klaatu sensed that it had never done so. It was quite alive.

Klaatu eased the hammer into a pendular swing at his side, testing its feel. Adding a little throttle, he worked the arc into a full battle roundhouse, yanking himself up off his feet in short hops as the hammerhead cycled on the edge of escape velocity.

"Hey boss," shouted Klaatu with a playful whoop. "Look at me!"

Sam turned grudgingly, annoyed at Klaatu's fleeting attention span, but stopped mid-torque.

"You found her! You found her!"

Sam ducked as Klaatu's eccentric got out of hand and sent him sprawling into the safety net piled in the corner. The hammer looped high through the air, hesitated thoughtfully, and plunged for Sam in defiance of classical ballistics.

Sam muttered an affectionate enticement as the hammer peaked, and stood with his feet wide-set and his arms outstretched to receive his old friend. The hammer flashed to him in an instant, but settled into his grip easily, like a puppy looking for a skritch behind the ears.

"Rosamunda," he cooed warmly. "My little Rosamunda. How have you been, my friend? I am sorry to neglect you so, but we are back together again. And I have work for you, work you'll like!"

Rosamunda positively glowed in Sam's arms, and Klaatu smiled sheepishly at Sam's open display of affection. Sam never displayed his emotions, at least not his nobler ones, and Klaatu felt unease at this little scene. Klaatu thrived on Sam's violent emotions, and never really considered the possibility that Sam had a gentler side. However, as a hedge against Sam's mellow mood depleting his psychic reserves, Klaatu edged towards the generator. As he did, he was disturbed to find an unfamiliar emotion rising within himself, an affection for the generator he had never known before.

Mentor, still nestling the hammer in his arms, waded through the clutter to the Workbench. A low-pitched subsonic hum rose from deep inside Sam, a hum that Klaatu felt rather than heard. The rumble blurred his vision temporarily as it lifted in pitch to an audible bass and his skull fell out of resonance. Sam began to sway as he stood there before the Workbench, modulating the monotone by quarter steps in time with his body. The tune lifted subtly around and through an incantation that had no words, in a language spoken only by rocks and trees.

The hammer still cuddled in Sam's arms, seeming to coo in a fluting counterpoint to Sam's bass accompaniment. Together they rocked, gently swaying ever more quickly, the tune ever more lilting. Klaatu felt a drunken, lightly euphoric warmth burbling out from his marrows, and found himself swaying selflessly with the lilt.

Sam's lair, usually a dimly lighted affair, brightened with the tune, taking on a rosy tint that made the furniture wince. The fire in the pit sputtered to an embarrassed, albeit resentful, silence as the glow of this enamored couple outshone its feeble combustions. The glow, however, did not come from Sam and Rosamunda in the geographical sense, but rather in the causal. It was the air itself, every loving molecule of it, that took on their harmony and reflected it back upon this little world.

Sam moved finally from the spot, first one foot slowly and then another more positively, turning grandly in a delicious pirouette. Sam held the hammer away from his body, delicately, like a father's first real look at his newborn, and smiled broadly. Lifting the warhead high, and singing out a full-throated cry that sounded to Klaatu like a yodeling grindstone, Sam whipped this living hammer into a swooping arc that whistled with a menacing mercilessness and a disarming joy de vivre.

Sam Danced with Rosamunda, a violently maniacal Dance that flung them both about their common center, sweeping the air clean of Sam's dismal perturbations like a broom catching cobwebs. Around and round they went, Rosamunda reaching high and low, Sam chortling a wildly musical chant that was melodious at the same time that it was inhuman.

Klaatu, torn between joining in the Dance and protecting himself from the hammer, settled on hitching a ride in the hood on the back of Sam's flying robe. Together, the three of them, bound in this merry-go-round of light and motion and music, looked pretty silly. In fact, Klaatu had about decided to bail out when Sam suddenly shifted gears. Klaatu sensed the surge of wrath in Sam's blood and held on tight.

Sam's face hardened to a resolute evangelical grimace as he urged the orbit of the hammer into the vertical. Down on the left of his body, and then down on the right, over his head and then down harder and harder until Sam's grip reached the limit of his palm skin. Sam turned his head to the Workbench as though to signal that he was ready, tilting it forward in determination, and then brought his heavy shoulders square away with his head and the Workbench.

Sam stepped slowly but deliberately towards the Workbench, each swing of the hammer bringing him relentlessly closer to the massive beams of the bench. His song had stopped by now, but the hammer gathered power from the world around it. Klaatu felt the chill and saw the dimming of the glow as the hammer absorbed power, gaining mass rather than speed, and knew that the hammer pulled Sam even as Sam drove the hammer. Closer and closer with each inexorable step, Sam drew a measured bead on the center of the heavily timbered Workbench. One last step and . . .

WHAM! The cries of the Dust shrieked through the air.

WHAM! Again and again, like a sneeze that would not quit. WHAM! . . . WHAM!! . . . WHAM!!! . . . WHAM!!!!

The cries faded.

It was immensely quiet, thought Klaatu, except for the ringing in his ears. After at least a minute, Klaatu rubbed his eyes to help them adjust to the darkness that had again overtaken the cave, and peeked warily over Sam's shoulders. Things were again as they were before the Dance, except that the Dust was completely gone. And Sam was crying.

"It held!" cried Sam through his tears of rapture, "The Workbench held!"

Sam sank visibly as the tension flowed from his body, the hammer dropping to his side, slipping lightly from his fingers to the floor.

"It held."

Sam sobbed gently in relief and release, mopping the tears with his cloak sleeve. The hammer wilted visibly. Sam stumbled uncertainly to the fire pit, which had sprung anew with a sooty flame, and rubbed himself to warm the body that had been stripped of anima in the Dance. Klaatu climbed down from Sam's hood, looked around the dim-again cave, and snuggled up to the fire to shake his own chill. Sam thought for a long moment.

"I think we are going to see the end of this." He spoke right through Klaatu. "And soon."

Sam filled his friendly pipe slowly, lighting it with a glowing twig. Drawing deeply a few times, Sam relaxed himself into deep concentration. These events felt solid in his mind, very real and massive. There was no doubt about them. But somewhere on the other end of them a world hung impaled by the force that he had unleashed and Sam had to be dead certain about his next move.

Sam settled squat-legged by the fire pit. Scowling deeply into the coals, elbows on knees, chin in palms and his beloved pipe in his teeth, Sam slowed himself to a glower that did not move in time.

The pipe had cooled an hour now, and began to squirm discretely to relieve the kinks. Sam had not moved in that time, nor had the thoughtful pipe, so Sam jerked a little when he realized its predicament.

"Sorry little fellow," he soothed, "I was lost in my thoughts."

Sam rapped out the dottle against his palm into the fire, rubbed the pipe deeply, and nestled it into its favorite nock in the sideboard.

"Are you feeling better, Boss?"

Klaatu certainly felt better. Whenever Sam went into one of his trances Klaatu slipped into Limbo, a semi-aware state that was neither life nor death, but was the worst of both.

"Yes. Yes, I am all right. How about you?" asked Sam with real concern in his voice.

"Me?" Klaatu was astounded.

Sam never worried about Klaatu because he was Sam's inverted Id. If Sam felt good, Klaatu felt good. If Sam was hurting, Klaatu hurt. There was nothing to learn so Sam had never asked. Until now.

"Well, yes. I guess I am in one piece."

Klaatu hesitated for a moment to choose his words carefully, but getting nowhere, he finally said simply, "What was that all about, Boss?"

"That," said Sam in satisfaction, "was Good."

CHAPTER 25

Hate and Fear

"Whoopee Peppers!!! We did it, Klaatu! We DID it!!" Deep breath.

"Take that Gabriel, you misbegotten daughter of six devils!" This last impaled on the universal fist of defiance.

Sam Mentor shouted out with uncharacteristic abandon and jumped with both feet flat-footed, whapping the dirt floor of the cave into a dusty maelstrom that joined in the festivities. Stomp! Whomp! Bamp! And Stomp! again.

Blasted with Mentor's unrestrained life, Klaatu sprang from tabletop to ceiling to coat tree, out the door and back again, flailed by Mentor's mindlessly rampant Id. He whooped and yelped like a box full of puppies, only dimly aware why, but thoroughly enjoying himself.

"Damn!" heaved Sam.

He bounced to a stop like a down-throttled earth compactor, caught his breath, and grinned from his solar plexus.

"DAMN!!"

Klaatu stopped mid-yelp, caught between Sam's word and its spirit. Sam's spirit won just as Klaatu crashed into the rack of pots defending the fire pit. The clatter caught Klaatu's fancy so he grabbed a handy pair of pans and beat them overhead together, ringing his eardrums to a tickle.

Sam joined in the parade, chanting "Damn! Damn! Damn and more Damn!" in off-tempo syncopation to Klaatu's brassy clanging. Yelp-Damn-Clang-Clang-Yelp-Damn-Yelp-Yelp-Clang! Sam was elated beyond all reason and Klaatu couldn't care less. He was having the time of his lives.

But when the wisp of a shadow caught his eye through the cave door, Sam stopped his stomp instantly. He silenced Klaatu with the classic shushing gesture that transcended the alien void between wizard and troll.

Sam softened to the doorway cautiously while Klaatu stood mid-whoop. As he watched, the shadow turned into a stark-edged puke-green overcasting canopy that bellied down to the treetops and churned the sky like a working ripe must.

Sam peeped through the doorway in a bent-knee crouch, ready to move quickly. Klaatu, joy de vivre still draining from his system, danced around a bit as he wound down, a grin on his muzzle. Sam grunted in apprehension, instantly taking the spring out of Klaatu's step, and reached instinctively for the supporting pillar just inside the way.

The air was dead still, The only sound was the creaking and grinding of the clouds themselves. It was not lightning or thunder, but rather a subsound verberation like a squeaky clean bottom on a wet bathtub, or a thick wet hawser binding a waterlogged dock post. The clouds were solid, liquid and menacing, reminding Sam of heavy cream swirling into black coffee. Sam watched for a clue, Klaatu sucked his thumb.

"Don't move!" hissed Sam. "The hounds! They've tracked us here!" Klaatu froze.

Sam stood just inside the doorway, exposed to the absolutely motionless atmosphere. He could not dare so much as a twitch. An eye blink would shatter the stillness and ring out to the Searchers like Klaatu's pot-banging. A movement of his eye would shine like a beacon in this oppressive humor.

The presence outside his cave drifted by, and looked directly into Sam's motionless face, searched it, scrutinized it, and drifted on. Sam relaxed a few muscles but moved nothing. The Searcher stopped! He could see nothing, but knew that it was there! It was looking right into his . . .

WHAM!!

Like a cannon shot in a culvert. Just one wham with no ring or after shock. Sam back-pedaled valiantly to keep his balance but fell onto his back in a second. Klaatu rolled into a heap under the desk and dug in.

Sam struggled to his elbows and looked between his toes at the middle-aged balding man standing in the entry, restraining two gracefully determined hounds.

"You've been busy, Sam."

The Rodinesque figure didn't move, nor did the hounds. The darkening sky rotated intensely behind the barely silhouetted mass of a man, giving Sam the feeling that the cave was turning past a frieze. The air was still still, in spite of the clouds, so thick that even the pit fire seemed sluggish. Klaatu open-eyed the apparition from his foxhole.

"Baanquer!! Three Hells, I thought I was a goner!" muttered Sam as he pulled himself to his feet. "Why can't you just knock!"

"Season's greetings to you too, Sam" said the silhouette, still not moving. "You are a hard person to find, Sam. Your petty spells and potions do work for some things. My little pets here would have missed you completely if you hadn't let your guard down."

The fire flashed into blue brilliance with those words, filling the pit to nearly the ceiling, and lighting the cave intensely. Sam could feel the coldness of the light and raised his hand in defense. The light shown through his hand, outlining his bones. Even Klaatu took a translucent turn. Turning back to the intruders, Sam saw that the light cast no shadow, nor did it illuminate the figure before him.

"Make a note, Klaatu," spat Sam out of the side of his mouth, "to set out the vermin traps tonight."

"You are fortunate, Sam Mentor, that I am in such a fine mood. Your insults mean nothing to me. There is to be no more Sam Mentor so your words weigh nothing."

The figure moved finally, but only to pet and stroke the hounds.

"You have done a fine job, my little pets. Do you know their names, Sam? They are called Hate and Fear. They worked very hard to find you, Sam, and they deserve a reward. I think I shall let them have you."

Instantly the hounds sprang across the three strides between their master and Sam's face, growling fiercely with blood red hate in their eyes and poison in their fangs. Klaatu shut his eyes tightly and covered his head with his arms, hoping only that his passing from this life would be quick and painless.

Sam didn't move to defend himself, nor to elude these terrors. He stood there casually, his eyes fixed on the shadowed figure as though the attacking hounds were mere dust devils. Then with an off-hand wave, Sam dismissed them and they were gone.

"Ah! Nice work, Sam. I underestimated you," charmed Baanquer. "But there are more where those came from. Could you do the same with a thousand, Sam Mentor?"

"Did you come here only to taunt and threaten me? Call your thousand if you must, Baanquer, and let's get on with it." Sam certainly looked confident at those odds.

"If not, state your business."

"My word! Aren't we testy today," said the visitor patronizingly. Klaatu felt a turgid surge of something new in his veins, hot emotion that plugged his veins like molten lead.

"But I am a busy man. I'll save that treat for another when. As I said, Sam Mentor, you are to be no more. That is written on the Stone. But until that happy day, I have a use for you. Will you cooperate?"

"You expect me to say yes!?" Sam was amused in spite of himself. "I have heard tales of your sense of humor, but they were understated."

"I understand your amusement, Sam. You have no choice but to do what I want, so it doesn't matter whether you want to cooperate or not. My only problem is how much of a spectacle you will make of yourself first. I would rather that the whole affair be done in a professional manner. Don't you think that would be best?"

"I know of the Stone, Baanquer. My time is not now, nor for a long time to come. And I will guide my destiny until that time as I have always done, at my own counsel and by no other's."

"Sam Mentor, surely you must know that you have redeemed your last day!"

The voice was more gentle than before, still overbearing but without the sharp edge to it. Sam was shaken. Klaatu was shaken.

"I . . . But that cannot . . ."

Sam realized too late that he betrayed his poise, but he had no choice. Whatever else he might be, the man in front of him never spoke anything but the absolute and precise truth. This man also knew the Stone, Sam himself had led him to it long ago. And this man was merciless.

"The Stone! I demand to see the Stone!!" shouted Sam, a cry creeping into his thinly demanding voice.

"As you wish, Sam," replied the voice, stiffened a bit by the tone of Sam's words but perhaps a bit more patient in understanding Sam's state of mind.

WHAM !! Like the first one.

"Is that really necessary!?" muttered Sam, knowing that it was not. "By the teeth of your cursed Hounds, that's an awful bong!"

"My trademark, Sam. It helps in ways that even you only suspect." Sam's silent and grudging response was a slant-eyed scowl at his guest.

"It's all here before you, Sam. Read the Stone and tell me that I am wrong."

Sam stood on the Stone, his reflection scarred by the inscriptions that told the indelible passing of time and events. Even as he looked at them, the leading edge of lives developed and crawled into place in a determined march that was the footprint of life. They each took their place and stopped. Irrevocably and immutably stopped. Forever.

Looking out along the Stone before him, Sam could see those marks that were ordained from the font of time, portending events that must happen, cannot be altered. There were only a few within sight span, some brighter than others, some nearer. Sam's mark shone bright and close and steady.

Sam turned about, glancing out at the expanse of the Stone to either side, an infinite plane in all directions, covered with the scratchings of living things in their trials and their follies. As he came about upon the past, Sam dropped his head to study the tracings of his most recent history, all of it both known and unknown to him until now. He had been here before many times in his early years as he struggled with the world, but he has been away from the Stone many years now, eons certainly. There was a day when he had finally come to terms with the world and abandoned his juvenile concern for history's judgment. He had not until now returned.

"Perhaps," he thought ruefully, "I should have been more diligent."

But now he must know! It just cannot be as he was told. He had hoarded Obs so carefully, planned his route so certainly! But there it is! To the left a little, in the meandering line crossing his own. There it is, just as he was told.

Sam leaned closer as it took on a pale glow for him, revealing its path over centuries. The myriad lines in the mesh of life inscribed in the Stone were a bewildering tangle. Reading them was simplified only slightly by their cooperation, but the reading was clear; the line that crossed his was long, long beyond reckoning. Sam studied the line intently, trying to find the kink, the twist that would reveal who or what it was.

The line only crossed Sam's, intersecting it but not combining or cutting. Whatever is was, it is still there and so is Sam. That's something. But as he followed the two paths, their mutual interaction was obvious. They would meet again.

"That's enough, Baanquer." Sam shook his head sharply once, straightening.

WHAM !!

Before Sam finished his capitulation, they were the cave again, staring at each other in the fire glow.

"How?" was all Sam could say.

"How?" Baanquer shifted his weight uneasily, as though about to do something personally repugnant.

"Sam, as I said, you've been busy. You have set in motion events that have no certain ending. You have taunted Hell Two, ripped the ether recklessly, and you have committed the unforgivable crime of surviving. Your being unbalances everything, Sam, and so you have been stripped of your allotted days. Tomorrow, at noon, you will have never been."

"Noon?" Sam was stunned. "But my work! My . . . My Obs! I have plenty of Obs! What about them?"

"You *had* plenty of credits, Sam. They're gone." The voice had melted to an almost compassionate tone.

"I thought you knew!"

"Gone?" Sam knew that if they were gone, they had been stolen. "Who did it! I'll get them back! Who is it!"

"Nobody has them, and you can't get them back. You know that Sam. They were smoked. They can't be reconstructed even if you knew who did it." The voice was genuinely compassionate there for a while, then it hardened.

"Sam, I thought you knew, but that doesn't prevent my doing what I came here to do. You would be in the same pickle even if you had known about tomorrow. And since none of that is my doing, I have no scruples in the matter. Sam, you were put up for sale and I bought you out. You're mine, Sam, every scraggy hair and scurvy curse."

Sam Stiffened. As the enormity of those words penetrated, his raging mind raced from denial to bargaining to acceptance and back again. Klaatu was out of control.

"I do not accept that," said Sam, just barely. Sam gathered his dignity, contained his rage, and in an unnaturally husky shaking voice repeated.

"I do not accept! I will credit you with no truth or power. You will go from this place!"

Sam knew that this was heresy! This man was never wrong, never devious. He had too much power to have that need. Mentor's visitor moved at last, stepping into the cave confidently. He walked up to Sam, facing him squarely.

"You will sit down and listen to me."

The voice was calm, as though it had never been used emotionally. It was a full and melodic voice, although certainly aged, and it warmed Sam compellingly. Sam stepped backwards to finger the stump that he knew was there and sat down.

Klaatu was still tuned to Sam's apprehension. The visitor's voice had not been directed at Klaatu, so he stood warily in the shadows, idling, while he pieced together the subliminal commands Sam leaked.

"That's better." A moment's thought accented Baanquer's next words, "We will get along well, Sam. I understand what is going through your mind, and I can help. Believe me, I can and will help. But you must do what I say, and do it irrevocably, or there is no hope for you. And maybe no hope for me."

The words washed over Sam like a cleansing hot spring, but Sam knew that was the effect of the mild hypnosis in the voice. Well done, thought Sam, as he tried to identify the elements of that voice. It continued.

"Sam, things as we know them are not to be. Maybe they were never meant to be. Most likely, they were only as we imagined them." Baanquer paused thoughtfully, not taking his gaze from Sam's squint.

"Whatever the case, at noon tomorrow something new will be. And that something is very real."

Sam concentrated on those shadowed eyes, sensing the import of the words, but still fighting their truth.

"Sam, we are not alone here. You know that as well as I do." He waited for Sam's nod before continuing.

"But what you don't know," pause, "and what I don't know either, is how our fates are entwined. That is why I bought you Sam Mentor; you are going to be the bait on my hook."

"Pffshheeech!" whistled Sam with an uphanded salute. "That's beautiful, just beautiful. You're going to dangle me before who knows what and then cash me in like a poker chip! That's a great way to spend your last day!" Sam skulked down into the sympathetic stump, his arms crossed defensively on his chest.

"Sam, you didn't hear me. I said that I can, and will help you out if . . ." Baanquer stopped, for the first time uncertain. " . . . If there is still an I. You have my word on that. If we be, so will be my boon."

Sam had a little trouble with that anachronism but figured it was positive in spirit. Sam spent a moment searching those shadowed eyes with vain and without thought.

"Do I have a choice?"

"Yes, you do, Sam. Go your own way. And at noon tomorrow, that's it."

"And if I do what you want?"

"Most likely, that's it as well. But perhaps there is a . . . a way." The voice betrayed no sign of anxiety. "We will both see the same fate."

"You do not have to do this. Why take any chance at all?" Sam knew that this man need take no risk, and as far as he knew had never taken the slightest. There was no need.

"I will take no chances, Sam. Chance implies that the outcome is in doubt, and that at least one of the outcomes is desirable and at least one undesirable. In this case, all outcomes are equally undesirable, so there is no chance involved. Merely a toting up of . . . imbalances. These imbalances have upset your life and they have upset mine. We will set things right again. But your question is whether you have any possible desirable outcomes." An answer was expected.

"Yes, it comes to that."

"No, Sam. There are none."

"Then let's do it and be done with it."

For the first time, perhaps the first in all time, Baanquer smiled. It was the sort of smile begot when tight shoes are slipped, or an inaccessible itch gets scratched. Not a grin certainly, but definitely a smile. On another the smile would not be noteworthy at all, but Baanquer passed through the ages largely indifferent to the arbitrary cacophony of the world and the smile was an intrusion on it. This simple smile stressed the reality surrounding them, warped it physically until it passed in relief.

"Yes, we will do it, Sam Mentor," said Baanquer, stepping to the center of the cave's center ring.

"Stand and join your eyes to mine that we may enter this endeavor and this pact honorably!"

Sam rose and moved to confront the man who feared nothing. Baanquer was not as tall as Sam by a knee, although more heavily built. He stood motionless as a mountain stands motionless. Sam stood still as a man stands still, uneasily. Their eyes met and locked.

Sam's cave misted and faded. He saw only those eyes as he plunged into their depths, falling through a maelstrom of light and movement as his mind met that of Baanquer. Sam knew that this was the gift that can be given only once, and that can never be returned.

This was Baanquer teaching Sam Mentor how to be alive for the first time.

CHAPTER 26

A Leak!

"Whoof!!"

"R-R-lumpff!"

Rubb's wheeled swivel chair recoiled off of the thick plastic carpet protector into the water cooler and mushed to a stop in the thick piled carpet, spinning a little. Rubb sniffed once deeply to set his head aright, and wiped his left eye with his right sleeve. The cloth was slick like satin, but not absorbent at all, and merely smeared the tears around.

"Dang hay fever," muttered Rubb. "Must be the climate here or something."

He hopped out of the chair and pulled it back to the desk where he worked at tying knots with one hand. He had been on the verge of his first left-handed sheepshank when the itchy nose hit. The knot unraveled instantly at the first sneeze, and the practice cord now draped loosely from the swag lamps in the corner.

Rubb popped his ears to relieve the pressure as he shuffled over to the lamps for the cord that he had relieved of its curtains. Things were pretty dull, outside of 3:05 PM, so Rubb had gotten into the habit of practicing his old show routine to pass the time. His finger dexterity had deteriorated more than he thought possible, so here he was going back to the basics, the tortuous and tedious drills he had first mastered at Sam Mentor's foot.

Lately Rubb caught himself lingering wistfully on those loving kicks of encouragement Sam lavished on his bumbling protégé' in those early simple days when the world was alive and danced exuberantly to his life play.

"The world is alive, my boy. All you have to do is play the right tune, or scratch it behind the ears." Mentor's words, many times over.

"Dead," thought Rubb in contrast. "Everything's dead here. No wonder I have so much trouble with the knots. The rope's dead. The chair's dead. Even the water! Ah yes, the water!"

Rubb whipped the unprotesting rope across the room in frustration and disgust, as though it were putrefying in his hand.

"That's why these Zerps are so vicious!" he said out loud. Then ruefully, "I'm not sure that even they are really alive."

"How's that?" prompted Slumpblock, rousing from his late morning nap on the couch.

"Oh. Nothing, I guess. I'm just a little homesick; a lot homesick. And tired." Rubb didn't move, but only stared at the rope on the floor in the corner.

"What are we doing here, Slumpblock?" said Rubb to the rope. "All we are is bait!"

"You're the bait." corrected Slumpblock.

Rubb didn't need that right now, although it was certainly true. Slumpblock was an accident, an oversight. But Rubb was here for a purpose, someone else's purpose, and everything was out of control.

"Sometimes I want to get caught up in the thousands that herd through here every day and make an end of it. But I know they'll just bring me back."

Rubb looked to Slumpblock for confirmation, but he was busy remodeling the desk again. This time it was an ejection seat built into the flopover table that swung out as a typewriter stand. He was having a problem getting the trigger just right. It would hang fire, then release just when he figured it was time to get off and take a look.

Rubb sulked back to the desk and climbed up into the deep plushy chair, slouching into a chin-on-the-chest funk.

"All we wanted to do was help," thought Rubb with a little crampy feeling in the corner of his eye. "We sure helped! Wow, thousands ripped to shreds, I'm stuck in a big box with some fool carpenter and Mentor's out somewhere doing One only knows what."

A defensive tear squeezed out of that cramp. Rubb kicked the air, turning the chair with a creak.

"He's not here, that's for sure. And he never will be!"

He grumbled darkly on that, not even daring to form words for the black feelings he felt toward everything.

"A lot of good that would do anyway," answered Rubb aloud to his own unspoken question. "I could damn this sinkhole into oblivion at home, but not here! Not in this dead world! Nothing works here!"

Slumpblock looked up at that.

"Well not yet maybe, but I'll get it here in a minute." He turned back to his work on the desk.

"I don't mean that! Not things! Me. My spells! This world just absorbs me, like . . . like punching warm putty. Like fighting a net."

This last was more a cry of pain than anger. Rubb's frustration at his own impotence was total and absolute.

Slumpblock, however, was in a world of his own, one that worked quite to his satisfaction. He puttered with that latch until it fairly snicked on and off voluntarily, honed to a gleam that invited a test.

"It must be nice to be able to get lost in metal and wood like that," thought Rubb. "Simple things are the nicest. And simple people too."

Slumpblock smiled in pride at the action, looked up at Rubb in triumph and darted off for some other piece of dead stuff without really seeing Rubb.

There was a lot of dead stuff lying about lately. Since the first daily battle the office had been rebuilt overnight. Neat as a pin it was, sometimes even better than before. Rubb hadn't really paid much attention to that fact until the quality of workmanship slipped a little. Then it slipped a lot. Gradually, over a period of several months certainly, the craftsmanship earned the title of shoddy. Leftover building materials, both new and old, were pushed into heaps here and there, providing good cover for the daily battle.

That was another thing. The battles between the Armee and the Zerp were becoming more of a real contest. Although the Zerp always won, it seemed to Rubb that their efforts were less spirited than at first, and those of the Armee more aggressive. Rubb would have been hard pressed to demonstrate that empirically, but after the initial shock of the yeoman like slaughter of the Armee, then the boredom of the sameness of it all, Rubb found himself taking a renewed interest in the fight.

In fact, Slumpblock even constructed a review stand behind Rubb's executive desk. The two of them formed the habit of taking a late brunch and settling in with a cool iced drink for the event. An occasional wager added a little interest. Although the Zerp always won, some sport derived from the preliminary coin toss to decide who had to lose by betting on the Armee. Still, it was a better show than at first, and improving.

Rubb was most unsettled by a subtle shift in the flow of battle. He noticed it when Slumpblock first built the review stand. Before that they watched the battle from under Rubb's desk because it always escaped the scrap unscratched. He gave that no weight until he studied the fracas from the vantage of the stand. The Armee clearly avoided carrying the fight to the desk, although it stood near the middle of one long wall of the office.

As a matter of fact, the Armee seemed to maneuver instinctively in such a way that the Zerp were finessed away from the desk. Rubb tried in vain to see just how that was done, but the effect was unmistakable; the desk and its inhabitants were uphill to the combatants who flowed around it as a stream avoids a hummock.

The fighters no longer noticed Rubb and Slumpblock, not that they ever paid much attention. In those early days they picked their targets from many options, Rubb included. Rubb had never actually been assaulted, but he figured that was because he was not much of a threat from under the desk. Now that he was a virtual sitting duck up in the stand, it was clear that he was being completely ignored.

Rubb had even tried to attract attention by throwing a few pieces of scrap at either side at random. Nothing. Rubb might as well have been throwing sticks at a shadow. Slumpblock, on the other hand, drew fire regularly until he finally retreated to his fort in the desk. Anymore he emerged only after the issue was virtually decided, and then decked out in a crash helmet and a suit of mail he had fabricated of many pop-top rings.

"Whoof!!" erupted Rubb.

"WHALF!"

They both stopped in their tracks for an instant. Just an instant, mind you, no more. Rubb thought that he had merely blinked at the sneeze. Slumpblock passed it off as the strobe effect of a quick power outage. But Rubb, on reflection, was certain that things actually stopped!

Now nothing in the room moved except Slumpblock and Rubb. Rubb had closed his eyes during the sneeze so he was not certain how he knew things had stopped.

"Did you see that?" Anticipating a reoccurrence, Rubb stared wide-eyed at a point about four feet in front of his nose so he could concentrate on his peripheral vision, knees bent and elbows cocked.

"See what? The lights? That happens all the time any more. Don't let it bother you." Slumpblock returned to the desk to lay out plans for the solarium.

"No, not the lights," said Rubb slowly, examining the room for a clue. "Something happened. I swear it! I didn't see it exactly, but things stopped just now. Didn't you see it?'

"But nothing was moving. How could it stop?" Slumpblock thought that was a grand analysis, and couldn't resist adding, "You must have shook something loose when you sneezed."

Rubb eased up a little, still scanning the room for clues. Seeing nothing out of the ordinary he shrugged and retrieved the practice cord from the corner. Wrapping the cord absently around his hand, he moseyed back to the chair, climbed aboard and set about his drills again.

Still disturbed about the incident, Rubb absently whipped up a left-handed sheepshank knot six or eight times straight while he mulled things over. The cord caressed his hands as he worked and when the work was done, snuggled contentedly back into Rubb's pocket as Rubb fell asleep.

CHAPTER 27

Double Cross

"You slop-slimy tailing of a two-headed Rotworm!!!" Gus was incensed. "By a thousand lice teeth that was a rounder!"

Gabriel moved not a whit, nor did she tingle.

"What are you trying to do to me, you misconceived sprout of a fireplug! I did everything you said, everything!"

Gus stomped back and forth, whapped the floor with his heel in rage and frustration, then kicked an ottoman. The stool tumbled muffily across the office and rolled up against Gabriel's stump. Gabriel didn't move but managed to acknowledge the seat in spite of having no eyes. Her attention returned to Gus, again without a trace of movement. That trick infuriated Gus even more.

"AAAghghghggggpgpgppffff!! . . ."

Gus was over the edge, flailing his arms and legs like a jerky puppet on a string and a stick. He whipped his fist overhead and down, he stomped the floor and kicked the furniture.

"I'm done for. You know that? I'm done for! You said if I did what you wanted you'd take care of Mentor. Well I did my part! Wow, did I do it! I got me the meanest, sneakiest, toughest old wolf in all Eard looking to fry my hide and you just stand there like it's tough tacos."

Gabriel considered that and seemed to agree.

"Don't you think it's about time you did something!? Anything! Just do something!"

Gabriel made no visible attempt to respond.

Gus stomped about some more until he ran out of steam. He circled about himself a few times, like a puppy unwinding before a nap, and flopped into a flowered easy chair in the corner behind Gabriel. Gus just wilted, heaving to catch his breath. His eyes glowered at Gabriel as though he could slash this abomination by eye skance alone, searching savagely for whatever it was that Gabriel used for eyes.

Gabriel did not move.

"Well say something!" Gus was not happy. "What do I do now? You're Mr. Know-It-All. What in the Fates do I do now?"

Gabriel moved a little, just a little. She loosened her grip on the parquet floor, allowing the carpet to relax a bit, and turned slowly towards Gus. The carpet squirmed in relief and tried to wiggle out of harm's way but Gabriel's grip snapped shut on the poor rug before it could escape.

Gabriel now faced Gus, if face is the word to use for a thing like Gabriel who had the features of a beanbag. She did have an incredible maw that was given to grins when she chose to display one. Other than that, when her mouth was closed you could only tell her front from her back by the tilt of the tine-tipped arm growing out of what you expect to be the forehead, slopey though it was.

That grin crept slowly across Gabriel's mouth gash, her crystal teeth beginning to show by the reflected highlights of the windows and chandelier. Her jaw dropped open. Well actually, the top of her head dropped up, exposing more of her teeth by the moment.

"You are done, Gus," said Gabriel finally.

Gabriel's voice was very slow and deep, aggravatingly grampish. It gurgled up out of her throat rather more like bubbling mud than anything vocal.

"And I'm out of here."

Gabriel's enunciation was good, as mud goes, certainly good enough for Gus to understand. She turned to go.

"What!! No! You can't do this! Wait! What do you mean I'm done?! You can't leave me! Mentor will . . . !"

Gabriel snapped upright and whipped around, focusing her attention on Gus. There was no doubt about her attention.

"I can't?"

The voice was suddenly mellow and patronizing, still deep-pitched but not at all muddy.

"I do what I do, Gus. I see no cants; only doos. I do what I am moved to do. You may do what you like, and I will do as I do." It was clear that Gabriel would not debate the point but she did wait.

"But you said . . ."

"I lied. That is one of the things I do."

"But that's not fair! We made a deal. You said if I set up Mentor for you I'd be rich! You said I could have anything I wanted. You promised!" Gus was fairly crying in frustration.

"Fair is a balance. Your reality was not balanced; it is now. That is fair."

"But you promised!"

"Promised? You mean that I am obligated? In what way?" Gabriel's voice was indifferent, with a little wry humor.

"You said if I set up Mentor for you that it would be the end of him. Well, he's still . . ."

"That is not the end of Sam Mentor, but that will be the end of Sam Mentor. Not quite yet, Gus, but he will end. Does that satisfy my obligation?" Sarcastically.

"But what if he gets me first?! What do I do then?"

Gus knew that Sam would indeed get him first, and he knew that he would be able to do nothing without Gabriel to back him up.

"You are not listening, Gus. I said you are done. It does not matter whether Sam gets to you or not. Either way, Gus ends."

Gus was dumbfounded, disbelieving. His eyes searched frantically back and forth over the span of Gabriel's surface, looking for any clue that these words were not true. He found none.

"You tricked me! You told me it would be the end of Mentor but instead it's going to be the end of me. That's it, isn't it!" Gus was past denial and into defiance. "You tricked me!"

"It is going to be the end of you, Gus, but not at my doing. I would have liked to trick you, Gus; you deserve it. But you have dealt your own destruction." Gabriel hesitated, relaxing only a moment for the carpet to stretch its kinks a bit. "Your fate was fixed before I touched upon your services. I only used you a little while I had a chance."

"ButBut." Gus swallowed. "But you said I could have anything I wanted! What about that?!" Gus apparently still believed that he could appeal to Gabriel's sense of honor.

"I did not lie about that, Gus. There is no need to lie. You will have everything you want."

Gus was beside himself in rage and frustration. Here he was talking to some fool spook, he was facing catastrophe at the hands of the most vengeful wizard in Eard, he had been lied to and tricked into this predicament, and he couldn't get a straight answer on anything. Gus was not at ease with the world.

"I'm not taking this very well, Gabriel." Gus was strikingly composed. Gabriel took renewed interest.

"Yes, that is true. Can I help?" That was not sarcastic.

Gus sensed the change in Gabriel's voice. She really was offering to help!

"Yes." Gus felt he would only get one chance at this and paused to get the words right. "What in Eard is going on around here? What are you doing and what am I doing and what's what?" Gus wasn't at all happy with the result.

"Gus," began Gabriel, amused but deliberate, "I was sent to pull the plug."

CHAPTER 28

Reality Check

"A hopeless mess!"

One shrugged shoulderlessly, outside of time. "Only those dreary Real blobs could have begotten a mess like this!"

One thought the affair settled once and for all, but here he was again trying to unravel the tangled backlash of the indiscriminate meddling of those impossibly wet things that drilled their petty little burrows through space and time without a thought of the havoc they cause.

"Can't they leave me alone?" One paused rhetorically but not temporally.

"No, I supposed that they cannot." responded he to himself simultaneously. "They are, after all, Real."

One spoke to no one, for there was no other One. Nor did One even think to One's self in the way that you or I think we think. One was aware that a thought had been thunk without the lead time imposed by chemical synapse, a fact that made One's world very immediate. And all very obvious inasmuch as One, perhaps only One, understood that causality did not flow from causer to causee; it puddled in the low spots and exerted a static pressure on all events equally in all directions. Any apparent flow of causality was simply a function of the observer's orientation.

"And these poor wet things," mused One, "feel the pressure only from their time side. No wonder they're so incompetent."

WHAM!!

One was not amused.

"Baanquer, for your sake and mine, will you stop doing that."

One did not turn to Baanquer as One has no behind, but Baanquer's presence started and One's attention was forced. One didn't like being forced and said so.

"Once more and you're smoke!"

"Uh, sorry."

Baanquer dropped his eyes, unnecessarily since One had no eyes right now and Baanquer's eyes had nothing from which to drop. But the classic act of subjugation couldn't hurt. Baanquer had been summoned and that bode ill. That always bode ill.

"You called?" Baanquer hoped to get this over with and get out of here as quickly as possible, although quickly didn't mean exactly the same thing with One that it does in a timey place.

"Yes, I called. And you know why. You have made a muddling fine mess of things in your Real little province. I thought you understood that things were to be set aright."

"I know. But I am working on it right now. Things are under control and it will be wrapped up in no time at all."

Baanquer winced at his unfortunate choice of words. He had been sent on this job in the first place because One had no time at all, and the problem was nothing if not time.

"Is that all?"

"No, that is not all! Tell me about the Imbalance. Why are things sloshing about so?"

"Oh, that. Well as you know, Real does that sometimes. It sticks to things and slides around when you least expect it. I must admit that I underestimated just how viscous Real is, but everything is working out the way I planned. More slowly than I planned, but exactly the way I planned."

"Yes, Real is tricky." One's tone expressed suspicion that a little Real clung to Baanquer yet. "But the Imbalance, it has gotten out of hand. You are sure that it is not too late to rectify events?"

The question told Baanquer that One knew it was too late. He hesitated a bit and shuffled a bit. He knew that the Imbalance was great, more than great, but he felt that he could pull it out with the help of Gabriel. Apparently not. One had no need to ask a question like that; it was only a courtesy.

"Well, ah, sure. I think I can do it." Wow was that cool! Come on Baanquer, he thought, get your act together!

"Yes. I mean No! It is not too late. I just need a little more time." Baanquer winced again.

"Time!! I have no time to give! You want time? Go back to Real where you belong and play games with those wet things of yours. They have nothing but time."

One paused in a way that Baanquer could appreciate, but One did not need to pause for effect; Baanquer was quite paying attention.

"I did not send you to play with time or to upend Real," said One. "I sent you to make a few minor adjustments in the ether and you muck about ripping Real like you owned it. Now I want you to do as I want and do it in your now. Is that clear?"

"Yes, yes. That's clear. I understand what you want. It is just that Real was not what I expected. It was not what you told me it would be."

" . . . not what you told me?!!" One really did pause this time.

Baanquer was One's own reflection, his Other I if you will, and had at his disposal all of One's wisdom. How could it be that Baanquer had misconceived Real when One himself was the conceiver! One had imposed his will on the Other Side and the result was Baanquer, One's salient into Real. Imperfect? Yes, Baanquer left a lot to be desired, but then Real imposed its own imprint on everything in the vicinity and Baanquer could not be held completely responsible. Baanquer took on an independent and unpredictable existence of his own when he budded off into Real, one of those unfortunate consequences of time.

Ah yes, time! That was the problem! Time moves. Time, of all eleven dimensions, is the one that moves. Damn! Time moved and the result was a little proper motion skewing Baanquer's Real injection. Well, it was one of those oversights that happen; One would just have to make the best of it.

One's attitude towards Baanquer in all of this mess was that of an exasperated parent towards a wayward child. Baanquer was not a child certainly, but he liked to play at Real like a child might play at tin soldiers. Perhaps this was One's own playfulness emerging through Baanquer.

"No! That can not be!"

One did not speak, but these last thoughts were allowed to Baanquer.

"One does not play, and Baanquer can not play!"

"Play? Wow! If you think that's play over there, you should try it yourself."

One thought that was exactly what he had been doing in sending Baanquer.

"If not play, then what?" asked One. "I see you chasing these wet things, working little incantations and scaring them. How do you account for the fact that things are worse now than when you were sent?"

"Worse? I would not say things are worse. Things are coming to a point, and to be honest I am not certain what is on the other side of that point. But the problem you sent me to solve will be solved. There was a flux of Nice, and there still is. I know what caused it, and it will end if I can complete my plans. But beyond the point? I do not know."

"Your plans! What plans?! You have muddied the waters beyond my understanding and you call that plans?"

One would be in a rage if he had hormones and plumbing like the wet things, but as it was he could only convey intense irk.

"Why did you not simply do as I told you? Surely that was not so difficult a task?"

"But you must understand something in offset, One. These wet things have power. It is a wild sort of power, unpredictable and barely manageable, but power nonetheless. That is what caused the flux of Nice in the first place; they did it!"

"They? The wet ones?! How can that be!"

"There is a quality to the wet ones that draws from Real, and particularly from time. There are individuals who have learned to control that quality and direct it. They live in it and revel in it. Nice flows with them and bucks them, but it always must interact with them and they with it." Baanquer warmed to his subjects as he saw One's anger subside with understanding.

"The flux was at their direction."

"They are pushing Real about?! They can do that?" One had to internalize that realization.

"Then what of your plans? Can you control them at all?"

"That is what I was not prepared for. They are very difficult to control. In fact, my plans have finally come to rest on that fact; they cannot be controlled. That is why it will take more time to reach fruition. These wet ones, as you call them, will work out the solution themselves with a little coaching and persuasion, but they will not be forced." Baanquer felt he had made his point, but had to add:

"There is still that point on which everything will turn. I cannot see beyond it."

"I can see your problem, Baanquer, and I can offer you no solution. You may be correct in your plans but I can not counsel you on that either. You have my leave to do as you see fit. Whatever else you do, keep an eye on the Stone! Remember the Stone."

"Yes, the Stone."

That was it. One thought timelessly about the conversation for a moment, then went about other business. Baanquer thought to himself temporally.

"Wow! Was that close!"

CHAPTER 29

Dust?

This isn't going to be easy, but it will help if you don't think. Just listen.

It's funny about Dust. There really isn't such a thing as Dust, only dust. Dust, capital Dust, isn't a thing so much as a concept like army is a concept, or beach is a concept. You cannot pick up a beach. If you try all you get is sand.

Dust is like that. If you get too close, if you try to touch it and examine it, it's gone. It's skin flakes and insect parts, rubbed dirt and itty-bitty broken things that you can recognize, but it's no longer dust in the collective sense.

But if you get caught in a dust storm, you sure get hit by something. Was it the wind or the dust? Or was it only the combination that was a dust storm, but not either one by itself?

Dust is not alive, although it probably was and will be again. When it's alive, however, it is not dust. It is only dust when it's dead. When dust was alive it moved and ate and metabolized like any other live stuff. Dead stuff, the stuff of dust, does not do any of these live things. It's dead. But don't be concerned about that stuff, it will all live again sooner or later. That's the whole point of dust, it's the ultimate recyclate.

But Dust is another matter. Dust, our Dust, is alive. It lives by the harmony of its elements, the way a school of fish moves by the communal action of its elements. The school of fish is not alive, however, only the individual fish are alive. With Dust it's the other way around; Dust is alive, but each dust is dead. Got that?

It's important that you understand how Dust fits into the story. The concept is simple enough; live things attract attention. That's mostly what alive means. Dead things do not leave vapor trails through the ether, nor do they deplete the life resources of a when or a where if they depart. Live things carry about them a vital quality that derives from and ties to every other live thing, both here and not here. It is this tie that is the basis for all power of one live thing over another.

Philosophers have always had a problem with action at a distance because the idea that one thing can influence another without touching it somehow is logically absurd. If thing A is in fact influenced by thing B, then the vehicle of that influence is merely an extension of thing A, or perhaps B. The fact that we can't see that extension is beside the point. Whatever it is, it's there.

Now that's true about dead things; dead things cannot influence each other without touching somehow. Live things are different. Live things are alive because they are little puddles of the essence of everything else. Just being something, dead or alive, conveys a taste of that beingness to all other things. Sometimes that beingness coalesces into a blob that takes on life because it has to. It is forced out of deadness because the only quality that all dead things have in common that can coalesce into anything is beingness. Get enough of beingness in one spot and you have life. Get enough dust in one spot and you have Dust.

So what does all of that have to do with the story? Sam had to move fast if he was going to help Rubb and save himself. Because all live things are tied together, like an infinitely complex spider web, any move he made would attract attention. His experience with Gabriel, Baanquer and Gus told him that he was attracting far too much attention. The only way to move without attracting attention was to send something to do his bidding in his stead, something dead. But, Klaatu aside, dead things are not very good at doing things. That's the major drawback to dead.

So Sam needed something that was alive to him that was not tied to all other living things, that was dead to all other life. So he needed some live thing that did not draw life from all other live things and so did not have ties that would draw attention.

Thus the Dust. Dust drew its life from Sam alone, and had ties to Sam only. It drew no life and carried no life. It was dead to the world, but it would do Sam's bidding and Sam's alone.

CHAPTER 30

Dust!

Rubb was a little hesitant to try that again. His desk never skritched back before and Rubb was not even sure that it did just now. He thought it did, but he was not sure. At least not sure enough to try that again.

He had wasted hours working over a set of blocks. The blocks were little, about the size of his thumb and the shape of bricks, but hollow and white with two knobs on each. He was trying to make a little building out of them, like the one he could see across the street, but the knobs made the blocks so tipsy that he couldn't stack them more than two or three high before they fell over in a clatter. No matter what he did they would not stick or stack. The little devils seemed to squirm in his fingers but they were not alive. Something alien to him would not let him assemble them according to their obvious interlocking design.

He tried to glue them together with some of Slumpblock's mucilage but it would not stick to the smooth blocks. Pounding on them with his shoe only scattered pointy shards of shattered blocks all over the office. Rubb found that frustrating but not surprising. Not the shattered blocks exactly, but the fact that he had so much trouble just getting along in the land of the Zerp. Even these little toys seemed to be aligned against him in a passive but mean-spirited way.

It was a lot like his days with the vaudeville troupe. In the off-hours Rubb tried to teach one of the brighter actors how to do a few of his basic tricks, like levitation or opening. But it was no use, those people had no awareness, no life! The world was no more than a lump to them, to be stomped on when the need arose, but otherwise dead. If they had to make a tool, their first thought was to hit it, or put it in fire. Hit it and cook it! All they had to do was to ask, but they didn't seem to understand that. They didn't really See the world.

After months of slogging through every day without his friends, Rubb knew how that brand of ignorance felt. This world was very hard to See, and many times Rubb felt the urge to pound it and braze it. Now that he was in the same fix, he noticed in himself a little understanding and compassion for those simpler folk. But just the same, why wouldn't these blasted blocks behave! That was the word he was looking for in his musings, behave. Nothing here behaved like it should. Small wonder these Zerp are so mean when they have such a time of it in this raw dead world.

Rubb was reminded of Sam Mentor's remarks when he blasted through this office billowing brocade drapes and obscenities. He didn't fit in this world either. And things just wouldn't behave.

What was that!? Rubb's attention popped back to the pile of little blocks at his knees where he sat cross-legged. He thought he heard a little plick just then. And something moved! Bugs? Rubb watched closely for a minute, then two. Nothing moved. Dismissing that as a slip of his psyche, Rubb turned his attention back to the desk that just now skritched his back.

Rubb had gotten quite fond of the desk over the months. There was this spot in the middle of his back that he couldn't quite reach by hand, a spot that always itched when he got frustrated. Lately it itched a lot. The desk was just the right height to skritch his back with the corner and now had only three square corners.

Rubb had reached his regular point of frustration with the little blocks and went to the desk for relief. He sorta snuggled up to it backwards, anticipating the delicious relief, when the desk skritched him! Rubb leapt at the touch, flying halfway up the opposite wall. His first thought was that Pentecost had skewered him to throw him to the same fate so many thousands of his kin had met. But there was no one there, not even Slumpblock.

Could he have imagined It? Yes, indeed he could; he was losing his grip on a lot of things. He first thought of going back to the desk and trying it one more time. But what if it didn't skritch him? That would only confirm his worst fear, that he was hallucinating.

On the other hand, what was he to do if it did skritch him back? All that meant was there was one more force to contend with around here and he had plenty to worry about, thank you. A skritching desk was relatively minor and Rubb didn't see a need to confront the desk, or anything else, when in order to confront it he would have to turn his back on it.

Still, it was a desk, a Zerp desk in Zerpland, and it surely skritched him. Something sure did, and there was nothing else present. No question about it. If Rubb had gotten skritched, the desk did it.

Rubb watched the desk closely and then farly, trying to catch it moving. His eyes started to burn and then weep from holding them open so long, blurring his little world like a heat mirage. It didn't budge at all. Blast! Rubb blinked just then and he was sure that the desk twitched in that piece of a second! Blast it all! Rubb kicked the desk in frustration and felt better for it.

Rubb had enough for now. Between the blocks and the hay fever and the skritchy desk and the 3:05 and what all, he was getting just plain mean. The desk could get up and walk out the door for all he cared. Go and be done with it, he would say. And those ridiculous little blocks! What were they good for any . . . !

Rubb stopped in his tracks so suddenly that the rug rumpled up ahead of him and toppled the little brick building into a heap of little hollow white bricks with knobs on them.

He blinked, took out a hanky and cleared his eyes, deliberately turning away from the pile of bricks. When he was ready he turned back to the ruins. The blocks were still in their disheveled heap.

"I saw that!" he shouted at the bricks, thinking that it was Slumpblock playing another of his tricks.

"I saw that building. I know you're here somewhere! Come out and let me see you, you devil."

"Whuzzat?"

Slumpblock rattled out from under a pile of battle debris in a corner at the far end of the office, in the direction behind Rubb.

"You want something?"

Slumpblock had fallen asleep while digging through war's ravages looking for something to use as a compressor for the air conditioning unit in his desk.

Rubb looked back at Slumpblock and then back to the pile of bricks. How could Slumpblock have done that?! He swore he had seen an exquisite little building made of those obstinate little bricks, in the exact image of the building across the way. Nobody could have made that model so quickly and traversed the room twice without Rubb's seeing it. Even if Slumpblock was playing tricks, how could he have known that Rubb was trying to make a model of that particular building? He had spoken to no one for hours, he didn't even . . . Mentor!!!

"Sam! Is that you? Sam!"

Slumpblock scurried back into the junk pile, thinking they were being attacked by some new menace. Rubb was prancing about the room looking high and low for some sign of Sam.

"Where are you?! Sam!!"

Rubb scrambled frantically over and under every cranny and closet in the office, under the huge desk, in the chandelier, behind the pictures on the wall, in the plastic potted plant, and then back over them all again. Nothing.

After some time Rubb slowed his search, then stopped.

Disappointment was not the word. Even the word devastated was probably optimistic. Rubb was in a total and abject pit of despair. He was simply not up to this roller coaster assault on his emotions; massive frustration, then wild anticipation, then despair. The psychic whiplash had wrung Rubb out like his socks that were drying in the sun over the back of a chair.

"You all right boss?" Rubb's anguish was apparent to Slumpblock even from across the room.

"Yes, I guess so. No. No, I'm not!"

Rubb suddenly drop-kicked the pile of blocks viciously. So viciously that they splashed over the office with a clatter and whistle as their hollows caught the air and their nubby surface warped their trajectories.

It was the first truly vicious thing Rubb had ever done in all time and it felt good. So good, in fact, he took another kick at the closest thing he could draw a bead on, Slumpblock.

Slumpblock ducked, luckily, squatting like a sumo wrestler while Rubb ballisticated over Slumpblock's back, following his foot. Rubb landed on his back a few feet out and just laid there. He didn't move a muscle.

"You all right Boss?" Slumpblock was nothing if not redundant.

"Ssshhh!!"

Rubb shushed Slumpblock through his teeth, still not moving a muscle, his eyes fixed on the ceiling. Slumpblock looked up reflexively, saw nothing, and looked back at Rubb who was still staring at the ceiling. Rubb was not glazed; he was looking at something with an animal intensity that unnerved Slumpblock more than a little. Slumpblock eased back, palms out, fingers up and elbows out. Rubb had been under some stress lately, witness the scattered blocks, and Slumpblock was afraid Rubb may have finally locked up the shop.

"Boss, I think maybe . . ."

"SSSHHHH!!!"

Slumpblock froze. He turned his head slowly towards the ceiling but kept his eyes on Rubb, not sure in which direction lay the greater peril. He finally had to let his eyes snap back into his head. It took him a second to refocus on the flat white expanse of the ceiling.

"Do you see it!" whispered Rubb, very softly and slowly.

Slumpblock looked down at Rubb, who hadn't moved, then back up at the ceiling. He looked hard and looked hard again.

"No," he replied, very softly and slowly.

"Not there!" spat Rubb, sotto voce, "There!"

Slumpblock, only a bit mortified, twisted his neck to bring his head down to the floor. Seeing nothing, he twisted more, then gangled his way to his back next to Rubb, head to shoulder and ear to ear. He sure felt dumb doing this and was about to say so when a floater caught his eye. Its purposeful progress stood out from the Brownian movement of the dust still lingering from Rubb's pratfall. It drifted lazily above, leaving a faint vapor trail that turned upon itself, drafting a nebulous block script in an unsteady childish hand.

Slumpblock started to read the letters aloud. "B . . . B . . . U . . ."

"Will you shut UP!" snarled Rubb. "I've got to get all of this and you're not helping!" This last out of the side of his mouth, his only acknowledgment of Slumpblock's presence.

Slumpblock mouthed the letters to himself, continuing where he left off. "R,E,L,B,U,O,R,T." Then another line, "N,I,M,I." Slumpblock stopped there, puzzled.

He snuck a look at Rubb who was entranced by the hazy display which had dissipated raggedly in a capillary sort of way. Apparently Rubb was translating that haze, his lips moving as he deciphered the letters, then the words, then the sentences.

Slumpblock looked up again to see what he was missing only to miss it. Great white arcs wiped overhead as the smeary runes evaporated into air like a nest of gnats in a gust. The wiping stopped with an abrupt fingernail-on-a-blackboard screech. Rubb didn't moved a muscle or blink.

The room hushed, although there had been no noise, settling into a heavy still mugginess, the greenish sort that precedes an evil summer storm. Light slowed in the mug, and defocused any details that lacked the determination to punch through, as though the texture and timbre of touchable things were melting away in a corrosive bath, leaving only nubs and stumps of real stuff. Slumpblock grabbed the floor and held on. Rubb didn't move.

In a minute or two the writing returned, this time in no form that Slumpblock could recognize. A squiggle here crossed a lumpy thing there. Curvy things danced and touched daintily, surged away in revulsion and jousted guardedly, each with the other, slowly filling the space above them with a manic jungle gym interstiched with incomprehensible runic characters and a throbbing excited presence. The smoky structure was alive!

Rubb still had not moved through all of this. Wait! There, he moved! Slumpblock abandoned the vaporous superstructure for a closer look at Rubb who was nodding, his eyes still blankly unfocused so as to see the whole display peripherally. Blank as he was, Rubb was clearly nodding.

Rubb's face, eyes rounded into focused attention, suddenly blanched, then fearlocked. Stark, jugular fear. Slumpblock looked up reflexively to meet the terror, and found the room empty again. No letters, no jungle gym; just white ceiling.

They both laid there silently, Slumpblock waiting for Rubb's next move and Rubb resting his eyes to allay the piercing pain. Neither said a word. Then Rubb stirred.

"We're done for," mumbled Rubb.

Now it was Slumpblock's turn to be terrorized. He leapt to his feet and dashed to his makeshift arsenal of secondhand pikes and bashers, anticipating an attack from the Zerp. He checked the clock on the wall over Rubb's desk. It was not 3:05 p.m.

Slumpblock sorta slowed to a stumble as he realized there was no immediate danger, but backed defensively to the weapon rack anyway.

Rubb slowly rolled over to his stomach as though he suffered a monumental hangover. He lifted his shoulders to a sway-backed pushup, pulled his knees up underneath his weight, then rolled onto his back again. Two more tries yielded an uneasy sort of balance. After thinking about it for a full minute, Rubb pulled himself erect at the drapes. Rubb lifted his eyes to Slumpblock and impaled him with terrazzo eyes buried in an ashen face.

"Wow!" breathed Slumpblock. "You look like terrazzo! You okay?"

Slumpblock asked this in the sense of 'Is that a live grenade?' rather than out of any real concern for Rubb's well-being. He held his position two strides away from Rubb, back to the wall.

"No! No, I'm not okay. Okay?!!" Viciously. Rubb was not even trying to be civil.

"No. I'm sorry, Slumpblock." Rubb powered down two clicks and did try after a moment. "It's just that . . ." Very long pause as Rubb lost himself in thought, " . . . have you ever heard of The Stone?"

In spite of his question, Rubb was not really in touch with Slumpblock right now and turned away, without waiting for an answer. He had pronounced the word Stone so morbidly that Slumpblock knew it was capitalized. Not expecting an answer, Rubb didn't notice Slumpblock's response.

Slumpblock rocked like he had been blindsided with a beam. "He knows!" thought Slumpblock in panic. "How could he? That . . . that stuff?"

Slumpblock looked up involuntarily. The air was clean. He looked back at Rubb who was still lost in troubled thought, paying no attention.

Slumpblock saw that he had not been noticed. He composed himself deftly and answered, "No. No, I don't think so," in as mannered a voice as he could. His hand, however, flitted behind him for a basher while his eyes measured Rubb for the requisite heft. He selected a piano leg.

"Huh?" said Rubb. "Oh yeah. Good. Thanks."

Rubb went back to his funk leaning stiff-armed against the wall, elbows locked and head down in the classic cookie tossing stance. Slumpblock relaxed a bit, then a lot. Rubb was out of it, although he had not yet lost it, and apparently hadn't noticed Slumpblock at all.

"Tomorrow." Rubb said this over and over again, shaking his head slowly in disbelief.

"How can that be? To-*mor*-row!"

Rubb steadied himself, straightened his back, jerked his jersey tunic a bit to no apparent end, turned shakily with his weight on his heels and tilted stiff-leggedly over to his chair. In spite of all that he sat down gracefully enough, maintaining his dignity throughout. He stared straight ahead blankly, hands on his knees.

Slumpblock relaxed his grip on the piano leg, leaned it quietly against an entrenchment, and wandered over to Rubb as though nothing had happened. Rubb turned towards him, a little recognition in his eyes. Rubb shifted his weight forward, gripping the chair arms to keep it from rolling about on the hard transparent protector on the carpet. He almost got up from the chair, then thought better of it.

"Slumpblock?" Rubb blinked a few times. "Slumpblock! Where did you come from?" Rubb looked around to orient himself and finally reached for a bottle of the industrial chemical they had both grown fond of lately. "Here, old friend. Let me pour you a drink."

Slumpblock needed one right now, but didn't dare. "If he knows," thought Slumpblock, "I'll need all my wits about me."

This was more prudent than you might at first think. Although he liked the stuff immensely, Slumpblock had virtually no tolerance for it; one good glug would punch his ticket.

Rubb, while he didn't really like it, could soak it up like water. In fact, Rubb had quite a reputation among the household help because of the quantity they had to replace every day. At that moment he recalled his drinking contests with Pentecost Watts. Warm recollections they were, not the least because Rubb always won. Pentecost never seemed to mind, however, at least not by the time Rubb had an insurmountable lead. Pentecost had been a great sport about that. Wow, has he changed!

"No thanks, Boss. But you'd better have one. Go ahead without me."

Slumpblock watched closely, but not obviously, as Rubb drained the bottle, belched only a little, wobbled less, dimmed and fell to sleep about that quickly. The hurt and frustrated scowl lingered on his face, growing deeper as he slept.

Slumpblock scowled back at Rubb. He sat on Rubb's desk, between the penholder and a lamp with a stained-glass shade, scowling at Rubb as though he could read Rubb's dreams if he tried hard enough.

"Great! This is just great," thought Slumpblock. "Now what!? Here I am, locked up with this emotional soap bubble, my cover's blown, something heavy happened and I can't even guess what's going on."

Slumpblock slid off the desk, belly down, and moved quietly to Communications Central in the corner under the pile of rags, insulation and carpet remnants he had fashioned into an anechoic refuge. Here, while Rubb was asleep, he could conduct business unobserved. He needed help now so he had to chance Rubb's awakening. He squirmed into the heap, pulled loose debris into the opening after himself, and stilled his breathing while he concentrated on the point of the crystal tine before him. It was long and slim, fully half his own height, and mounted point upward in a hard fist-sized gob of something that had once been soft and probably alive. He raised his arms upward, slapped his hands together three times overhead and crossed his eyes, just as he had been told. He sure felt silly, but this last episode with Rubb was just what he had been warned about. He prepared for contact.

"Hey Gabe!!" hollered Slumpblock as hard as he could. "Hey! It's me, Slumpblock! I gotta talk to you! Now!"

His voice whumped into the rags and puffy stuff, leaving not a trace. He hollered some more, even unto hoarseness, pausing after each string for a response. Hearing nothing repeatedly, he repeated his plea, varying the order of the words randomly until he had tried them all.

Communications Central was well dampened and Rubb was well asleep so Slumpblock need not have worried about waking him. It was a good thing, for the crystal tine began to ring like a rubbed goblet. The note rose in pitch and volume until even the rags rang sympathetically. Just about the time Slumpblock found his ears hurting, the note began to waver up and down slowly, then more and more quickly until it was a piercing discordant trill.

He decided to move out when he started to shake like the rags. Just then the one-noted tune stopped instantly, with no echo or afterglow. He watched the tine closely, noticing it move a little, then a lot. The gob into which it was set wriggled and stretched a while to get out the kinks, then opened wide a gash of a mouth that was ringed with tiny tines like the one mounted on its top. Slumpblock inched away in revulsion but kept his eyes fast upon it. Finally it spoke, in a voice all out of proportion to it size.

"This better be good," it warned. "You were told what would happen if you failed."

"Yes, I know, Gabe. But I got what you wanted!" Slumpblock was terrified, not really knowing if this was what Gabriel wanted. "I did just like you said!"

"Well?"

Slumpblock retold the story, everything from Rubb kicking the little bricks to the vaporous calligraphy. He ended with Rubb's last words, 'Let me pour you a drink.'

"You clearly heard him say he was done for?" asked the grotesque little gob with a blend of satisfaction and surprise. "He said he was done for? Tomorrow?"

"Yeah, that's it. That's just what he said. That was what you wanted wasn't it? Do I get paid now? I'd sure like to get out of this dump."

"You have done right in calling me. It seems that our Mister Rubb fell into the trap. Too bad he didn't offer more of a fight, just for the fun of it. But that's nothing now, the job is done." The gob turned more fully towards Slumpblock, then said, "Yes my friend, you will get all that's coming to you, but you will get it tomorrow when Rubb gets his, like everyone else."

"But . . ."

"Tomorrow!"

The rag pile suffered only a little from static cling at Gabe's vanish. Slumpblock stared at the empty spot at his feet for a moment, then crawled outside. Rubb was still asleep at his desk, his face still scowling. Slumpblock sighed a little, thought about what he would do tomorrow when he was paid off, and snuggled up asleep against the rag pile. He noticed the neat little brick building standing in the corner of the room next to Rubb, just like the one through the window across the street, but thought nothing of it.

CHAPTER 31

The Ends

This is the final installment in the saga of Rubb and his mentor, Sam Mentor. If they don't mess things up again, this will also be the last of the story so we can be done with it and go on to something more profitable.

Overall, things have not gone well for Rubb and Sam. Rubb is imprisoned in a palatial penthouse by Pentecost Watts, a dropout from life who made it to the top through the machinations of a mysterious man called Stump. Rubb has just learned from Sam that something dreadful is going to happen, and soon.

Sam Mentor is fighting for his very existence, threatened by Gus the Phrogg on the one hand and by One on the other. One, a largely disinterested but extremely powerful player in this game, manifests himself through his spin-off ego Baanquer, a shrewd but so far ineffectual imposition on Real who bedevils our heroes unconscionably in his efforts to restore a balance to things at the behest of One.

Baanquer's messenger in this quest is Gabriel, a free-lance problem who looks as much like a bean bag as anything. Gabriel's role in this affair is not yet entirely clear, but with a little luck we'll know by the end of this chapter. Slumpblock, one of Rubb's own kind, whom he trusted without reservation, has turned out to be a real rat. He'll get his. In fact, a lot of folks will get theirs, including Rubb and Sam. Now let's get on with it.

. . .

"Gus!!" Sam Mentor stared in momentary surprise at his good luck in catching Gus unawares, then masked it immediately when he remembered why he had come.

"You son of a sewer slug!" imposed Sam. "Prepare to meet the destiny you have bargained for, for you will bargain no more!"

That sounded so good that Sam smiled, no leered, both in contempt and satisfaction, relishing the revenge he was about to take on his betrayer.

Sam prepared to unleash that most terrible of strokes, the Full Frontal Anathema, an instantaneous discharge of a lifetime's accumulation of cabalistic moxie focused on one small target. It had taken Sam centuries to hoard this weapon and it would take centuries to replace it. But, as Sam had only one day left, the point was moot.

The Anathema is the ultimate weapon in any wizard's repertoire, one to be garnered against the inevitable day with no alternatives. Its power derived from the practice of wizardry itself, little tears and traces scuffed from the stuff of spells, clinging to the wizard like lint on a pant leg. It was not used lightly because it not only attracted a lot of ethereal attention, it also left the wizard completely defenseless. In this business, interstiched as it is by the two-edged sword of mutually assured destruction, and peopled with a generally opportunistic lot, unleashing an Anathema amounted to doom for the leashor as well as the leashee.

Once spoken, a word is a devilish thing to undo, at least with any style. In like way there is no way to recall an Anathema; once loosed things become as if they had always been. Since the new events have in effect already happened, any ramifications have a strong impetus to stay put and are the very dickens to dislodge. In fact they have never been undone, either in this time or any other.

The leashee, Gus, faced a doom so terrible that even Sam dared not dwell on it overlong. You see, there are many Real places out there (witness our story) that slide against each other like shucked oysters in a tub, but dry. There are also tight places in between those slivers of Real, grinding cracks that are neither here nor there, forgotten by everything and by everyone and beyond any knowing. Anything wedged into such an evil place is in a timeless limbo and stays there eternally beyond reach in the way a windblown whisper is beyond the reach of red, or the black squishy oily stuff of long dead bugs is beyond the reach of song. There is very little fuss involved actually; the victim simply becomes not, as far as we are ever to know.

An Anathema put you there, pounded into a crevice like hemp caulk in a hull chink. There is no room in those tight places for time to ooze; the victim's last experience is the only experience possible, forever. Gus' last moment, his perpetual moment, would be as terrible as Sam could contrive.

There were many times that tempted Sam to use the Anathema, and many people who probably deserved it, but he had always quelled himself waiting for the right time, the right target. It was ironic that the right time would turn out to be his last time.

Sam raised both arms above his head theatrically, palms down and fingers outstretched in a craggy splay that allowed the fractured light from Gus' Tiffany lamp to play dramatically on his honed and polished nails. His robe began to smoke about the hem, wafting oily wisps of evil upwards on a demonic draught that rumpled the atmosphere. The troubled air began to rumble with the accumulating hate that Sam assembled for the annihilation of this sniveling bug splat called Gus. The worlds were due for a thorough cleansing and Gus would be a good start for it.

Sam whirled about his center of gravity, round and around slowly then faster, over then under, each turn winding up the threads of his hate, extracting them from the ether itself and spindling them more and more tightly as he wove his cocoon of vengeance.

To better draw every Hatewhip from everything he had ever touched, the very warp and woof of his misspent life, Sam set his head at an ungodly angle to his frame, as if he had been hanged. The technique, known in the trade as a Spitball, unbalanced his mass and forced those evil windings to focus their impact on Gus like a shaped charge. As a result, however, Sam precessed loopily around the room like a wobbly top.

Gus felt there was something amiss but to him Sam was just a blur and a breeze. That took some of the fun out of it for Sam since anticipation is the larger part of revenge. Sam dearly wanted Gus to remember his moment of doom forever, and remember even longer the face of Sam the Beneficent.

Fully charged, Sam wheeled to a stop facing Gus. He coolly set the exquisitely delicate hair trigger on the Anathema and drew a bead on Gus. Sam locked eyes with Gus, or rather forked them to accommodate Gus' wide-set orbs. "On three," paced Sam to himself.

"One . . . Two . . ."

"Oh, Hi Sam," said Gus cheerfully. "How's tricks."

Gus looked up only momentarily, smiled at Sam with more sincerity than Sam thought possible for a cad, and went back to his desk work with a happy hum.

"Whoa!" Sam jerked, desperately trying to gather the Hatewhips that had already loosened. "Hold it!!" Sam cursed while trying to wrangle both the whips and his composure.

Sam had dreamed so long of launching Gus into eternal terror that he almost lost it seeing that Gus was anything but terror stricken. He had but one bolt after all, and he daren't waste his last shot only to wed Gus to his never ending fate with a never ending smile. There was also a moral issue involved; blasting Gus into eternal bliss is the sort of faux pas that his professional colleagues would snigger about until their own doomsdays.

Gathering his whips and his wits, Sam imposed himself on Gus's attention with a colorful Lotus Blossom starburst that exploded under his desk. Gus, sensing evil afoot, turned to Sam by default.

"You have one second and one word left to your life," raged Sam through a gargoylean visage he borrowed for the occasion. "Use them now to prepare for eternal pain (Zzzap!), abject sorrow (Crash! CRASH!!), and dismal despair more desperate than your darkest nightmare (Sizzle-izzle . . . Ka-BOOM!)."

Nice work, thought Sam.

Sam leaped to twice his size, flaring leathery black spike-tipped wings that whipped the orange smoke belching from his blazing nostrils. He let out a screech that shamed a thousand blackboards and bared glistening talons that dripped blood. Poised to strike, Sam set the Anathema for ground zero.

"Die!" screamed Sam, "Die again and again forever and ever!!" This time it took and Gus was terrified indeed. He jerked this way and that, seeking haven, but time stopped too soon for Gus as Sam pulled the trigger.

A light crystalline ting-a-ling lingered a few moments in the room. The room, however, was empty, twice.

.   .   .

"Golly, that Rubb is a jerk," thought Slumpblock, "and I'm not gonna take it any more." This is a Slumpblock we haven't seen.

Slumpblock had it with all that "Yes, Boss" and "No, Boss" drivel he had to spout at Rubb to keep his part of the deal. It was all he could do to put up with Rubb's moods and complaints all day every day. He had a smoldering urge for revenge ever since the day Rubb fell asleep in the middle of Slumpblock's rendition of the Eardian Anthem. As he crept up on Rubb sleeping at his desk, he saw his opportunity ripening. He didn't need this self-doubting wimp anymore; his mission was over and tomorrow was payday!

Slumpblock stole stealthily around Rubb's desk and gave a mean little kick to the hindmost wheel of Rubb's tilted office chair, then scattered. Rubb jerked from the belly trying to right himself even before he woke up. The chair slipped under him and he crashed to his back, half under his desk and half not.

"Whoof!!" puffed Rubb when he hit the floor. Actually, Rubb didn't hit the floor so much as whump it; the carpet was obscenely deep, he didn't fall all that far and he wasn't all that heavy. The whoof was more a function of surprise than impact. He did, however, take note of Slumpblock's merriment and vented his upended dignity.

"Aw, Slumpblock. You didn't have to do that, did you?"

"You See!!" shouted Slumpblock, his merriment spoilt. "You just lie there like a dead fish! Why don't you get up a take a swing at me, or . . . or . . . something!?"

Rubb rolled over to his belly and pulled himself out from under the desk, wrestling with the swivel chair a bit.

"Something is bothering you, isn't it?"

Slumpblock turned and toppled his head into the wall, pounding it overhead with the fisted pad of his palm.

"Why me? . . . Why me?"

"Because you didn't have a choice. Remember?"

The voice was deep, like bubbling mud with a lilting crystal overtone in the background. It was not Rubb's. Rubb, thinking it *was* bubbling mud, looked down at his feet instinctively, tugged on his pant legs and lifted himself up on his tippy-toes. Slumpblock, in contrast, froze.

"Allow me," blurped the voice. "My friend seems to be at a loss. My name is Gabriel. And you are Rubb." It was not a question.

Rubb turned the wrong way looking for the source and reared back when he found it, dropping both his pant cuffs and his jaw.

"This is new!" thought he himselfly.

"Uh, yes. Yes, Rubb." Rubb stared at the mess before him unto discourtesy. "Yes. Uh, would you like a seat?"

He gestured towards the couch against the wall next to Slumpblock. Slumpblock had stopped pounding by now and lowered his head to see out from under his right armpit.

Gabriel did not move so much as a wrinkle, although he burbled a little on idle. Slumpblock did not move either, preferring to go into light shock. Rubb, having no real experience to back him up on this one, strode over to Gabriel with his hand out in greeting in spite of the obvious lack of anything handy.

"Yessir! Rubb, that's me. What can I do for you."

Gabriel did not move. Rubb wiped his hand on his hip, stepped back twice and ventured:

"You're new around here, aren't you?"

This time Gabe moved, opening that crystalline maw just a little. He didn't really speak at Rubb as the gash seemed to have no ends, but the words were directional nonetheless.

"It is time."

Rubb was puzzled at that. Then he recalled Sam's vaporous warning about tomorrow's calamity. Until now Rubb hadn't fully appreciated Sam's gift for understatement; this thing was calamity squared. But there was business at hand.

"No! No! Wait!" he blurted out. "Not until tomorrow! Sam said not until tomorrow!!"

Rubb jumped and stamped and beat the air with cute but frustrated little fists. His voice turned decidedly whiny and he actually managed to squeeze out a tear or two. Rubb figured it couldn't hurt to try a tantrum and sometimes it worked.

"I see you have been warned. Sam is clever, more so than I thought possible. Too bad it is as nothing." Gabe hesitated while he chose his words. "Sam forgot to mention that it is my tomorrow, not yours."

Now Gabriel really did turn, first to Slumpblock who by now was reduced to sniveling in the corner, then to Rubb.

"They are waiting. We must go now."

"No! What about my Obs! Yeah, my Obs, that's it! Sam said . . ."

"I know nothing of your accumulations and they are of no worth where we are going. As for Sam, he has his own problems to solve; he cannot help you. Your Obs mean little and Sam's petty posturings even less. NOW!"

Blurpp!

That pretty well settled things for when Slumpblock finally peeped out between his clam-shelled arms they were gone. Without hesitation or look back, he strode for the door and swung it wide on his freedom. Between here and there, however, stood Pentecost Darn-Watts silhouetted against a haze of back-lighted smoke, his feet wide-set and his fists on his hips.

Glass chimes rang incongruously somewhere but Slumpblock had no time for that. He stopped on his heels and leaped for cover back into the office. The last image etched on his mind was the clock on the wall. The little hand was on three and the big hand was on the one.

.   .   .

Pentecost Darn-Watts strode down the hallway towards Rubb's office. He was smiling and singing lightly as he strode, something to the effect that a policeman's lot was not a happy one. He glanced at the wall clock. Three oh-four.

"Right on time," he hummed during the second chorus, "Right on time de time time time!"

This little refrain echoed louder than he expected and he looked back down the hallway behind him with a little embarrassment. Seeing no one he relaxed, picked up the tune and his pace.

Pentecost had made this trek too many times to count now, dozens of times certainly, hundreds probably. A thousand? Maybe. Whatever, it had always been profitable. Lordy, had it been profitable! Today he would make his final killing, one for the books. And then? Who knows, but he was going to have fun exploring the whole world to find out.

In fact, it was so easy that he was considering retiring undefeated. He sure didn't need any more money and the routine here was getting a little monotonous. Maybe in a year or two.

In quiet moments he still marveled to himself at how things had turned out; one day he was your basic drunk and the next he was the richest and the most powerful man in the world.

"Stump!" he said aloud. Then to himself again, "That was his name, Stump. I sure owe that guy a favor! I wonder what ever happened to him . . ."

"Awww . . . Who knows and who cares!" he said aloud again, without a thought of eavesdroppers. "Hells fire, I'm rich and I own the store! And in one more minute I'm a zillion richer. Take that, Stump!"

While empiricists consider a zillion woefully vague, Pentecost was right conceptually. The Thud had been a windfall for him and he was definitely rich, beyond counting likely as not. He had an absolute monopoly over the only source of Thud, which in turn was the only known specific for the Intelligence virus. Without the Thud all of the Executives would burn out in a matter of days, terribly aged and withered by rampant braininess. They had all seen it happen and they were all eager to pay any price Pentecost asked for just one more Thudfest.

And this was the beauty of the deal; the Thud just kept rolling into his lap. Every day at 3:05 hundreds of the little rascals would pour out of Rubb's executive suite. All he had to do was round them up and ship them out. No money invested, no risk, no overhead, no nothing. Just pure profit. But there was more pressing business now and his attention snapped back to the work at hand.

Pentecost strode to a determined stop in front of Rubb's office and looked over the preparations. Rubb's office was the biggest one in the building, big enough to hold the hundreds of Thud that poured into it at this time every day. The men were all in place, barricades in order, nets ready, the smoke screen wafting down the hallway. The technique of capturing the Thud was down to a science anymore and preparations were always the same. However, Pentecost recalled uneasily how the men used to take up stations inside the room. Now they were set up outside, in the hallway.

Little by little, it seemed, the Thud were getting harder and harder to overwhelm so his men had taken up their positions outside the doorway, at the narrowest point of their escape. That should hold the Thud for the time being but he also noticed that his men did not seem particularly confident of their prospects.

He checked everything one more time and nodded with satisfaction. Even though he didn't actually touch the squirmy little devils any more, he still thrilled to the chase. It was exactly 3:05 when the doors opened.

There stood one wide-eyed little Thud, with the room behind echoing in its emptiness. Pentecost looked at the Thud as though expecting an explanation. The Thud looked at Pentecost as though surprised.

Pentecost looked at his watch again, tapped it sharply a few times for encouragement and glanced up at the high hallway clock. 3:05.

The little Thud jumped backwards, twisted like a dropped cat and jumped behind a large cast iron radiator in the office against the opposite wall.

Pentecost ignored the lone Thud for the moment and studied the vast office suspiciously. He looked back at his troops, turning his head no more than necessary, then returned his eyes quickly to the room. It was silent, quiet enough to hear the light but strained gasping of the lone Thud behind the radiator. The clock moved once, to 3:06.

Everything seemed in order, save his apprehension about several hundred late Thud, so he took a deep breath, set his face on resolute and turned bravely to his men.

"Chaaaarge!" It was a pretty convincing order. Pentecost led his troops unto glory with one giant step into the office. "Inside! We'll ambush them from . . . !"

But the men were fearfrozen in place. Well, not frozen exactly, and it was not fear either; no one moved so much as a lash or a shadow. They were alive, Pentecost was sure of that because they were not glazed or matte, but they did not move and they certainly did not charge.

Pentecost wondered at that for only a moment, however, as his momentum carried him irretrievably through the trajectory he had set for himself. He realized too late that he had leaped into a void so absolutely black that eyesight failed of purchase, as did fingers and toes. There was no office and no hallway, no Thud and no soldiers, no voice and no sound, no floor but no falling, no ceiling but no up, no movement in space and as far as he could tell no movement of his joints; just Pentecost Darn-Watts and a crystalline ring all around him, like glass singing.

.   .   .

"Hello, what have we here!?" The old man stopped in mid-stroke. "My hair can wait," he thought, setting aside the two rocks.

He studied the rhythmic undulations in the grass off to his right, puzzling over its compelling attraction; that particular movement jangled a familiar note in his frizzled brain. He leaned over closer, within arm reach of the budding lump of earth, trying to connect it with something very important way back deep in his tattered memories.

"Confound it!!" he muttered aloud.

The dirt stopped mounding, as if listening.

That was important! He knew that was important! But why?! Blast it all! He couldn't do a thing with his head anymore!

He shook his head violently, then again. That helped. Something seemed to bubble up from the depths of the disassociated mass of axons and dendrons that once was a Brain. And an Executive too! Don't forget that. That's important. But the old man lost the thought again, whatever it was, and still had only a slipping feeling that the mound was important. It began to move again.

The old man relaxed a little, settled back against the tree and reached for the rocks. The mound, pausing as if to make one last lurch for the record, splashed open in a dirty little spray of rubble and dried grass. In the center of the earthwound stood Slumpblock, big as you please and ready for a fight.

"Th . . . Th . . ." The old man was not startled, as his nervous system had deteriorated far beyond anything that could be called a jerk, but the creature before him stimulated the last lump of gray matter in his brain that could still compile a syllogism. His eyes widened, his pulse quickened and he tried to vocalize the surging burst of thought that went right to his tongue.

"Thud!!! Thud! They've come back! Thud! Ohhh, Thud!"

The old man began to cry in joy and relief, then almost forgot why he cried. With a beaming grin on his wrinkled face, he leaned over to the Thud who *was* startled, and took it into his arms. Holding it tight to his breast, the old man rocked slowly to a simple tune that he hummed, one that he had learned so long ago that it could never be forgotten.

Slumpblock squirmed considerably but could not break the grip of the old man who poured every strength he had into his grasping arms. Slumpblock, who had no idea what was going on, yelped for help.

"Yhelp!!"

The old man tightened his grip of endearment, squeezing another whoop from the Thud. In desperation the Slumpblock spent his last breath on the only names that came to mind, the last two people he saw before his world turned black and he had clawed his way into this predicament.

"Rubb! Rubb!," and then thinking better of it, "Pentecost, save me! Help, Pentecost!"

The old man stopped instantly. His eyes searched those of the Thud he held up at arm's length. His head cleared a little as he struggled to assemble a sentence.

"What did you say?" asked the old man, very intently.

The Thud froze in his hands, afraid to move.

"Pentecost. Pentecost Watts. Is that what you said? Pentecost Darn-Watts?"

"No," Said Slumpblock tentatively, still not sure what was riding on his answer. "No, I . . . I said Pentecost, just Pentecost."

"You know Pentecost?" The old man was percolating with hate and fear at the name. "You know him and you live?"

"Well, yes." The answer seemed obvious to Slumpblock.

"Take me to him! I must see him one more time. You must take me to him before the Powerdowners come." The old man shook at these words, shaking Slumpblock as well.

"You don't know how important it is! I must tell him in time! Do you understand at all? I must tell him before it's too late!"

The old man was livid, just short of violent, when a deep voice with the soothing coolness of creek bed mud rumbled behind him.

"You will have a chance to tell him later, Stump. We must go now. Come."

Stump turned just quickly enough to catch the gleam of crystal teeth set in mush, but no more. Slumpblock found himself suspended in mid air. Stump was gone in less time than it took for the universe to notice that Slumpblock should have fallen. Before it did, however, a hand, Stump's hand, grabbed him by the scruff and yanked.

.   .   .

Well! A lot has happened to our little repertory group. And it's clear that there is only one common denominator. Not so clear, however, is how all of this will fall out.

Will Rubb ever return to his semi-beloved East Eard? Will Sam Mentor, his resources spent on the Full Frontal Anathema, find peace at last knowing that his life was completely wasted? Will Gus the Moneymonger get his come-uppance? Will Pentecost and/or Slumpblock get his/theirs? And what about Stump?

Sorta, no, yes, no/yes, and who knows.

CHAPTER 32

Resolution

You know this place, the Library where this tale began. The Books are still here, much as we left them, although we have disheveled the dust a bit. The Scribe has stopped by since to chronicle the most recent doings of things that move, and has gone again.

There is still a ripping good fire in the place, still cold and noiseless,

The Watchers still stand, silent and unblinking. Oh yes, the Watchers are still here and by now they know you well. Do not move suddenly and do not stare at them.

We have returned to the Library because there are no more pieces to the story you have traced; the thread has run out. It may be that any course you could have chosen would bring us to this same point. The confluence of all recorded impact is here, at this point, the point set by Baanquer's contrivance. We cannot see beyond it and no Book records it. Even the Stone is blank.

We have come here for enlightenment on that point, although if the truth were known, Baanquer himself is mystified by the void beyond. He knows his intentions regarding the point and has played his hand deliberately, according to the odds. But in the end, results will turn on the draw.

A heavy-posted high back chair sits to the side of the fireplace facing into the seating array. It is not cushioned, in stark contrast to the other posh furniture, and uncomfortable in spite of its quality. The furniture is arrayed to focus on this chair.

On this highback, legs crossed at the ankles and hands folded nervously between his knees, sits Rubb, quite alone save for the Watchers who hardly count as company.

Rubb had sat there long enough to feel the chair. All creatures have bones where they sit, probably so they don't sit too long. Rubb qualified as one of these and squirmed a little to ease the stiffness, slowly so as not to draw the eye of a Watcher. As far as Rubb could tell his every move was monitored, so he moved very little.

Rubb's concern about the Watchers was well-advised inasmuch as that is all Watchers do, but it was probably also wasted. Their black eyes showed no white and Rubb found it impossible to tell if he was indeed being watched. Each eye, particularly that of the flyer, was bottomless obsidian that seemed to look in every direction at once, like Santa-Follows-You.

Once or twice he toggled his glance quickly between the beasts to catch their eyes moving, like trying to catch yourself in a mirror not looking at you. The only result was more meanness, however it was he came to know that, so he soon broke off the game.

There was certainly no breeze in this room, hadn't been since it started, but Rubb goosebumped at a chill across the nape of his neck. A light crystalline tingle like wind chimes completed the illusion of breeze. The fire flared a little and danced under duress but it was no hotter or noisier than before. Slowly and quietly at first, then louder, a deep subsonic chuckle rumbled up behind.

"Mumbumbplebum. Bumplepumburpledump . . . Humph!"

Rubb, by this time ready to welcome any company who might stand proof against the Watchers, turned quickly about in greeting.

"Am I glad . . ." and stopped. Gabriel!!

"I do not know. But that is hardly important." Deep rumbly muddy voice. "Are you ready?"

"Ready!?" Rubb didn't like the ring of that! "What ready! Nobody said anything about ready!"

"You are here to be tried. You have unsettled things, things you should have left alone. You have attracted the attention of those best avoided. Your crimes are high and many. Think about your defense."

"Crimes! CRIMES!!"

Rubb's hollering raised a little dust, prompting him to check back in with old Harpy-on-the-Mantel. It had not moved any more than the mantel but he did feel the intensity of its sharpened attention.

"Uh . . . crimes?"

"Oh yes, my little friend. You have gotten about so, into places you ought not. You cannot go on. You are guilty. This trial will only determine your fate."

"Guilty? Guilty of what! What did I do?" Rubb began to slip down off of the chair, confrontation in his veins.

"Shush!"

That was a pretty good shush for a mouth as wide as Gabriel's that precluded a pucker.

"Listen! It begins."

Rubb froze mid-slide. Goosebumps returned as he turned slowly to face what he did not want to see. When he did see, he could not believe.

"SAM!"

The black thing on the mantel moved this time, shrugging off a little dust clump that lilted down, highlighted by the cold light of the fire.

"Sam!" More subdued and in a stage whisper. "Is that you?"

Rubb felt the black beast's only eye focus more narrowly on his throat, sensed its tightening sinews.

"Yes," observed Sam Mentor absently. "It's me. Say, have you taken a look at this carpet. It's really very remarkable." Sam faced away from Rubb, examining the carpet. "If you look closely you can see it moo . . ."

Sam stopped shy of the end of his sentence and rocked up on his tippy-toes like he had been stuck with a pin, shoulders back, back arched, elbows and knees cocked. " . . . oops!"

Sam froze when the words finally registered, the name Rubb emblazoned across his mind even before he fully grasped the situation.

Rubb!! Can it be!?

He took a moment to compose his words and turned in controlled dignity.

"You imbecile! You unconscionable bumbler!! Look what you've done! I knew you dwarfs would be the end of me!" Sam really dumped a load on Rubb. "How can one lump of Sop cause so much trouble so fast. You've ruined me! I'm done . . . finished!!"

Rubb stopped mid-slide again, noticed his vulnerability, dropped quickly to the floor and skittered behind the legs of the chair.

"Now wait a minute, Sam," he started. "I didn't . . ."

"Wait, my tamales!" Sam, absolutely livid with rage, paused to roll up his sleeves and set his feet. "This is my last day and it's all your fault! If this is to be my last, it will also be yours! Prepare your last thought for you are doomed!!"

"Stop." There was no urgency in the voice and there was no command, only mud.

Sam did stop, at his own amazement, and turned to Gabriel who fixed Sam eyelessly. Sam did not doubt that Gabriel expected obedience, but he had also pledged to himself that before this affair was ended Rubb would be low grade runny goop fit only for dust suppression. He raised his arms again, mouthed some vile incantation and whipped a spray of tinselly stuff all over Rubb and the chair. Rubb cringed hands over head, recognizing Sam's fearsome Whomp[3], and did in fact think his last thought.

Having thought that, he thought again, to wit: "That didn't hurt as much as I expected." Then, "Check it out!" He opened his eyes to meet Sam's.

Sam could only stare at Rubb and Rubb stared back, both confounded. Sam rarely missed and then only under the influence. But now Sam was quite sober and, if it were possible, even more enraged. Sam grabbed for another handful of tinsel from the purse at his sash.

"Sam," mumbled Gabriel, again with no urgency, "Put away your tricks. They will do you no good here."

Just then a seam in the tinsel bag parted and the pixy dust ran out all over Sam's shoe. Rubb giggled. Sam lost it.

"AAGGGGHHHGGGGLLEEEEEOOOOO!!"

Sam flew to attack Rubb with hands and feet flying, blood in his eyes and murder in his heart.

"Shush!" bubbled Gabriel with a happy urgency.

Sam smacked splat in mid air like he had hit a wall, then dropped awkwardly to the floor jelly side down. He did not move, nor did Rubb.

"You don't want to miss this."

Baanquer stood solidly at the center of the room, awaiting attention with mild amusement. He is a large person, heavily muscled and boned, thick-maned and ruddy. He might have been a stone smith once, or pulled barges for a living. One could imagine his having wrought this room bare-handed from some primordial forest. He was now aged and sensitive and wise, and might as easily have painted the landscapes or engineered the tools in this room.

His feet were set wide, his arms folded. His belly potted just enough to convey substantial means without that jiggly hint of overindulgence or underuse. He wore no jewelry but the gold lame' jump suit picked up a sparkling mosaic of the starburst on which he stood. He stood barefoot. The jump suit, by the way, fit.

Sam recognized Baanquer at once, as did Gabriel from his words. Rubb, with little more than the jump suit by which to measure the man, started to giggle again but stopped prudently at Baanquer's sharp quick eye.

"You are guilty, my stalwart friends," began Baanquer, getting right down to it. "Tell me why you should not now suffer your fates. Take your time."

He glanced pointedly to the Watcher on the mantel and then to the position of the window light on the wall. Sam and Rubb both followed his eyes to the light fall in time to see it jump one click. Baanquer smiled indulgently at some inside joke.

"ButButBu . . ." sputtered Rubb.

Sam slapped his hand over Rubb's mouth before he could do something stupid and pushed him to the rear. Rubb continued his muffled bubububbing which tickled Sam's palm to distraction. Sam held firm.

"Baanquer," began Sam solicitously. "You and I have been through all of this before. You know why I am here. It is only because some scoundrel has stolen my life. I don't know who and I don't know why, but it is not at my fault. Therefore, I should not suffer for the actions of others." Sam stopped, pleased so far, and continued.

"This Son of Sop, however, has done nothing but tear up the ether and scorn the devils themselves. It all started when he blasted unbidden into my very home. We would not be here if he . . ."

Rubb listened in accelerating disbelief as he caught Sam's drift. He stopped bubbing and struggled to tear Sam's wrap-around palm from his face.

"Waamph!!"

Rubb struggled and kicked, finally biting Sam's hand. Sam let go right away but Rubb lost the opportunity when he gagged a little on the taste. Sam cursed the little mumbly dump. Rubb spit a little twice, then continued.

"What!!" Sputtersputter. "You . . . You . . . ! You're as guilty as me, you traitor!!" That in a pitch too high. He cleared his throat and continued in a lower register.

"You helped every step of the way." Much better he thought. "You called up all your old demons and sent me off to Six Hells and back!! You and that slop you call beer. I should have known you couldn't be trusted when I saw that anchor chained to your leg. And I walked right into it! Boy, did I walk into it!"

Rubb caught his breath and was winding up again when Sam jumped back in.

"Guilty? Me?" Sam had an little innocent shtick that didn't work very well. "Why this . . . this Shaman practically begged me to help him. In fact, he . . ."

"Enough! We all know what you did, both of you." It was a sterner Baanquer, no longer indulgent. "I thought that we might be done with this in a more orderly manner. I can see that you will be more trouble than this affair warrants. But, if you must . . ."

He turned his head aside deliberately and introduced the first witness with a theatrical sweep of his hand. All eyes followed, even, had anyone been watching, the Watchers.

"Gus!" That was Sam.

"Gus?" Rubb.

"Gus." said Baanquer mildly.

Gus blinked at finding himself dropped into this hostile company without warning. He was agitated, obviously expecting something painful and/or terminal, but he was not surprised. He knew exactly why he was here. Sam recognized Gus, of course, but Rubb was still mystified by it all.

"Generalissimo Ultissimo Schwartz, sole proprietor of all Eard," continued Baanquer. "This is where it all started."

"Wait a minute! You can't blame this all on me!"

Gus jerked from one set of eyes to another, panic and pleading in his own.

"It's those Eards that did it, that's who! They gave away the store; all I had to do was get in the way. If you have to blame anyone, blame those shiftless Eards!"

"There is considerable truth in what you say, Gus. The Eards are a shiftless lot. Their wastrel ways are recognized far beyond that little world and their loutishness is epic."

Baanquer let his gaze linger on Rubb's head uncomfortably long, just enough to squirm Rubb a little and lay a shot across the others' collective bow.

"But I did not say you were to blame for all of this, Gus, I said that it all started with you." Baanquer paused, Gus fixed by his knowing eyes. "However, you are not entirely blameless either, Gus. Tell us about your war casualties."

Gus blanched.

"What about them! How do you know about them?"

Gus knew that it did indeed start with the war casualties, or rather the lack of them. But Gus found he could not refrain from speaking about them; he was being forced to tell the truth. Contrary to his meager will and his devious bent he began:

"There never was a war."

NoNo! he thought, don't tell them! But he could not help himself.

"There was no war and there were no casualties. Those soldiers just . . . evaporated. I had an arrangement with . . . with One. One did all the dirty work in exchange for betraying Sam Mentor!" Gasps all around, including Baanquer!

Sam clenched his teeth, baring them in anger, and growled a little. He shifted his weight forward, as if to attack Gus but was restrained by Baanquer's hand waving summary dismissal. This was more for the show than anything; Sam knew Gus had treachery in his heart when they had confronted each other in Gus's office. Still, it never hurt to take the moral high road in situations like this.

The remarkable thing was Baanquer himself. He was clearly not prepared for that answer. One!! Consternation was written all over Baanquer's face, although he recovered quickly. He stared at Gus while he pondered his next move. Dammit! Gus was supposed to finger Pentecost, not One. What was One doing in all of this? One didn't know a thing that was going on, did he? Why would One upbraid me for this mess when he knew all along what was going on!?

Baanquer pondered these questions over and under until someone cleared a throat as encouragement to get on with it. The mantel Watcher glanced from one dog to the other and raised its eye heavenward. Baanquer looked about sheepishly, scrunched his back to relieve the tension and in a voice with a tad of squeak in it said:

"All right then, Pentecost, tell us your role in all of this."

"Pentecost!" That was Rubb.

"Pentecost?" Mentor and Gus simultaneously.

"Pentecost," said Baanquer, with some resignation. "A Man."

He was getting a little confused himself, in spite of the fact that he had engineered it, and was beginning to wish it would all go away. It was far too late for that now, even for himself, but he could not allay his uneasiness about One. What was he up to?

"Well?"

"Unnmmph," he began with his throat. "Well, I'm not really sure where to begin."

This was true enough. Baanquer had put no imperative on his words yet. Noticing Rubb, however, jump-started Pentecost's memory.

"I guess it all started when Rubb walked up to me in the park. We got to be friends and drinking buddies, you know. And so I got arrested and then I got this neat job and office and all and then these Thuds just dumped all over me. I didn't do anything."

"Thuds?" interrupted Baanquer. "I'm not sure everyone present is familiar with the term. Just what is a Thud?"

"Why, Rubb there. He's a Thud. Everybody knows that. Like I said, they just dumped on like a basket of fish. Hundreds of thuds! Honest. What else could I do?"

The pitch of Pentecost's voice had risen about as far as it could go, so he stopped.

"I'll ask the questions, Pentecost. And the question I put to you is this: Exactly what did you do?"

"I sold them, of course. What else do you do with a Thud?"

Gasps all around, Although some were too obviously only polite imitations of real concerned surprise. Everyone was covering themselves very professionally.

"Tell me this," continued Baanquer. "You can sell only to one who is willing to buy. What did your buyers do with hundreds of these . . . uh . . . Thuds, as you call them?"

Baanquer had a vested interest in the proceedings and was anxious to hear this answer on the off chance it didn't match the one he knew. Pentecost hesitated overlong on that question, inadvertently giving undue weight to his answer. Baanquer was compelled to turn the screw on Pentecost.

"Okayokay! So they eat them, what's the big deal. They just came barreling in like they were getting off the train. If we didn't do something they would have overrun the place!" Pentecost looked about from shocked face to disgusted face and back.

"Hell's Fire, we used to pull them out of the ground like turnips!"

The onlookers momentarily forgot to gasp, genuinely stunned for the most part and for the first time. A nervous cough got the chorus rolling again.

"GASP!!" Nice chorus, finally.

"And why, my charming man, do your kind eat the Thud?"

"Me? I don't eat them. Never did. I don't know why they eat them."

Not even Pentecost bought that. His eyes wandered upwards and for the first time rested on the Mantel Harpy. The predator's interest centered unequivocally on this uneasy thing called a Man.

"Try again, harder." Baanquer torqued Pentecost a good one. Pentecost, caught between the Black Menace on the mantelpiece and Baanquer's psychic onslaught, responded quickly.

"Okay! They eat them . . . because of some disease they have. They sorta dry up or something if they don't eat Thuds every day. That's why they were so valuable; no Thud and they dry up and blow away. Something like that."

Pentecost stopped only to find that he was expected to continue.

"Well," he added, "if you don't believe me, why don't you get that old guy that got me that job in the first place. His name was . . . was . . ."

"Stump. My name is Stump."

And indeed it was Stump, sitting with his legs crossed on the carpet by the fireplace. His eyes were alert and his smile in good working order. He was old, definitely old, but spry and springy. Stump seemed to be the only one to this point who wasn't surprised or afraid at being here.

"Ah yes, Stump. I'm glad you could make it. I was afraid you were dead by now."

Baanquer strode straight to Stump through the now considerable crowd that parted for him like the Red Sea and helped him to his feet. "Come, join our little soiree."

"Thank you, Baanky." Gasp! "But I'm afraid you are right, I am dead."

GASP!!

"I thought I might stop by and see if I could be of assistance." Will the wonders never cease!?

"Well, yes," replied Baanquer. "Things are a bit muddled. Do you mind. You had quite a hand in it all."

"Yes," said Stump with a chuckle. "I guess I did. Let me get my thoughts together and you can ask me whatever you like."

He settled into one of the overstuffed brocaded settees, squirmed a little to free himself from the nap and signaled to begin.

"First of all," said Baanquer without a trace of his former sternness. "Why do Men eat Thuds?"

"That's the easy question. I made them that way."

Gasp! A little jaded.

"Please go on." For the first time Baanquer seemed to be enjoying himself.

"Well, as you know, I discovered the virus that made Men different from all of the other creatures, the bug that made them intelligent. The Stump A Varietal virus they called it, after me. But it gets out of hand in certain people. Burns us out in no time. You see, intelligence is just a matter of the rate at which the mind works, and the virus put us full blast. And then, of course, we went phhtt."

"Phhtt?" in unison.

"Phhtt!" confirmed Stump in no uncertain terms. "Like a flashbulb. And the only cure, really no cure at all, is the Thud. If you caught the virus, eating Thud slows you down enough to do useful work, at least for a while. No Thud, phhtt."

"And Pentecost?"

"Pentecost is immune. The virus, as you have probably figured out for yourself, doesn't work on Pentecost. Lots of things don't work on Pentecost. That's why I chose him."

"Chose?" Mock incredulity. "What for?" Baanquer knew exactly what for, and relished the dramatic anticipation in the room.

"What for!" exploded Stump in equally mock surprise. "Why, to be the anchor, of course! We needed someone who could hold down our end of the tunnel without eating it!" Stump smiled directionally to Baanquer, both amused at their secret game.

"As you may have noticed, Pentecost's mind is a wall," he continued. "He couldn't catch the disease so he didn't need the treatment. That virus didn't give him so much as a headache!"

Stump grinned triumphantly to his audience, then reconsidered. They had responded with dull confused mutterings that can be easily imagined.

"If there are no further questions, I think we can . . ."

"Sir?" It was Rubb.

"Sir, if I may." Rubb turned to Pentecost. "You bastard! You . . ."

"That will be quite enough, Rubb. You are correct in your assessment of the situation into which you fell. But you must remember that you did jump into it, quite voluntarily and even more noisily. You blasted yourself all over creation and literally woke the dead. You and this Sam Mentor of yours! We shall hear your stories soon enough. After that, if you still feel the need, you will have your turn."

That didn't really satisfy Rubb but he took the better course and held his peace for now. He did, however, continue to glare at Pentecost until he finally turned away, pretending to pick a nit.

Rubb had to admit that he had undertaken his quest in spite of the risks, perhaps even because of them. But taking a calculated risk was one thing, being double-crossed and used by a friend was another. He knew he had been finagled into this somehow, set up for it long before there was an inkling of trouble. Before he and Sam had made their pact with the devils. And maybe even before he won the Prime Ministership in that . . .

"The lottery!" exploded Rubb, directly at Stump who startled. "You fixed the lottery too! That's where this all began! That's why I'm here!" Now Rubb was really ticked.

"No Rubb," said Stump mildly. "I didn't do that. It was a stroke of genius, looking back at it now, but I didn't do it."

Stump was so certain and unflapped about the point that Rubb conceded it.

"Then who . . . ?"

Baanquer cleared his throat. "I might be able to clarify things a bit." He eyed each one in the room in turn while he chose his words. "Yes, I fixed that lottery, Rubb. As a matter of fact, I even put you out of work so you would have to accept the position." Baanquer stared levelly at Rubb with no sign of guilt or guile.

"For the rest of you who may have lost track of things, I chose Rubb for this . . . this adventure . . . because he has in abundance one very rare quality that was essential to its success: he has a conscience."

Gasps all around, probably genuine.

He paused to smile benignly upon Rubb, who blushed for maybe the first time in his life, and continued.

"The plan was to make you Prime Minister of Eard. In that way you would inevitably have to confront the problem of the war. But from that point on, Rubb, you were largely on your own. You and Sam had me guessing a few times, but you performed magnificently!" Baanquer paused to see if they were buying it. It seemed that they were.

Rubb still smiled broadly, embarrassed at being exposed as a nice guy. Sam even tried to cover a little rising good humor within by scratching his nose. He did not have to try very hard or very long, however, as he quickly recalled that his days were numbered (that is, to just one) and by his own admission it was all because of Baanquer's meddling. Baanquer and this man who called himself Stump!

"Now just a minute!" exploded Sam in his return to reality. "Here we are in this tomb, elbow to chin with the most unscrupulous scoundrels in two worlds, and you want us to feel good about being played for fools!! We are facing the end of the world and you compliment us on how well we let ourselves be used!"

During all of this Sam was surreptitiously winding up his Id for a final shot to take out Baanquer. Rubb noticed the tell-tale glow behind Sam's ears and the peculiar warble in his speech, as though he were riding over cobbles in an iron-tyrd coach. Baanquer seem not to notice, or care, while the rest of the company suspected nothing.

"Well, I will have none of that!" continued Sam. "I have been savaged by your irresponsible diddling, Baanquer, and it is time for an end to it! I demand that you put things aright and depart forthwith!"

Sam thought his speech pretty grand and maybe even effective. The others seemed to agree, as long as they were on the sidelines, and nodded so. Baanquer made no perceptible response. Sam, encouraged and with nothing to lose, continued.

"I am not afraid of your reputation, Baanquer, and this grandstand light and mirror show of yours really does nothing for it. Show what you are made of and . . . !"

At this point Sam Frisbee-whipped his right arm back-handedly at Baanquer, his palm open and fingers crooked to focus the flaming Maque on Baanquer's belly.

"Stop this!!"

Sputt. Nothing happened.

Baanquer did not enjoy seeing Sam embarrass himself in public. Everyone in the room, including the Watchers, turned to Baanquer with Sam's Maque Attack, then back to Sam when nothing happened.

Baanquer did not blink but he did smile to one side, to Stump's side. Sam was mortified at the fizzle and looked like he might cry.

"Ah, but you see, Sam, things are to be set aright, as you say. Things are not as they should be? Agreed. And you will have your way, your rightness, Sam. Although I have no idea if it is what you had in mind, things will be definitely set aright. And soon."

Baanquer paused as he surveyed the room face by face, stopping momentarily to smile at Stump again. He moved easily to one of the devil dogs in a corner and stroked what was most likely its head. The beast did not move or take its eyes from its charge, but it did relax in a manner so subtle that the room itself relaxed. The people in the room were something else. The patch of light on the wall advanced one inaudible click. Baanquer turned back into the room suddenly.

"Now if there are no more questions, we should be done with this in short order." He raised his hand as though to pull down on a chain.

"WAIT!!" Everyone in the room, very sincerely.

"Yes?"

Baanquer, again amused, lowered his hand only a little, then a lot. He joined his hands behind his back and stood expectantly.

"Yes?" he repeated.

"But what did I do?" Rubb was quickest on the draw, with emphasis on the do. "What was so terrible about trying to stop a war or stop Pentecost or stop eating Eards or Thuds or anything else?!"

"Yeah!" That was Sam. "And not only that . . ."

Sam tailed off pretty quickly as Baanquer's rage flared to incandescence almost instantly. The Mantel Harpy shielded its one good eye with a wing, peeping out under it. One of the dogs soiled the carpet.

"What did you do?" Baanquer kept his controlled cool but there was no doubt about the intensity of his feelings. "DO!?!" he repeated in wild amazement. This was no private joke with Stump or anyone else!

Baanquer finally broke form and stormed around the room a few times, arms waving wildly overhead in wonderment and despair and exasperation. Gus jumped aside quickly to allow passage and Rubb scampered to a defensive position under his chair. After a few circuits Baanquer stopped suddenly and whipped about to fix them all with lowered brow and flaming eyes. No one moved.

"I'll tell you what you did! You and this accomplice of yours!" Sam winced. "You ripped a gaping wound in Real that will not heal until the Six Hells are drained. You have yanked the chain of every damned demon in the Pits and loosed most of their safely dead familiars! Your meddling scarred every loving living thing in at least two worlds and probably several more I haven't had time to tend. Everything has changed! Everything is different now; nothing of your world remains as it was. And you dare to ask what you did?!"

Baanquer paused while his eyes speared both Sam and Rubb several times in turn, his chest heaving. When his wrath settled somewhat he gestured tiredly to their rear.

"Behold."

"Mmmmmmm. M?" It was tall dark-haired Cyd, the devil of Speed!

"Oh, no!" thought Sam and Rubb as one. But there was more.

"May I help you?" murmured Cisly solicitously, a high tech gleam flashing from her flowing chrome mane.

"What! What!" said the oversized Bookend.

"Slash!" said Thumduk, the butcher. He didn't say it so much as conceptualize it with his sabre and sweat. They all got the idea.

" . . ." Rheostat, always the diplomat, said nothing. The Chianti bottle rocked a little and the candle flame sputtered once, but outside of that . . . nothing. The bottle was, however, full.

"Speak up, my friends!" Baanquer waded into the fray, directing traffic like a ringmaster and gladhanding like a game show host. "You have nothing to be modest about."

When he reached Rheostat he popped out the candle, glugged down a mighty draught and set it back in its place. The bottle was still full.

"Thank you," said Baanquer. "Now who will be first. Cyd? Yes, Cyd. Tell us about your experience with these two hooligans so we can see who is guilty and who is not."

"Mmmmee?" murmured Cyd modestly. "Mmmy yes! It was mmost unmmmannerly of themmm! I was so surprised that sommme of mmmy mmmost mmmiserable souls got away. I had the devils' ownn timme finnnding themmm!"

Rubb and Sam both looked away in embarrassment. Interrupting a devil during its most private of entertainments was the unforgivable faux pas.

"Ah! You see?" said Baanquer like a barrister to a jury. "And you, Thumduk. Tell us your story."

"Slash! Slash, slish, SLASH!!"

Old hairy-backed Thumduk whipped the sabre skillfully but violently, just overhead and too near their tummies. He whirled and danced in counterbalanced abandon as he sliced the air into singing ribbons. The Butcher knew that a raw bald-faced threat of violence, up front and full throttle, saved many words of explanation. This was no exception. Thumduk, who had no face, was as bald-faced as you can get. He was also congenitally short on words. The combination worked.

"Uh, Thank you." Baanquer noticed that the tummy button on his jump suit had been cleaved neatly without disturbing the thread.

"You have made your point. That will be all for now."

Everyone relaxed a lot as Thumduk braked to a stop and stood at ease, massive arms folded across his sweaty chest, feet spread solidly. Pentecost hitched up his pants as he tried to tie a knot in his severed suspender straps. Rubb sucked his thumb. Gabriel giggled, setting the top of his grin to rattling like a teapot lid, all the way around.

"Ah, lovely Cisly! So nice of you to come." Baanquer bowed slightly and kissed her hand graciously. If chrome blushes, Cisly blushed. "Do you have anything to add?"

"Thank you so very much, Baanquer. It is indeed a pleasure to be here. And, if I may impose upon your patience, I think I can add my modest experience to your deliberations." Cisly didn't really talk so much as whistle, like Mariah over polished edges, and trailed a vaporous slipstream in spite of the stagnancy of the air.

"Yes, it's true, I must say." Cisly turned to Rubb and Sam. "These ragamuffins have been of late a constant thorn to me. I must apologize for my temper, but their deportment has been simply horrid. I am completely discombobulated at this whole affair."

"Can you tell us, my dear Cisly," said Baanquer both unctuously and solicitously, "exactly what Rubb and Sam did."

"My familiar," whistled Cisly, "dropped a litter!"

"It what?" said Baanquer.

"Oh, no!!" thought Rubb and Sam, again alike.

They both knew that when a familiar bears young, its facility is dissipated among the young, leaving the familiar powerless. Familiars never really get pregnant; they just sorta pop sometimes, usually only when its master decides.

"My lovely dragon, Dickins. When they blew through Hell, my Dickins was so startled she dropped a litter! They squandered her for a lark! It will take eons to build another!"

"You see, my little terrorists, you have been rather a bother in Hell. Would you like to hear more?"

"More! More!" chanted the crowd, really getting into it. Even the devils found these revelations irresistible. Sam and Rubb were absolutely miserable.

"What about you, Bookend!"

"What? What?" shouted Bookend. "Yes! Yes! It was just awful! They did it! End them now!! They did it!"

Baanquer just smiled. There was no point in questioning Bookend when it got into one of these toots. But Bookend never lied; if it said they were guilty, they were guilty. Sam and Rubb knew this and raised no challenge.

"Any last word from you, Rheostat?"

"Yes!" said Rheostat, rocking a little in agitation. "There is no question about their guilt. Turn them off now and end this affair!"

Baanquer glanced from eye to eye as each nodded their agreement. Even Gabriel, who had no eye, assented on cue. Pentecost, who saw that he might at last be rid of this nuisance Rubb, voted thumbs down. Gus shook a little but he said nothing.

"Then it is done!"

NO!! WAIT!

There was no sound, no words were spoken, but everyone stopped to refocus their vision. The stagnant air in the room seemed to shift lazily into clumps and lines that bespoke purpose.

It was the Dust! The haze in the room wasn't dust; it was Dust! It tickertaped deliberately in and out amongst the assembly, spelling out its story for each. The room was absolutely quiet, like a silent movie theatre, as each read the story that unfolded before them.

"We have listened to these proceedings with interest. There are a few things all of you must know. May we?"

"Of course," said Baanquer tiredly, looking up for guidance and forbearance. Most of the others jumped at the sudden sound, then read on.

"In the beginning," began the Dust, "things were indeed as Baanquer states. Gus' war upset the balance of things, all things as you know them." The Dust paused into a little huddlepuff to gather its thoughts, then sprayed out again to continue.

"The point that you all miss is the List. Gus unwittingly favored us all by sending those Eards off to war. Each of them carried a little fluff of Eau de Eard to that wet world. Little by little the life of Eard accumulated until it was downhill to Zerpland. That's where Baanquer came in!"

Baanquer became cross-eyed glaring at the words forming one by one in front of his nose, fuming more and more at each. Gabriel smiled broadly. Rubb, who had met the Dust before, still thought the skywriting was a neat trick. Sam was relieved to see his old friends again but didn't get the drift of things. The devils could not see the words. Gus saw his case worsening while Pentecost could only think "Zerpland?".

"Rubb blew it all open," continued the Dust. "With a little help from Sam, of course. Rubb blew a hole clean through from Eard to Zerpland. That's how Rubb and Sam will save us all!"

"Hunh?" Everyone, including Baanquer.

The Dust settled into a satisfied little mound on the mantelpiece while their audience stood stunned. But the Dust wrote no more. The Dust was now merely dust.

"Thank you, my little friends." Sam broke the silence with his heartfelt farewell to the last intimate he had.

Baanquer, not certain what to make of this development but determined that there would certainly be an end to it, reached up.

"Since there is nothing more to say," Baanquer gripped a beaded chain that hung from above and YANK!! pulled the plug. "I'll see you on the other side."

"Oh no!!" As one. "Nooooooo!!!"

Quiet.

Anticipating their fate, no one spoke even if they could.

There were unanswered questions, to be sure. Sam's question, more or less, was "I'll get the Xzplrt who stole my Obs!"

Rubb's was not nearly so focused, "What's going on? Eau de Eard?"

Gus? Gus just muddled a panicky "Why me? Gabriel did it! Why me?"

Pentecost still plotted. "If I can catch Baanquer in private, I think we can cut a deal. 50% up front . . . no 40%."

Even Baanquer had his private concern. "What is One up to?"

And Stump! Stump, with more questions than anyone in spite of his death. "Why did they choose me? How did I know what was the right thing to do, and why did it work? Or rather, will it work? And when it does, will I ever know it?"

Gabriel was perhaps the most composed of all the company. "I gotta see this!" she thought.

Each looked into the eyes of every other, but confounded in their speech and thoughts, they did not speak.

They all heard the lonely clankclunk coming from somewhere deep below them, definitely metallic with liquid overtones.

There was no other sound or movement for an agonizing moment. A low swishing gurggly sound swept up through the room, surrounding them with the feel and the rush of a Bloo tornado. It whipped around them and through them, churning the ether until the room looked like a watery reflection in the galloping windowpanes of a speeding train, out of control but still clearly there.

Each one of our little company could still see into the eyes of the others and sought them desperately to relive their terror, but to no effect. Only Baanquer's eyes smiled, the others were in unbridled panic.

A musical tinklyring imposed itself on the maelstrom, then disappeared as quickly as it arose, while the storm itself abated dramatically, suddenly. There was a moment of complete silence, then a clear aquiline glug-glug-glug-glug leaped quickly up the scale;

"do-ray-me-fa . . ." followed by the docile murmur of flowing, fulfilling water.

Baanquer turned to Gabriel, patted her on the bean and said, "Thank you again, my misbegotten friend. Until we meet again . . . ?"

There were no other witnesses.

CHAPTER 33

Epilogue

Well, my dear readers, that is hardly a satisfactory ending to our story, is it? All shadows and mirrors, signifying nothing. Well, you may be assured that it is indeed the end of the story, but not the whole of it.

Was that the end of Sam and Rubb? Most decidedly so, I'm afraid. Not fair, you say? That is hardly your call; we have traced this Impact flow as it is. I am about to stop.

In all fairness, however, you have been persistent, if not entirely credulous, in following me to this point and you deserve some satisfaction. As your reward I shall allow you to look in upon our friends one last time.

I will, however, entertain no more complaints about fairness.

. . .

Ms. Machd and Foster Pokorni never made it together. Foster remained in government service and was ultimately very successful. In fact, after rising to the very topmost position of authority in the Office of Opportunity, Peace and Security, he was appointed to a cabinet position by the administration. By a real administration, that is, not the Administration. The Administration ended with the end of the Thud. The Thud ended when Baanquer pulled the plug that restored the balance of Nice in the universe. Once the Thud disappeared, the Brains quickly burned out and the Administration computer collapsed.

Real people took over the administration by default and after a brutal readjustment period, recognized Foster's hard-nosed managerial style. Foster, who actually looked like a shark many mornings, tore through the old bureaucracy like a shark and whipped it into pretty good shape in pretty short order.

On the basis of that performance he was nominated to run for President. He might have won but for being shot in a second-story motel room on election night by his girlfriend's husband.

Ms. Machd lived out her days peaceably enough. She hated every minute teaching kindergarten and hated the little brats even more. She was devoted to the job, though mostly by default, and did well at all times. She taught kindergarten until the day she retired to a cozy bungalow on a chilly and windy seacoast. She writes and illustrates children's books to support herself.

She still thinks of Foster from time to time, though the aged image is faded, and is still capable of sighing wistfully at the thought of what might have been. Foster was her only real emotional involvement ever, aside from the dishrag collection of her childhood, and was her only cherished memory.

Ms. Machd lives on that lonely seacoast still, I understand, occasionally entertaining a student from years past and smoking fish that wash up on the beach.

. . .

Gabriel is an enigma. There has never been anything like her. Considering she is the only one ever, there is not likely to be another. That does not concern Gabriel in the least and most others are comfortable with the fact.

Gabriel got into this affair on a bet and stayed for her own amusement, mostly. She enjoys the emotional milieu of Real and found the dramatic overtones refreshing. Gabe works behind the scenes, like a theater company stage manager, and only occasionally gets to take a bow. Being a meddler by trade, she is a natural henchthing for Baanquer who employs her for many of his dirtier projects.

Nothing sticks to Gabriel. Baanquer/One are powerless to force Gabriel in the same way that grease won't stick to water. Because she can act with impunity, Gabriel is absolutely free to do as she pleases. That is why she is feared so.

Actually, Gabriel rarely does anything capriciously. She sells her services to the highest bidder because she is the only one who can do it. She does it thoroughly and reliably, and is paid well for it. In that regard she is absolutely predictable. The downside is that she also has other clients with other frequently overlapping interests. She also has her own agenda. She also has her own finely tuned sense of priorities. And she cannot be controlled or sanctioned or coerced. Her clients cannot buy results, only probabilities, but she is the only game in town.

What did she do in all of this? She plunked Slumpblock in the right place at the right time. Slumpblock was a traitor in the purest sense. Gabriel offered fame and money to Slumpblock to betray Rubb and Slumpblock took it without a blink.

And what did Slumpblock do? Slumpblock made one call, to Gabriel when Sam's Dust penetrated the ether to Rubb. Slumpblock didn't know what that meant but Gabriel sure did. It meant that something was going to happen fast and it was time for Gabriel to set the trigger.

Gabriel, perhaps more than anyone, knew what was going down but she didn't know when. That was the one piece she couldn't know because of her ease of movement between times. Those who move easily through any medium have a problem dealing with it; the medium establishes the physical baseline and the psychological zero. Real people don't notice air except in a storm, which by definition is a perturbation of the medium, and fish don't notice water. Gabriel didn't notice time, except in a Whenstorm, and needed moles like Slumpblock for her early warning system. That was Slumpblock's only function, to call home. And he was all too ready to oblige, a circumstance for which he paid dearly.

.   .   .

Baanquer and One are a little confused about the nature and thrust of their relationship. Baanquer, as you recall, budded off from One at One's instigation; One has no presence in Real and so had to send a Real copy, sort of.

Imagine if you will this situation: light streaming through a transparent medium that is stressed in such a way that the light is polarized, casting a phase-contrasted shadow-pattern onto a screen. You can see the result, the pattern, and it is definitely real. But wherein lies the reality? Does the essence of the pattern lie in the light, the medium, the stress or the screen. Lacking any one of these there is no shadow.

Is the shadow the same as the stressed medium? Certainly in some way it is, at least in that it closely reflects every intimate detail, revealing perhaps more than the unaugmented medium itself. But they are two different things entirely.

If you imagine that the screen is Eard or Zerpland, and the medium is One, the shadow is Baanquer. The stress is the imbalance that prompted One to act, to relieve the stress.

Now, you may ask, where did the stress come from? All that magic moxie that clung to the Thud as they percolated into Zerpland? No, that relieved the stress!

You can see a little problem here. The stress must have built up long before all of this sordid business we have just witnessed. In fact, the stress is what caught One's attention in the first place. Here's what happened, close as I can figure it.

You see, Sam, Rubb and the other magicians extract their power from the Out There. They don't know it but that's how they do it. They know how to want it to be so, and want it so much that they just sort of soak up Nice and wad it up for magic. To Nice, a wizard is downhill. That is what magic is, real honest to gosh magic, concentrated Nice puddling in the soul of a wizard.

A spell or an incantation works like a snare, winding up shreds and wisps of Nice that are always coming loose here and there. If you could see wizardry at work it would look like a paper cone-handle whisking up threads of cotton candy spinning from one world or another.

Nice is out there for the taking; it doesn't belong to anyone. The problem, and the impetus for our story, is that the Eards were sopping up more than most folks because they are lazier than most. That's why they go into magic in the first place. At the same time, the Zerp throw off more than most worlds because of the Administration, the Executives, the Brains, the Stump A Varietal virus, etc. The net result is a flow of Nice from the Zerp to the Eards. It is not necessarily the same Nice, you understand, just the net Nice.

Sometimes Nice is badly used by the magician, squandered or ill-spent, and sometimes it is used very well, very well indeed. Most of the time, however, magicians use their hoards of Nice to do the dishes or laundry, muffle a complaining in-law or keep out mosquitoes. Pretty mundane stuff that they hardly think about. In Eard, magic is an everyday thing like playing the stock market or cheating on taxes. Everyone does it all the time without thinking, certainly without awareness of the consequences. But all of that offhand diddling with the cosmic supply of Nice adds up. This constant drain of Nice into Eard caused the imbalance, the stress.

The corrective action was to let Nice flow back from Eard to Zerpland, slowly through the Thud at first and then all at once through the hole Rubb blew between the two. Baanquer didn't know that Eard was soaking up Nice; only that he was sent into Real by One to set things aright and restore balance.

The heavies in all of this, although they did not know it at the time, were Sam and Rubb. These two, being probably the most powerful and certainly the most profligate of all Eard's wizards, sucked more than their share of Nice from the rest of Real. The Zerps were the unwilling victims, losing Nice to the magicians.

From the Zerps' standpoint Gus is the real hero, although they hadn't a clue! He started the non-war that sent thousands of Thud to Zerpland, taking loads of Nice with them, and ultimately restoring the universe to its former chaotic balance.

.   .   .

Ah yes. Pentecost. Pentecost Darn-Watts. Pentecost presents a bit of a problem in this story. He is the archetypal protagonist and at the same time the incompetent bungler. He was a willing co-conspirator in the travails of Sam and Rubb as well as a self-made jerk in his own right. He was used and misused in the most outrageous manners, and paid the ultimate price for it. The problem is that I did all of that to Pentecost without giving it much thought at all. I treated this character very badly indeed, with worse to come, and not a shred of an excuse for doing so. There may be no more tragic creature in all literature, excepting possibly Kong. I rather think I should do something to redeem our honor in this matter and extricate Pentecost at the same time.

Of the two the former is the more feasible, this being my story. The latter is more difficult as I may have painted Pentecost and myself into a literary corner. Let's see how this turns out.

We must first review a few Pentecostal points, not the least of which is that Pentecost was the Choosee. He didn't know it at the choosing and probably never did figure it out. Stump the Chooser didn't know it either. Well, Stump knew that he had set the snare that would choose some unsuspecting victim but he had no inkling that it would be Pentecost. Stump also knew what fate was in store for his victim, at least in a general sort of way, and set the trigger anyway.

In fairness to Stump it was not a random thing at all. His trap was set to entangle the first one who already had the trait needed to set his plan in motion, one who had the Immunity. Stump had no control over the role that trait would play in the events that unfolded, nor for Pentecost's luckless possession of it. He only identified the probability that events would demand the complicity of one in politically high places who was Immune, one who had somehow evaded the effects of the Stump A Varietal virus that endowed intelligence. That is to say, this highly placed person had to be an unsuspecting patsy who had no need to eat Thud. We'll get back to Stump later. For now all we need to know is that Pentecost was chosen to be that patsy.

And what was it that Pentecost was to do? His sole role in the story was to keep Rubb alive and in one piece long enough to anchor the hole that he, Rubb, had blown through the ether. This allowed the rest of the displaced Thud/Eards to follow, draining the magic from Eard into Zerpland. That is why he, Pentecost, had to be Immune to the virus that ravaged the highly placed Executives and Brains who had to eat Thud to survive. Pentecost's Immunity insured Rubb's survival.

Why did Pentecost have to be high-placed? After all, what difference did it make where in Zerpland all of that magic emerged? First of all, the shock treatment had to be applied to the center of the problem, the Executives, in massive overwhelming doses. That is also the reason that Baanquer allowed the displaced Thud to accumulate so before springing his plan; he was waiting to build up enough potential for a knockout punch.

Secondly, the Executives, through the medium of the Administration computer and its attending Brains, controlled distribution of all commodities throughout Zerpland. Dumping a cheap supply of Thuds in their laps by the thousands, certainly more than they could ever use locally, insured that the Executives would see to their distribution Zerp wide. Rubb, however, had to stay put.

Lastly, Baanquer was not at all sure that this whole scheme would work and operated in damage control mode for the most part. He figured if it didn't work, the fewer who knew about it the better. That in turn meant that those few knowing people would have to be proportionately more powerful.

Did Stump know about Baanquer's plan? Probably, at least in a statistical way. But Stump is dead now so we will never know for sure.

. . .

Devils, as a rule, operate outside Real, spending what in Hell passes for time tending to themselves and their admittedly arcane entertainments. Occasionally they can be goaded into what we would call bedevilment but only as a last resort, and then only if there is merriment to be had. From their point of view all contact with Real is an intrusion by Real; devils have no initiative or ambition in our direction.

To be completely fair with these otherwise vile creatures, devils are quite honorable in the sense that they are completely true to themselves. They can be counted upon absolutely to look out for No. 1 to the exclusion of all other considerations. Understanding that, they are reasonably easy to deal with. If you assume, however, that they will behave with even a smattering of compassion for another, you lose.

Otherwise they are a benign lot, guilty of little more than body odor. When there is a problem, it usually centers around the black cast to their humor; few outside their ranks fully appreciate the fun.

You must view the devils' involvement in our story in that light. Sam and Rubb bashed in on them and they reacted in the only way they knew how, like prodded snakes. Once Sam and Rubb got their attention, the devils were simply in it for the fun, their brand of fun, and for any profit that might be had to boot. End of story.

They had their fun and their profits, both mostly at Sam's expense, and lost interest almost immediately. They simply went on to more devilishly amusing pastimes. On the whole they were disappointed with their Real experience, much preferring greasy and/or cold things. They have given the affair no thought since.

For their trouble, however, they did pick up all of Sam's Obs at bargain rates. Most were ancient and, through the magic of compound interest, uncommonly potent. Devils don't need Obs, of course, but they are a generally accepted hard exchange medium that can work miracles in a confrontation with the occasional Real power. Rubb lost all of his Obs as well but since he had relatively few, and those were mortgaged to the eaves anyway, he suffered little for it.

Sam and Rubb had set out originally to contact Baanquer about the Zerp and their war, reasoning correctly that they were interconnected somehow. Their invocation, however, hit Hell like an Eardquake. From the devils' point of view, and the intrusion certainly entitles them to it, being so rudely roused was like a thorough thumping with a dense heavy waterlogged thing. That's the wrong way to open dialogue with a devil. Events slud downhill from there.

In retaliation the devils played right into Baanquer's plan (although none of them knew it at the time) and provided the instrument for the salvation of both Eard and Zerpland. That is, in granting Rubb and Sam's demand to find the Zerp, the devils blasted Rubb through the hole that drained Eard. And that, in the end, proved to be that.

Whatever else, the few devils in our story have pretty much settled back into their dark routine and should present few problems for Real.

.   .   .

Penelope never really had a thing for Rubb. Rubb never occurred to her as anything more than found money, something to cash in and spend. On her scale of personal values, Rubb fell between lottery winnings and miscounted change.

You see, one of the prerequisites for wizardhood is the ability to focus entirely on one thought so intensely that it is yanked from the virtual into the accomplished. To outsiders the result looks like magic, an event that pops into and then maybe out of reality. But to the wizard it feels like passing through puberty instantly; it's still the same person before and after but profoundly and permanently changed. It was this wizardly intensity that did it.

Rubb focused that intensity on Penelope for only a moment, when she showed him what little kindness he found in Zerpland, and was permanently scarred for his trouble. He could not forget her in the same way that you cannot rescind your adulthood, she was part of him forever like fire is part of tempered steel. The fact that she was a killer was irrelevant to Rubb.

At his rational best Rubb realized the futility but in matters of the heart he was no more rational than any other smitten fool. The tragedy was only compounded by the metaphysical gulf between them, not to mention their difference in heights. But they would never meet again, probably for the best, and Rubb would never forget her. Rubb remembered Penelope fondly forever afterwards, in spite of her duplicity and ultimate attack, and as it turned out she was the only real love in his very long life.

Actually, love is probably not the correct word to describe the situation. Rubb missed her, no doubt about that, but it was more in the order of missing parts, like the way you bump into furniture when you rearrange a room. The old habit is an ingrained part of you and when the room changed that part is missing, inversely speaking.

Penelope, however, never looked back, preferring instead to devote her life to out MA!-ing MA! After the disappointment of having a live Thud and instant wealth in her grasp only to loose it, Penelope turned into a slob in pretty short order. She took to eating pies like MA! and spent her days hollering at her little brother who eventually swore better than she.

MA! dropped dead of a heart attack many years later, mostly due to eating too much. In fact, at the time she was grazing through a lunch cart of jelly Bismarcks at an outdoor food fair revival. She hit the asphalt dead and bounced no more than a bag of chilled shot.

All of that disappears into the haze of time now and Rubb never knew any of it. All he had were his memories of the longhaired Type II with the smile and the musical voice. That, thought Rubb quite correctly, was rather a lot.

. . .

Sam and Rubb? Let's look in on them one last time.

Klaatu looked up from his dinner absently, his eye caught by Sam's sudden movement in the corner, but he resumed eating, concerned only that the rocks were crunchier than usual. Halfway through the next mouthful he leaped to his feet in full startle. His plateful of sautéed geodes splashed to the floor of the cave and rattled randomly about a bit, quickly coming to rest unmoving. The rocks failed to scurry for cover as the rules specified but Klaatu didn't bother to think that through. Sam!!

Sam jackknifed from his proneness with a start and a bellyjerk, feet and head up, butt down. Still dazed but sitting upright under his own power, Sam pushed his head around to check where it was.

"Klaatu? Klaatu! Is that you? Is that really you?!"

Sam lumbered over onto all fours and pulled himself up by the shredded remains of the dragnet still partly draped over the rafters.

"Klaatu! By the Black lords you're a grand sight! It's really you!"

Quickly realizing that he was not dead, Sam grabbed each of his accessible body parts to confirm that he had left nothing behind. Satisfied, he turned to steady himself on his The Bench, fully expecting it to be there, and fell flat on his face as it was not.

"Zounds!! Where has that blasted The Bench got to?! Klaatu! Help me up. We've got work to do!"

Klaatu could see Sam's spirits rising meteorically but felt odd that he felt nothing of it. It was odd that he didn't feel Sam's rage and it was odd that he felt no compulsion in Sam's words. Not used to independent thought, Klaatu found it still odder that he even thought it odd. While he sorted that out he bent to picking up the unresisting stones.

"Klaatu!! You come here this . . ." Sam's screech was cut short when Rubb blasted out of nowhere and flattened Sam on the second bounce.

"Whooof!"

They tumbled to a stop against the polished granite wall that was the door to the Flang. The Wall was cold and smooth and unmitigated granite.

Each looked at the other for a moment, both stunned at the sight, and then grabbed each other in the warmest teddy bear hugs ever. They said nothing for a little while, each overcome with relief and gladness and comfort and giving.

"I'm so happy you're alive, Sam. You're alive and here in one piece! What happened to us? What's going on?"

Rubb didn't even try to hide his tears of joy. Nor, to his eternal credit, did Sam.

"Rubb! Dear Rubb. You're back! Oh, what would I have done without you. Just let me look at you!"

Sam held Rubb out at arm's length and looked at him. Simultaneously Sam and Rubb awoke suddenly to the same realization, each by now looking pretty foolish to the other.

"Oh NOOOoooo!!" they exclaimed unanimously. "We're nice!!"

Sam covered his eyes in humiliation, mumbling something about being expelled from the lodge. Rubb could only shiver in shock at the prospect of terminal niceness. Sam leaped into action, panicking through his cabinet for some effective specific for nice.

"Klaatu!! Where are all of my potions! What have you done with them?! They're not here!"

Klaatu had no time to answer, a happy circumstance in that he had no response. In compound, Klaatu found he really had no inclination to give Sam an answer even if he had one.

"Again," thought Klaatu in amazement, "Sam's rage does not rouse me."

By now Sam was stomping and crashing back and forth through the cave, discovering one loss after another. His robes, his library, even his cauldron!

"I'm ruined," sobbed Sam. "Everything's gone!!"

Clouds suddenly loomed and the cave darkened. A voice from everywhere boomed into the cave.

"Sam! Sam!! You can't use the force. You are a wizard no more. Central has been shut down. Your license has expired, permanently."

Baanquer!

"There is no more magic in Eard. There is no more Sam the Wizard. Not even a Sam the Barely Adequate Meddler. Quit making so much noise and get a real job!"

There was a very long silent pause, then the voice resumed. "You too, Rubb." Then silence.

"Butbut," rebutted Rubb. "That can't be! No more magic?!" Rubb looked at Sam and Sam looked at Rubb in terror and disbelievement and frustration and finally realization.

"Then that's why all of my magic stuff is gone?"

"Yes."

"Where did it go?" said Sam suspiciously.

Sam knew that magic is as palpable as tree sap or rock and is never really used up, only transmogrified. It can be used again and again, like recycled water, if you can find it and if you know how. Sam knew how.

"Remember the Zerp?" asked Baanquer in response.

"The Zerp!? You mean in Zerpland?" sputtered Sam in disbelief. "What in 62 dimensions is it doing there! They don't know how to use it! And I can't get there without it. What kind of a deal is that?!"

"A very good deal, the way I see it. I'm finally done with this mess and you can't get into any more trouble." Baanquer smiled audibly. "Good-bye."

The clouds scuttered instantly and Baanquer disconnected with a sharp sputt, the effect decidedly terminal. The sun shown again.

"Well, that's that," mumbled Rubb. "We're done. That's what he meant when he said we would end today. We're done."

And in fact they were. Sam and Rubb, civilians now, took up meaningful (that is, salaried) occupations; Sam as a classical thespian and Rubb as a media consultant in the political arena.

Thenceforward, neither Sam nor Rubb made any noticeable impact, either jointly or severally, on anything of even marginal consequence, in their world or any other.

About the Author

My experience in writing a book draws from a quarter century in public schools, and a quarter century in insurance marketing. Writing insurance sales training materials is a great foundation for writing humouous fiction. Also, reading the daily newspaper thoroughly provides a wealth of source material.

I read fiction and non-fiction voraciously. Most fiction I find great fun but too often lacking in a satisfying resolution to the story. Hence my story which satisfies me immensely, and I hope you as well.

I am a native born and raised Iowan, but totally urban. I admire farmers but I cannot cope with anything agricultural but the eating. I have four children, all long since out on their own. I am now retired.